# Vampire's Secret

## IMMORTAL PROTECTOR

### BOOK TWO

# STEPHANIE FLYNN

Small Fish Publishing

USA

First edition
Cover design by Stephanie Flynn
ISBN eBook: 978-1-952372-59-9
ISBN Paperback: 978-1-952372-58-2
ISBN Hardcover: 978-1-952372-64-3
ISBN Large Print: 978-1-952372-65-0

Library of Congress Control Number: 2022912353

# Also By Stephanie Flynn

Find my catalog at StephanieFlynn.com

**Immortal Protector series**

0.5 Vampire's Distraction

1 Vampire's Deception

2 Vampire's Secret

3 Vampire's Promise

3.5 Elf Bound

4 Vampire's Demand


**Immortal Protector Side Tales**

Deer Holiday

Love Claws

Depths of the Heart


**Matchmaker in Time series**

0.5 Minutes to Live

1 Seconds to Act

2 Hours to Arrive

3 Days to Hide

4 Years to Savor

**Pirates in Time series**

1 Pirate's Prize

2 Pirate's Treasure

3 Pirate's Plunder

**Time Travel Romance Shorts**

Fateful Time

One Crazy Time

If you like your urban fantasy without the romance, too, check out Stephanie Flynn's other name, Marie Flynn!

# I

# Naked Tease

**Daisy**

DRESSED IN MY UNIFORM, I swiped condensation off the bathroom mirror. Oliver Rockwell's luxurious bathroom was like nothing I'd ever experienced before, but damn, the four showerheads were like trying to swim upstream at Niagara Falls. Unlike my vampire boyfriend, I required air to survive. Speaking of the sexiest devil to walk the earth, I'd left a naked Oliver slumbering on his king-sized bed, where I'd rather be right now, but my boss required me to report early for my afternoon shift to meet my new partner. Again.

I pulled my hair into a low ponytail, and the sexiest sight caught the corner of my eye. Oliver was leaning against the bathroom doorframe wearing absolutely nothing but a lopsided grin and my sun ring. In his hands, he held a tray carrying a plate of scrambled eggs, buttered toast, and crispy bacon. A mug of steaming coffee and a single rose finished the surprise. Naked breakfast as previously promised, but I'd missed the show.

My face heated at his miles of lean muscle, smooth skin, and a dusting of soft dark hair over his chest and trailing down low. His manscape was always on point, just like when he sported a beard. It was always trimmed and soft. The hair on his head was another story—typically shaggy, sometimes gelled into submission. After defeating a battalion's worth of murderous pillows and performing Olympic-level gymnastics on his mattress all night, Oliver currently sported a sexy bedhead style. It suited him.

"How did you make this so fast?" I asked, amazed, and reached for a wavy slice of bacon. I hadn't heard the sizzle as it cooked, so I could divorce this breakfast staple from my previous comparison of my boyfriend frying in the sunlight. Besides, with his ring voluntarily returned, courtesy of Soren, I didn't have to worry about that nightmare ever again.

"Next time you'll have to watch." Teasingly, he pulled the tray just out of reach and set it on a nearby chest of drawers. I hungrily followed him for a crispy slice and picked one off the pile. The crunch was divine.

I stepped up to his chest and walked my fingers from his abs up to his firm pecs and teased a nipple, which hardened under my touch. Other things quickly hardened. "And the kitchen's clean, too?" I asked sweetly.

"Every little inch." Oliver groaned with pleasure.

I finished the slice and glided my hands up over his shoulders to the nape of his neck. "There is absolutely nothing sexier than a hot steaming plate of food and a gorgeous man who cleans up." *Pinch me.* I must be dreaming, I thought.

"Ouch," he said sarcastically and gripped my arms, holding them in place. "I was made in a cave, not born in one. And for that, I'm going to show you just how much of a gentleman I can be."

"Sounds like there's a promise in there."

Oliver leaned close, pale gray eyes mesmerizing, nose touching mine in a gentle tickle. His lips teased mine, urging me to give in to his irresistible charm. "Clear your schedule."

"The whole shift?"

"Regulations dictate breaks at regular intervals, so yeah, I'm going to need all night."

"So, sex is a job for you?" I playfully asked.

"I take my duties very seriously." His hands nestled against my face. "And when my queen needs a breather, I will feed her chocolate-dipped strawberries and tequila. If those aren't enticing to you, then anything else you could ever want is also on the menu."

How was I supposed to resist this guy? He knew he was sexy as hell, too, and I loved his confidence. "I'm tempted to stay and warm your bed, but my boss would rain fiery hell upon me if I called off today. I'm meeting my new partner. You remember how Kayla ended?" Nerves returning, I released Oliver's neck and picked up another cooling slice of bacon.

My understanding boyfriend wasn't disappointed with my rejection. Suddenly serious, he adjusted the collar of my EMS-embroidered polo and picked a fuzzy off my shoulder. In the process, his fingers brushed my necklace, and the vervain protection sizzled his skin, but he didn't flinch. "I have a feeling your new partner will be your best friend."

With vampires, elves, and witches running amok in our small town, I envied his optimism. Megan had been my best friend, and I didn't think I could survive losing my favorite person again. To keep the mood light and my nerves at bay, I dryly said, "I wish."

Oliver leaned forward as if to kiss me, but I pressed a finger against his eager lips. "Only one way to find out," he said against my finger, distorting his speech.

I laughed. "You are too much."

"Better than not enough."

"True." I dropped my finger in favor of another piece of bacon. Oliver leaned against me, hard length ready for another long session testing the durability of his bed frame and the hearing of his niece.

Not wanting to be late, his niece was the perfect change of subject. "Did Nicole see you make breakfast?"

His human, AARP-card-carrying niece might suffer a heart attack seeing Oliver in his full glory. Technically, she was his great-great-great-grandniece or something, which was still wild to wrap my brain around.

I chomped on the toast, and his lips found my neck. "I wore a towel for her. She's seen enough of me in her day."

I tipped my head back and chewed, eyes closed. Soft butterfly kisses tickled my exposed skin, stopping at the neckline of my polo. His fingers found the hem of my shirt, but I grabbed his hands to stop him. "Slow down, stallion. As incredibly alluring as you are, and extremely difficult as it is to resist, my patients and my mortgage depend on me. So your libido will have to wait until after work. But I do have something for you," I said while re-tucking my work shirt.

"Well, what a coincidence, because I do, too." Oliver gestured down low, and his hard length bobbed its morning hello.

Sometimes I envied his carefree lifestyle. With immortality, he felt no hurry to experience life—no desire to climb the corporate ladder to prove himself, no urge to have children to pass on a legacy, no craving to explore the world, because it was always there. He always had time, and later would always be available. Oliver didn't struggle with any of that, or at least he hadn't told me about it.

For the rest of us, life was too short. As the years ticked by, faces changed in the mirror, and new aches popped up in joints. I was only thirty years old, but I felt the pressure of my mortality far more since falling in love with an immortal vampire. I didn't want to think about twenty, thirty years into the future. One day I'd be just like Nicole—up in years, graying, with more wrinkles than a T-shirt from the dryer, limping with a bad hip—a bad hip that could snap if Oliver slightly changed angle with his eager thrust. If he'd even still want me. And in public, I'd receive all the dirty looks or be mistaken for his grandmother.

I was too young to worry about being too old, but Oliver would be perfect forever, and he would outlive me. Someday I had to say goodbye, and because we weren't going to grow old and die together, I had to live each day to its fullest and not dwell on the future that wouldn't come. That was a task all by itself. Enough depressing thoughts for one day.

I smiled wistfully, trying to hide my gloomy brain-train, and I pulled open a dresser drawer. I lifted out the package, wrapped in plain brown paper and tied with twine, and offered it to him. "Here. This'll make our lives easier."

Oliver accepted the gift while I forked up a bite of eggs—fluffy, yellow, salted *perfection*. Always perfect. Considering he couldn't eat human food, he was a great chef.

"Easy is good." With a wink, Oliver tore through the gift wrap and laughed at the box in his hand. "What do you expect me to do with this?"

I lifted the box's lid and handed him the sleek new phone I'd already set up. "I can call you, and vice versa. I already loaded my phone number onto it. You need to figure out how to call and text. Just don't break it. They're surprisingly fragile things. Welcome to the twenty-first century."

Oliver turned the black device over in his hands. "When I grew up, I manually plowed and sowed the fields with my dad and brother. Our irrigation system was rudimentary and unreliable, so we'd pray for rain against the drought, and worry about having enough to eat over the winter. We rationed the meager supplies we had, while the cold January winds whistled through the gaps in the cabin's walls. I wouldn't wish an existence like that on anyone."

Replacing my phone and learning a slightly different layout annoyed me to no end. I couldn't imagine having to adapt to all the insane changes to society since he'd been alive. Oliver was a rock, a constant, in a world of change and uncertainty, and he would go on through the centuries, long after I was gone.

Fighting back the bleak thoughts again, I said, "Cell phones can be intimidating, but they're surprisingly intuitive. The power button's over—"

"There's a reason I drive a car manufactured in the 1960s, live in the house I built in the 1880s, and always dress in my finest," Oliver said, interrupting my lesson. "I am only comfortable with luxury, which naturally commands..."

"Longevity," I surmised bleakly.

"Dependability. As for your phone here, I've gotten by for a hundred and eighty years without one, but I know how to use it, and I'll carry it for you."

He wanted things that would last, and that wasn't me.

Oliver touched my jaw, tipping my chin up, so I'd meet his gaze. "What's on your mind?"

"Nothing. It's nothing." More specifically, nothing I could do anything about. There was no use spoiling both our moods. I tried my best smile, but I didn't convince him.

"Daisy, talk to me. Whatever it is, we can fix it."

I shook my head. Things were so great right now. I didn't want to ruin them, and as far as I was concerned, there was no fixing this problem.

Oliver insisted. "Please talk to me."

The more he pushed, the harder it was for me to avoid the conversation—the truth of what made me unworthy, the real reason for my gloom. But I'd already made up my mind, and I'd never discussed it with him. I sighed. "It's just...I..."

Oliver patiently waited. "Take a deep breath and let it out."

"I love you, and I want things between us to stay just like this. I don't want things to change."

My sexy vampire smiled. "Is that it? Consider it done."

He didn't understand. Why was it so hard to be straight? "When Soren bit my throat, I was terrified. Spell or not, I truly thought he was a monster straight from the horror movies. I'd never felt so scared in my life. And I know the two of you are different, but I...I can't be like him. And from our very short interaction, I can't be like Evangeline. I can't take the chance that I'm not...like you. What I'm trying to say is I don't want to be a vampire. Ever." That meant the gloom would infect us both.

Oliver bent to meet my wavering gaze. "I agree."

I expected him to insist on a discussion about my turning soon, or to offer me some sort of platitude to make me feel better and attempt a conversation when we had more time. "What?"

"I don't want you to be a vampire either, so things won't change between us."

Oliver hadn't considered our differences as much as I had. "That's just the thing. They will change. If you were human, I'd selfishly say to mourn me in misery until you die, but you're not. You're going to outlive me. I can't ask you to suffer for an *eternity* in misery, and I know assuming you'll love me literally forever is unrealistic and selfish, too. So when the time comes, I want you to move on and be happy without me. These are the thoughts cycling through my brain every day, unable to stay quiet."

Oliver took my hands in his. "I didn't realize the extent of your fears, but you don't have to struggle with this alone. I know—I've been around a long while, and I've faced it and avoided it. We must accept there is a time limit to our relationship, but when the time comes—a long, long, long time from now—I will still love you. I promise, Daisy, you are my forever, and that is never going to be in question." He squeezed and kissed my knuckles. "So we have fifty, sixty years before us. Promise me you won't worry about leaving me alone on this earth until after that long, long, long time."

As much as I wanted comfort from his words, I fixated on one that made it worse. "Sixty?" I choked back the emotion clogging my throat. "I'll be ninety years old, drooling in a nursing home, and you'll be just like you are now."

Oliver kissed my forehead. "There's no chance in hell you'll be in a nursing home. Don't worry about that."

I didn't get the relief I'd wanted, but my phone chimed with a text. I read the bubble of confusing words and frowned. I swiped my eyes clear and read it again. Shocked out of my depressing stupor, my voice returned. "Huh?"

"What is it?" Oliver said, worry in his tone.

"Dad wants to have a family meeting tomorrow night." I paused and stared at the words on my screen. "Lily's coming." I hadn't seen my sister in way too long, but Dad and I weren't on good terms, to say the least, ever since he'd partnered with Mr. Newton Reed in his lab. Hopefully, he wasn't resting in peace.

"Remember, he had been under a spell, just like Soren. Underneath all he's done, he's still your dad. He loves you, and he wants to see you, so what's wrong?" Oliver rubbed my shoulders.

I gazed into his gray eyes, concerned over Dad's intentions but intrigued beyond belief. "You're invited."

"Huh?" Oliver said, mirroring my reaction.

"It's tomorrow, dinnertime. Maybe he wants to apologize for creating a weapon to annihilate vampirekind."

Oliver frowned skeptically. "After locking vampires in his lab and experimenting on them, he eventually discovered I don't eat human food, right?"

"Dinner always accompanies drinks."

Oliver smiled. "Why didn't you say so? After you graciously destroyed what was left of his experiments, he can't hurt me, but I'll make sure he doesn't hurt you."

Honestly, I was grateful to have a powerful vampire by my side, because I suspected whatever apology Dad planned to offer was getting thrown back in his face. And Oliver could stop me from doing something I regretted.

# 2

# The Next Replacement

**Daisy**

I SECURED MY PURSE and keys in the locker room at Borealis Medical Center, while curiosity and nerves battled within. I trusted my boss to choose only the best candidate for the job, but I was positive questions about vampires, witches, and elves weren't on the application. At least, they hadn't been on mine. And after Kayla's cat-smuggling child story, I was certain they hadn't been on hers either.

My first partner and best friend, Megan, had been mauled by a vampire, and she died in front of me. My second? Not much better. While off duty at a party, Kayla sustained a vampire bite to the throat and was carted off by paramedics. Unsurprisingly, she promptly quit. Who was going to be the next victim riding shotgun with me?

Thankfully, with the witch's spell broken, Soren hadn't been leaving behind anymore of his meals. Perhaps my giving him the cure for a second chance actually resonated. But he wasn't the only vampire around. There was my bag-only boyfriend, Oliver. His ex-girlfriend, Evangeline, who escaped the lab. And I'd been told there were more vampires around than I cared to know. Three was plenty.

I'd struggled to accept this dangerous hidden world around me, even though I'd unknowingly dated an elf, currently loved a vampire, had two witch roommates, and my dad was a medical research scientist who tried to kill all vampires with a serum he personally developed. And when he'd first refused to do the job, my own mother was killed for it. Then he'd warned my sister to vanish for her own safety...but not me. That was a thorn in my side, but not my current problem.

The nerve-wracking identity of my next partner was. I didn't even know whether I should broach the dangerous subject matter with her at all. But would it be fair for her not to know? Seriously, an elf was a fellow paramedic.

On the way to the breakroom, I waved to nurses I recognized and received friendly smiles in return. Kevin Fontaine stood at a patient's bedside in the emergency room. His sweet smile and gentle manners relaxed the patient, reminding me of when he and Megan were all smiles before she'd died. I'd expected him to come to me after Megan's funeral, but people grieved differently, and I didn't want to push. So my urge to give him a hug would continue to be suppressed.

As I was almost through the department, Kevin patted the patient's shoulder and turned, catching my eye. I sent him a friendly smile and a wave, but this time he approached me. With his buzzed head and dark eyes, it was hard to remember he was only twenty-five years old. His maturity and seriousness made him feel wise beyond his years. "Daisy, I ran into your ex the other day."

"With your car?" I asked, never wanting to see Pierce again.

Kevin tilted his head. "He wanted to know how you're doing. I told him to ask you."

"I'd rather he didn't."

"So it wasn't a friendly break." Kevin eyed me as if he were battling with what to say next. "I, uh, I wanted to be at Megan's funeral. I bet the service was deeply moving. How are you holding up?"

And there it was, the sweet Kevin. "I was going to ask you the same."

"There are a lot of places around here with special memories." He smiled wistfully and glanced at a few nearby doors. I was well aware of his and Megan's closet activities, which were probably a constant reminder now. "And I've been meaning to ask you, what's it like out in the field? I know your department is a pay cut, but I'm curious if you get to do more than handle drug seekers and low blood sugars."

*More deadly.* "Honestly, I see a lot of the same, but the scenery always changes." Like whether a hungry vampire was lurking around or not. "So I think it's great, but I believe the position's been filled. I'm on my way to meet my new partner now. I just hope she's up for the task."

Kevin's eyes shifted to the side, as if tracking a patient's request. "Maybe another time then. I've got to go. Old man Reynolds needs his metformin."

I opened my mouth to tell him I'd put in the good word, but Kevin rushed off. The emergency room was always busy.

Inside the sparse breakroom, which consisted of a scratchy couch, a television mounted to the wall, a bookshelf, a messy bulletin board, and a coffee station, I poured myself a cup and checked the clock on the wall. I had a minute left before having to report to the boss's office, and my heart pounded in my ears. The Soren and Newton Reed problem had been solved, so statistically speaking, my new partner couldn't become Kayla 2.0. In which case, these nerves were a waste of brain matter, but an effective distraction from my depressing conversation with Oliver earlier. My life was too short. I didn't want to waste any of it being away from him. *We didn't always get what we wanted.*

With a sigh, I returned the carafe to the coffeepot and added creamer and sugar to my mug until it was almost beige and chewy. I held the mug in my chilly hands and sipped carefully, watching the second hand with reluctance. It ticked over far too fast, and I marched down the hallway and knocked on my boss's office door.

"Come in," his voice carried through.

One more deep exhale as I centered myself for the next innocent face, who wasn't aware of the danger she'd signed up for, and I pushed through the door. My boss sat upright at his desk. His gray comb-over needed a fresh styling, his silvery mustache was just a hair too long over his upper lip, and the cheery smile on his face only enhanced the need for a trim. I followed his excited gaze to my new partner.

According to my dad, I was destined to become a medical researcher like him. Of course, that wasn't going to happen now—R.I.P. med school—but there had been a few classes, biology specifically, where I did exceptionally well. I'd spent copious amounts of time in solitude with my microscope, watching an entire ecosystem too tiny to see with the naked eye. Organic chemistry could take a flying leap off a bridge for all I cared, among other subjects. Despite my many shortcomings, I definitely did *not* do arts, as my graded-on-a-curve doodles proved, and with my regular spikes of anxiety, I certainly did *not* do performance arts. As my jaw fell, I almost dropped my coffee. Like, literally.

Sitting in the chair across from my boss, who gracefully rose to introduce himself, my new partner wore department-issued blue polo and dark wash jeans, which was so strange to see, considering I'd only ever seen him naked or in a suit. And right now, all I could see standing before me was the naked man holding a breakfast tray adorned with a red rose. I barked in disbelief, "Oliver?"

My boyfriend looked at me like I was a stranger, except for the tiniest sly smile lifting one corner of his mouth. With hands fastened behind his back and shoulders squared, he stood bright-eyed and at-attention. One, how did he beat me down here? And two, he had no medical training, unless he counted his extensive experience puncturing carotid arteries...with his teeth.

I glanced at my cooling mug and then blinked. Had someone spiked the coffee? "Are you sure he's the right fit?"

My boss's brows rose eagerly, wrinkling his forehead. "Excellent. You've already met. Well, as I'm sure you're aware, he has an impressive resume. He joins us from Midwest Ambulance Station Four in Milwaukee, and his vast experience in the big city will be invaluable to our small town. Daisy, give our new team member a warm welcome."

I intended to protest further, but I couldn't properly put into words just how unqualified for the position Oliver Rockwell was without answering questions I didn't want to answer. And if Oliver had used me as a reference, I didn't want my reputation to be tarnished for two reasons. One—the pesky mortgage and two, the gut-punching student loans with their hands out.

Oliver tipped out his elbow for me to take, and out of habit, I cupped my hand around his strong forearm. He led us out of my boss's office, and I closed it behind us. Without a word, I dragged Oliver into a nearby closet for privacy. Shutting us inside, I spun around to face him. "You compelled him, didn't you?"

Oliver tapped his temples, confirming my suspicion. "Comes in handy."

He reached for my hand, but I pulled back. "You can't do this."

"Daisy, you'd said Kayla was in direct danger as your partner, and if dopey out there hired another Kayla to be at your side, I couldn't live with myself if something happened to you."

I couldn't believe this. Not only was he inserting himself into my professional life, but he assumed I was incapable of handling my job, a job he wasn't qualified for in the slightest. "I don't need a babysitter. What I need is a partner with medical training. You actually need to save lives here."

"My blood heals."

I gritted my teeth at the obvious problem, one that hadn't occurred to me with all the other angry noises in my head. "We have a massive conflict of interest."

Oliver folded his arms across his chest, taking offense. "I'm a grown adult with more self-control than humans—comes with age...and practice. I'm here to protect you."

I trusted Oliver. I loved him, but my ethics couldn't allow me to accept this. "From what? Your brother skipped town, and Mr. Reed is dead. I'm sure my dad is back to his normal research, which I'll confirm at his dinner. All of that is over now." I wanted to believe my words, but I didn't.

Oliver gave me a pointed look. "As long as vampires and elves exist, and Pierce is sniffing around, you're not truly safe. I'm the best bodyguard you could have."

A bodyguard could follow me around with an app. "I don't have a paramedic's license, and neither do you."

"Let me join you on one call, and if you aren't satisfied with my...performance...I'll quit, and you can petition the boss for someone qualified."

I squinted at his terms. "According to your resume, you're the most qualified candidate we've had."

Oliver tapped his temples again. The vampire could make my boss forget. I sighed. It wasn't fair of me to claim to trust him and then fight him on his word. Frustration poured through me, and I lifted my index finger in the air. "Just once."

"Deal." Oliver smiled and observed the cramped quarters. "This is a quiet closet, and look, the door has a lock."

"We're at work," I said as a knee-jerk reaction, still annoyed by this whole situation. Kevin and Megan made good use of the private areas of the emergency department, likely this very closet, but as much as I envied her at the time, I wasn't in the mood now.

"And there's nothing going on this minute. Just you and me and complete privacy." His beautiful eyes called to me. Since they didn't morph into a bright cherry red, he wasn't using compulsion on me. He promised he would never again.

Oliver's hands rested on my shoulders and slid down my back, drawing me closer. A shiver of nerves followed in his wake. I closed my eyes, and Oliver's lips found my sensitive ear. A tiny moan escaped my lips, and my mind conjured all sorts of desirable imagery involving his hands, his lips, and my thundering heart. My boyfriend, eager to get out of the doghouse, leaned in close, nose touching mine, lips pleading.

I wanted to give in, to feel the exhilaration of not getting caught, but Oliver hadn't rebalanced the scales yet. I pressed my finger against his lips, stopping him just as the overhead alarm sounded, and I leaned toward the door to hear the unit called. "That's us. Time to go and bring that A-game of yours."

"I wish I cooled off as fast as you," Oliver grumbled and adjusted himself.

"And that's why at work we keep things on ice."

I rushed out of the closet and down the corridor to the garage. Maybe now he'd get the hint. Just because we were spending copious amounts of time together for one call, we didn't have freedom from responsibilities. I still didn't know what Oliver did to manage his carefree and extravagant lifestyle, but clearly, he hadn't survived on wages in a long time, if ever.

I reached the rig's cab, but Oliver's butt was already in my driver's seat. I had to admit, his super speed was a useful benefit. "Oh, I don't think so. Move over."

His hands caressed the steering wheel forlornly. "One call was our deal, so this might be my only chance to drive this...this boxy beast of a thing. It's not my style, obviously, but I'm shaking with curiosity and delight." Oliver lifted a hand to show me. It did tremble.

"You can compel someone to let you drive anytime you want." I paused, rethinking the idea. "But not me, and not now."

"Whose free will should I alter for a little joyride?"

I sighed and marched around to the passenger seat. His excitement was infectious, but I bit back a smile. I had to be the levelheaded one. Lives were at stake, and I was in charge. I buckled in and handed him the rig's keys. "This isn't your Shelby. No sharp corners, and the rig's slower to stop."

"Duly noted." Oliver flipped on the sirens and lights with a goofy grin. "Always wanted to do that."

I glanced out the side window and used my hand to block my smile, pretending to scratch. Oliver was too cute. Frustrating as hell, but damned cute sometimes. He steered us through traffic, headed toward the address. Once I swallowed back the contagious smile, I asked, "If you've always wanted to drive this thing, why haven't you yet?"

Eyes on the road, Oliver said, "I don't take enjoyment from altering people's minds. It's frustrating when you forget who knows what. Remembering the lies you tell is exhausting, and correcting them only makes it worse. So I only use my compulsion when necessary." From what I'd seen of him, that was the truth. "And two, I didn't want to get caught in a real emergency situation without knowing the person at my side was capable." Oliver faced me and winked.

Heat rushed up my face. No pressure or anything. "Fair enough."

Oliver parked the ambo at the curb on the scene. Streetlights cast an eerie shadow across the field of tall grasses in front of a humming factory. We climbed out, and I carried equipment with me. There were no witnesses waving for our attention, and the victim wasn't standing up with her own flag either. We would need hours to search, or... I lifted the radio at my shoulder and pressed the call button. "Control, this is unit 9B on scene. We're going to need a K-9 unit to find the victim in this field."

"Standby," control relayed.

Oliver waved and shook his head.

"What?" I asked.

"Not necessary."

With an arched brow, I pressed the button. "Scratch that last request. Thanks." I looked at my partner for an explanation. "How are we going to find her?"

Oliver sent me a smug smile. "Easy. Follow me." Oliver vanished into the field.

"Show off," I grumbled under my breath. I wished I had that speed. It could be the difference between life and death in some cases. I grabbed the stretcher from the back and scanned the darkened field. Oliver's hands waved in the air about thirty yards away. I trudged through the uneven field, and Oliver rushed to my side to assist. I set the stretcher aside and approached the patient.

A woman about twenty years of age, wearing tight jogging clothes, sprawled on a patch of bent grass. I kneeled to assess the patient further. "Miss, can you hear me? Can you tell me your name?"

She didn't respond. My instincts told me to check her neck first. With a guilty glance at Oliver, I swiped away her thick ponytail. I found fang punctures with rivulets of blood running toward the ground. I checked her pulse as a formality, but she was already cold. Drained. Like the victim, my blood chilled.

If this wasn't Soren, we had another vampire on the loose. I stood up and asked the obvious of my new partner. "Did you follow the scent of her blood?"

"Didn't need to." Oliver gestured toward a tree, where a forty-something man wobbled over, wild-eyed and face drawn with distress. He wore jeans and a T-shirt, and in his hand was a disposable shopping bag. Unlikely to be the guilty party, he had to be a witness. Finally!

The witness, shaking with fear, stopped to see the victim. "You should've seen it. You won't believe me."

I bet I would.

"I was minding my own business when this woman came out of nowhere and buddied up next to her." He gestured to the victim. "I didn't think anything of it at first. You know, like they were friends or something, but the woman—perpetrator, the perp. You call her the perp, right?" Without an answer, the witness kept going. "She dragged this lady off the sidewalk by the neck. The neck! Who does that? She didn't scream or fight back, but it didn't look innocent either. So I yelled, you know, to save the damsel in distress, and the attacker ran off. A *woman* attacked this lady, and now she's running loose. Why didn't they send the cops yet? Why aren't you putting her on the cart? She's not... She's not de...?" he trailed off and pressed a fist to his mouth, unable to finish the obvious last word.

Dead.

This witness had no introduction to the hidden world. What could I possibly say to convince the guy it was an animal attack? "Can you describe the attacker, this woman?"

"Uh, yeah. Tall, thin. Her clothes were mismatched and didn't fit her right. Wild hair, like she slept in the woods. We don't have a homeless problem here. There are plenty of beds in the shelters—ask me how I know. Young though, early twenties? Late teens even? Was it drugs? It was drugs, wasn't it?"

Oliver approached the man and touched his shoulder for comfort. "Look at me."

The witness hadn't given his story to the police yet—for whatever that was worth. Still, he deserved to keep his full mind. "Oliver, you said you weren't going to do that unless absolutely necessary."

"We can't allow him to tell this story. Trust me. It's not something to gamble on."

Remembering what it was like to have my own memories returned, and realizing I had no control over many decisions, I reached for Oliver's arm. "You can't take away his free will."

"What?" the witness asked softly. "What are you talking about?"

Oliver ignored him. "You know what it's like to have it happen to you."

"Of course." I didn't know any different at the time, but afterward it had been a violation worse than any other.

"Then you know you're completely oblivious. No harm done."

After having my own memories tampered with several times—both by vampires and elves, and how many more I didn't know about yet—deliberately watching a man have his mind messed with was something I couldn't turn my back on. "There is harm, even if he doesn't know it until it's lifted—"

"It won't be," Oliver pressed. "Compulsion doesn't go away unless the vampire responsible releases it on purpose or dies. Or if the human in question becomes a vampire or a witch." Oliver eyed the guy critically. "I'm not going to release it."

And Oliver would never die. Now was not the time to be reminded of how short our time was. Pulling myself from that downhill mudslide, I recalled a contradiction. "How did I break free from Pierce's?"

"Elf compulsion isn't as strong."

That didn't answer the question, nor was it relevant to the witness. "From personal experience with the police, they aren't going to believe his story, anyway."

"From personal experience," Oliver mimicked, "when too many humans find out the truth, the consequences will be dire. With witches and elves lurking around, having another out-of-control vampire around is too big of a risk."

"Vampires? Elves?" the witness's voice rose with panic. "What are you talking about? There's a lady there who needs help! Why are you talking about comic-book stuff? Help her!" The man raked a hand through his disheveled hair and stared, on the verge of tears. Leaving him in this state would, at the minimum, get his police report torn up, like mine had been. I couldn't imagine the worst-case scenario that had Oliver spooked.

"Fine. Do it," I said, folding my arms over my chest, wondering if his blatant exposure of the hidden world was on purpose.

Oliver nodded, and he turned to the witness. "Look at me. What's your name?"

"Uh, Jared."

"Alright, Jared, I need you to look at me." The man did, and Oliver smiled. "You never saw any attack. You were walking home from the store and dropped your keys, but you found them. Go home."

Jared blinked and looked around. He smiled awkwardly. "I, uh, just lost my keys, but hey, I found them. I have to go home." He turned on his heel without a glance toward the victim and scooted back to the sidewalk.

Just like that, his mind wasn't his own. I sighed and then focused on the patient. Our dead patient. "Jared said the attacker was a woman, so at least we know Soren is innocent this time. Do you recognize his description?"

Oliver looked at the body. "She's just like all the others."

"She? My victim?" I followed his gaze to the jogger with the throat bitten out. Reminded me a little too much of myself.

"Soren didn't attack your victims. He was hunting the vampire responsible."

Since Oliver didn't name her, I had to know who she was. My known vampire list was very short—the disheveled woman in the lab, who drank Newt's blood for the cure of the vampire weapon, and escaped. Oliver's ex. "Evangeline?"

"You'd think after forty years of experimentation, she'd make a run back to Europe while she had the chance. Seems like she isn't ready to leave town yet."

"I'm afraid to ask what she wants."

Oliver collected my hand in his. "Me, too."

Sirens finally grew as they approached. I turned my head in their direction. "Are you going to compel all of them, too?" My tone was sharp and a little snarkier than I'd planned, but messing in someone's head felt so wrong.

"You remember the story I told you about the Peshtigo fire of 1871?"

Oliver had said the devastating fire was a punishment for witches and their heathen ways. But my roommate, Jamie Harris, had said witches were hunting vampires, and the fire got out of control. All I knew for sure was that many people had died, and the truth was buried with the bodies. "What does that have to do with this?"

"If too many humans become aware of the hidden world, knowing they're not at the top of the food chain sends them into a panic. Picture our friend Jared with a stake and a gun, less confused and more angry. Now picture dozens just like him. Chaos ensues. A growing group of humans in the throes of fear can and will do stupid things, like attack and kill those who are different from them, who they perceive to be a threat."

Vampires were a threat, but I didn't bother pointing that out. The trickle truth of history annoyed me. "Are you saying *humans* hunted both vampires and witches, and *that* led to the fire?"

"I was a human at the time, turned that night, but I pieced together the truth over the years while seeking my sun ring." He held up his ring-adorned hand. "Which I still very much appreciate. Thank you."

Warmth filled my chest, but I brushed it aside. I needed to know the truth. I made a motion with my hand to get him talking.

"The witches from Peshtigo and Marinette heard stories of vampire carnage, and together, they trapped a handful of nearby vampires. Deep in the woods of Peshtigo, the witches intended to burn them alive. When a couple of humans thought they saw heathen witches preparing to burn fellow humans, they amassed a pitchfork crew and intervened, freeing the vampires. It was a dirty battle. If it weren't for the fire and the strength of the witches' spells, the vampires would've slaughtered them all. Instead, humans, vampires, and witches perished as the drought caused the fire to get out of hand."

A vampire hunt gone wrong because of a misconception. Still, I had questions. "But no one recorded any vampire bodies. Your fangs are still teeth. They would've survived the blaze."

"Like sunlight, fire turns us to ash—teeth and clothing included. That's why witches insist on burning us instead of staking. No trace to be discovered. Vampires and witches have feuded since the dawn of vampirism. Elves tend to stay out of it, but witches will interfere with their lifestyle, so sometimes elves get their hands dirty. At all costs, we have to prevent a repeat of the pitchfork crew."

A police car rolled to a stop at the curb, blue and red lights flashing in the area. A pair of officers stepped out of their vehicle and approached.

"You're going to smooth this over too," I said as a statement with only a hint of question, as if pleading for him to leave these officers' minds alone, but I knew he couldn't.

"As I said, only when necessary." Oliver turned away from me and approached the woman and man team. "We've got a single female here, victim of a dog attack."

"We received a call. It was a woman attacking another," the man said, shining his flashlight in Oliver's face. "Where's the witness?"

Oliver shielded his sensitive eyes from the direct light. "It was a dog. The witness was blitzed out of his mind. Trust me, I'm the paramedic."

The woman officer shifted her hand to her hip, hovering over her pistol. "Of course, there's another dog attack," the woman said, scanning the area. "We never caught the dog."

And they never would.

# 3

# Facing the Evil

**Oliver**

I WAS STILL ITCHING from that awful polo I'd worn. Clothing manufacturers should be ashamed of themselves for subjecting people to that torture. Technically, that broke my first rule, but since people wore that material voluntarily, it got a pass. Now I could be myself, because a dinner invitation wasn't complete without a suit. My white dress shirt was unbuttoned at the throat and tie-free—about as casual as I was comfortable being.

Except I wasn't comfortable at all strolling up the pathway to Dr. Greg Barrett's house. We didn't have a great history, and Daisy on my arm seemed nervous. Regardless of the cause, I wanted her to relax. "You're beautiful."

She wore a pretty little black dress with the vervain and black nightshade necklace around her throat. Her brown waves cascaded around her shoulders. The sides were pulled back to expose her ears...and throat. She was so tempting, so stunning. I wanted to strip her down and take her right now. My cock tightened my pants.

"And you look just like yourself, handsome as ever." Daisy trembled beside me. I knew she yearned to see her sister again, but family drama had always been the bane of my existence. Except squabbles over politics were no match for developing a weapon designed to kill me and my kind. No matter how much the doctor might apologize, I could never forgive him. Just standing on his porch made me want to tear the door off its hinges and shred the man's throat. Instead, I swallowed my pride and smiled at Daisy like a proper gentleman.

I would do anything for her except walk away, leaving her vulnerable to manipulation, mistreatment, and danger. And that suited me just fine, because I loved her more than seeing the sunrise for the first time in almost two centuries, more than the finest top-shelf tequila, or my 1967 candy apple Shelby. Daisy was my everything. I would watch over her and protect her for all of her natural life.

Night had settled upon the city, and when Dr. Greg Barrett answered the door, warm light spilled over our feet. The last time we'd seen each other, I'd been frantically looking for Daisy, and he'd called me the scourge of the world and kicked me off his property. Clearly, he wasn't as afraid of me as he had been of Newt. But the witch had a flair for controlling people.

I had a different kind of flair.

Greg's friendly smile and proud chest had me baffled. He wore trousers and a short-sleeved button-up. He wasn't threatening in the slightest, but I couldn't trust him. "Come in, come in. I'm glad you could make it. You too, Oliver, welcome inside."

Even though I'd been included on the text invite, hearing a human knowingly invite me inside was so—foreign. I slowly reached my fingers toward the doorway, and the barrier had been dropped. Cautiously, I led Daisy inside and lifted my brows at the unexpected quality in the Barrett household. The floors were brushed tile, and above was a dangling fixture popular two decades ago. The entry table held photographs, which I wanted time to inspect, but her dad ushered us into a sitting room to the left. A tray of glasses, waiting to be filled and served, rested on an oak coffee table with storage underneath. On either side of the table were a couch and a pair of recliners, all of them clean and in new condition, and all of it a matching set. After seeing Daisy's eclectic mix of home furnishings, I didn't expect the visually impaired lab monkey to have a tasteful eye—even if his choices were dated now. I was the last person to judge the age of one's possessions.

I couldn't capture the scent or sound of a meal in preparation. I reached out with my heightened senses, seeking additional heartbeats or murmurs of people moving around, and I was certain we were the only ones here.

As if reading my mind, Daisy asked, "Is anyone else coming?"

"Just the three of us," Greg said, and gestured to the couch.

Ignoring the invitation, Daisy stiffened, and her face fell. "Lily's not coming?"

"I invited you here because I have a serious matter to discuss with you. Please have a seat."

Daisy didn't budge, and I stayed by her side. "You used Lily as a carrot on a string?" Daisy asked with an edge to her voice. "How could you?"

"Please sit, kitten. All will be explained in due time." The fake-friendly smile on his face angered me, and I cringed at the patronizing and offensive nickname. She wasn't small, harmless, or anyone's pet, but it said more about him than her. The more I learned about the man, the more I disliked him.

After a few seconds' staring contest, Daisy tugged me over to the couch, and we sat together. In front of us, the tray of drinks appeared innocuous, but had the scientist sprinkled in a special herb?

"Then start talking," she said.

Greg clapped his hands together as if excited for a presentation, and he tugged at his pants before sitting in a recliner across from us. "You'll be pleased to hear Mr. Reed's mess at PDI was taken care of. The official story is that a drunk ex-employee wanted revenge for being fired. The security guard didn't remember doing his job, which was chalked up to post-traumatic stress disorder. Like I said, no cameras." Greg smirked. He'd always known nefarious things happened behind those closed doors. My blood boiled at his depravity, and I wanted to punch the smug smile off his callous face. "Mr. Reed had been added to the employee database just in time to pass the story, and the brave young soul was commended for his efforts."

"That's a relief," Daisy said dryly.

I darted the man a warning glare. He had done us a minor favor by keeping the events under wraps, but he'd harmed his own daughter. Any decent father would've begged forgiveness immediately, but Greg's priorities were not the same as mine.

Perhaps I could prompt a heartfelt apology for her sake. Swallowing my pride, I said politely, "Thank you for taking care of the situation, Dr. Barrett. I'm sure your experiments have taught you that, like humans, vampires only want to live our own lives. Vampires agreed to remain in secret while doing the least harm possible, but like humans, there's always the rogue exception." The slightest change in Greg's face caught my eye, but it wasn't readable. "I'll admit that in the past, maintaining anonymity was a struggle, but with the advent of blood banks, we can peacefully coexist."

Daisy squeezed my hand in support.

Greg leaned back in the recliner across from us. Tension radiated from him. He steepled his fingers and made eye contact with us both before responding. "Every morning I woke up thinking the world was good and kind." He smiled superficially, and I happened to notice the use of the past tense. He gestured to Daisy, recognizing her still-present beliefs. Those were the things I loved most about her—that endless optimism and belief in second chances.

Look at me, I thought, giving this animal a second chance. Daisy was a good influence on my baser desires.

"I chose medical research," he continued, "because I didn't have an interest in maintaining a bedside facade for patients, but that didn't mean I lacked compassion. On the contrary, I dedicated my life to discovering new treatments to save lives or to make their struggles easier, more manageable. I could do more for people behind a microscope than holding their hand in a hospital bed." Greg leaned forward and knitted his fingers together.

"No one's faulting you for that, Dad," Daisy said. "I hold your beliefs in the highest esteem, too."

Daisy left the door wide open for her father to compliment her or apologize. I waited patiently with low expectations.

Another fake smile bent his lips. "That all changed when I met a man."

Baser desires told me to rip his throat out before he hurt her further, but I refrained. Barely. The things we put up with for the sake of family.

"With a flick of the wrist and some proof, of course, of his radical claims, this man opened my eyes to a world I never imagined real. He made me an offer I couldn't refuse—until I did, and we know how that turned out."

What kind of husband could be so dismissive of his wife's murder? Of the pain he inflicted on his daughter? I tensed, fighting back the urge to inflict great bodily harm.

I hadn't eaten for a while, and my bag-only preference was simply that—a preference.

Greg leaned forward and poured the amber liquid into the trio of glasses. "But that's all in the past. I'm back in control of my lab, and I'm going to continue working at PDI, saving patients from a different kind of threat to their health."

Once Newt had died, post-spell clarity should've caused Greg to wallow in guilt, change careers, or at a minimum, change employers to attempt to bury all the dark-and-dirty the lab had done. Finding out the face in the mirror had tortured people wasn't so easy to swallow. Dr. Greg Barrett seemed in very high spirits as he handed me a glass.

Never one to pass up a free drink, I reluctantly accepted. Greg handed Daisy a glass, too. Instinctively, I wanted to slap it away. Daisy sniffed before tasting, like she was just as skeptical and hesitant as I was, and I couldn't be prouder of her awareness.

To draw attention away from her uncertainty, I said to Greg, "Where you work is your own decision, which doesn't require a collective agreement. Since not only is there no Lily, but there's no dinner, tell me why you insisted on this meeting tonight."

Daisy squeezed my arm. I took it to mean she agreed with my haste.

Greg lifted one ankle and rested on the other knee. The casualness of his posture was incongruent with the whole evening. "Witches, like Mr. Reed, have a bone to pick with your species, and I don't know why. Please do help me understand."

"It's a long story," I said dismissively and declined to elaborate. His loyalties clearly remained with the witches. Even if I wanted to tell him the tale, he wouldn't change his mind.

After a long pause, Greg got the hint. "Well, since you insist on cutting our evening short, I asked you here tonight because I wanted to ease your concerns over my new direction. Daisy,

I can see you care deeply for Oliver here, so I wanted you both to know I will no longer be working on the vampire serum."

That was...pleasantly surprising. Maybe I'd been wrong about him all this time. No wonder Daisy was always so frustrated with him. I couldn't read him either. I lifted my untouched glass in a toast. "That's certainly good news. To new beginnings."

Greg raised his, followed by Daisy. While they both sipped, Daisy watched me as I tasted my drink. Mid-shelf bourbon. Not bad. I shared a reassuring look with Daisy and tuned into my body, just in case, but nothing adverse happened. No tingling or sharp pains. I shrugged, letting her know I was fine, and I swallowed down the rest, unwilling to let any liquor go to waste. Eased the craving to rip out his throat.

"Wait, you considered continuing the work on the serum?" Daisy asked.

"I decided carefully after a thorough analysis." He sipped again.

I wasn't a fan of his needing such a long time to decide not to murder my kind. Daisy slammed down the rest of her drink, and I didn't blame her. This was the quietest, most awkward roller coaster ride I'd been on.

Greg set his nearly full glass down on the tray. "Before we conclude this meeting, there is one more thing I need you to know, Daisy."

She returned her empty glass next to his and licked her lips. "What's that?"

"To protect your mother, I used her blood for the base of the weapon's recipe. Because of her immense value to the witch's plan, Mr. Reed only planned to torture her until I complied."

Daisy worked over the words. "Only torture? So her death was an accident?"

"Mr. Reed gave his orders, but somehow the vampires killed her. As much as I've grown fond of your fanged friend here, you carry within your veins your mother's blood."

I tensed, and I didn't believe he understood the word 'fond'. "Daisy's blood is the same—the base of the weapon."

Greg nodded as if proud I understood Daisy's danger. "Now you see, kitten, why *every* vampire will be hunting you."

Unlike scratchy polyester, I couldn't let this deliberate, disgusting break of my first rule go unpunished. Leaning forward in clear warning, I set my empty glass on the coffee table and exhaled. Greg shifted his legs and leaned forward, mirroring my posture, and I almost laughed. If the elder Barrett intended to fight, he had no chance against me at all, and I didn't figure the doctor to be suicidal.

We stared at each other in silent challenge, as if waiting for Daisy to give the go-ahead. I hadn't been more excited for a meal in a long while. Because of our great difference in strength, I'd allow the human the first move. Was it out of fairness? Nah. Was I being gentlemanly? Nah. Waiting for the attack made the fight much more pleasurable—for the short while it would last. As I waited, I ground my teeth together to release the tension.

The doctor blinked first, and while he reached into the coffee table's storage cabinet, I smirked in satisfaction. Greg retrieved a pistol and pointed it at my chest. A few good stings would only make the fight more fun. The idiot human knew that wouldn't kill me, only anger me uncontrollably, and I didn't want to get blood splatter on Daisy's cocktail dress. He was never considerate of his own daughter.

Shame.

Daisy gasped and yelled, "Dad, no!"

But Greg's sloppy aim had me shifting into defense. He squeezed the trigger, but I was faster. I shifted toward Daisy, covering her with my body, and the bullet only skimmed my biceps, a small, hot graze. It blew through the couch and *thumped* into the drywall behind us.

Daisy gripped my suit jacket tightly in her fist. "Dad...? What...? What's wrong with you?"

I was practicing the art of patience. I gritted my teeth and said, "Being in our world means you knew that wouldn't kill me. You ruined perfectly good wool, and you deliberately risked Daisy's life...again. Now I'm cranky."

Greg made no motion to flee for his own life, but he set the gun down on the table. Since he'd prepared this situation ahead of time, he must've prepared to die—suicide by vampire. Not original, but effective. Still, for all his bravado, it didn't make sense. I inhaled and counted to ten, not because I needed to breathe, but I found it to be a great calming exercise. If I didn't relax, Greg's death wouldn't be clean, and I didn't want to traumatize Daisy for life. My upper lip twitched.

Daisy scrambled for my flesh wound, fastening her palms over it. Her hand sprung back as if it stung her.

"What is it?" I asked.

She showed me her fingers coated in my blood, and she gripped my uninjured arm. "I know what you're thinking. I know you're mad. Please don't kill him. I can reason with him. Please."

Greg rose. "I'm sure you're dying to tear out my throat."

Damned right. I smirked, rising to meet the challenge. Greg collected the pistol once more, as if that would help him any.

Daisy leaped up and pressed her hands against my chest. She knew who the victor would be, and I appreciated her confidence. "Stop. Stop this. Dad, we can figure out a way to coexist, like Oliver said." She gazed into my eyes, pleading for mercy.

The barrel in his hand still aimed at me, regardless of Daisy's precarious position. I moved her to the side and gave her a quick squeeze, acknowledging her plea. He and I were beyond coexisting, but I would spare Daisy the sight of it and relish the hunt later.

Greg glared at me. "Witches inherently destroy vampires, and from the little I'd gleaned, elves aren't your friend either. So, I don't understand why you and Pierce have a truce or why you bother to stay in town. Either way, that's none of my business."

Finally, something we agreed on.

"But to finish what I said, I will no longer be working on the vampire serum, not because I've had a change of heart." Greg paused and smiled at his daughter. "No, I stopped because it's already perfect. You'll thank me later, kitten."

With a soft gasp, Daisy dragged me from the living room as if knowing how much danger I posed.

She had no idea.

# 4
# Avoiding the Monster

**Daisy**

Oliver parked the Shelby at the curb of his impressive house and walked alongside me up the pathway. An expected family dinner with drinks and apologies became an interrogation and attempted murder. Dad believed Oliver was a danger to me only because my dad made the vampire weapon from my mother's blood—my blood. But Oliver Rockwell was my love, my protector. He was stronger and faster than a human, and he'd never let anyone harm me. I trusted him. Rather than respect my relationship and trust Oliver too, my dad shot him in protest. All that did was anger Oliver and confirm my dad hated vampires.

I guess that meant holiday gatherings with family were out of the question now.

I rubbed my bare arms under the crisp blanket of nighttime stars, wishing to have Mom back. Stacey Barrett hadn't been home much, but as a successful real estate agent with her smiling face on billboards around town, she was an independent powerhouse of class and style. And she was cold, factual. She would have known what to do, but because of Dad, she was dead. Now, because of another mistake he made, keeping Dad alive from Oliver would be the biggest challenge of my life.

We stepped into the cozy light of the bed-and-breakfast, and Oliver headed straight for the bar. I could use another too.

Oliver shucked his suit jacket. "Dr. Barrett put a hole through my suit and dress shirt." Oliver fingered the coat damage and tossed it on the bar. "Flying my tailor up for a repair is no simple feat. The man is immune to the money I throw at him, and he rambles about his time being limited. I already knew your father hated me. There was no reason for this at all." Oliver poured himself tequila and used a fang to punch a hole in a blood bag to mix it. "You want one?"

"I'll take the clear half, thank you."

Oliver poured me a half a shot of tequila with a fresh slice of lime, set it on a coaster, and pushed it to me. Oliver drank down his red mixture and sighed with pleasure. I loved that sound. I sipped the drink he'd made me.

Holding the empty glass, Oliver pointed at his ruined suit jacket. "I should send your father the bill. Might give the old man a heart attack and let me off the hook."

I couldn't help it. I chuckled. Then I felt guilty for the damage my dad had caused. "I can replace it for you." Somehow.

Oliver smiled sweetly. "Thank you for offering, but it's not your mess to fix. Besides, it's only one of many suits. It's just the principle."

Great, because I didn't know which bill I'd have to skip to cover it, because like Dad, I didn't know how much custom-tailored suits cost either.

"I don't know what's going to happen, Daisy." Oliver set down his empty glass and approached me. "But I'll do my best to keep your father at arm's length. If he were anyone else, he wouldn't be breathing."

"I know." I couldn't imagine how frustrated Oliver was. He needed a distraction. "Let's go upstairs."

"I like your thinking."

We climbed up to his bedroom. I set my purse down and kicked off my heels. I pulled him toward me and unfastened a button near his smooth pecs. His restraint in the face of insult and literal injury was hot. He deserved to know how much I appreciated him. I reached for the next button and kissed the side of his neck—where he liked it most.

Oliver smiled. "What was that for?"

I freed another button. "I'll admit I had concerns about your lack of training, but your vampire skills can be handy. My worries were unfounded." Especially after the restraint he'd shown tonight.

Oliver smiled deviously. "So I passed the one-call test?"

With a lusty curve of my lips, feeling extra spicy in my little black dress, I said, "I would be proud to have you as my partner, and I was wrong to judge you."

"I haven't stayed alive for a hundred and eighty years by snacking on everything that moved, not that I wasn't tempted. Right now, something else is far more enticing." Oliver's lips found mine, and he kissed me with all the urgency and passion of our first time—when he'd pushed me up against my front door, and I'd wrapped my legs around him, feverishly needing to have him naked. At the time, I didn't know just how skilled he was. But I did now, and I shuddered with need.

As his hands moved over my body, my heart fluttered, and I reached for the next button on his shirt, moving faster and faster to expose his beautiful skin for my eyes to drink him in. Oliver's sweet lips found my neck. My pulse thundered along my veins, and my breaths came in shallow pants.

I slipped my hands along his strong arms, urging him closer, and Oliver sucked in a breath when I grazed his wound. I pulled back and frowned at the blood on my finger. "Shouldn't that be healed already?"

Oliver finished unbuttoning his shirt and flung it to the floor. Averting my hungry eyes from his luscious pecs, I frowned at a concerning bloody trickle down his biceps that marred his perfect skin.

"When I haven't fed on the fresh stuff for a while, all my abilities, healing included, aren't up to par. I should probably..." Oliver met my gaze with a hint of shame. That meant he had to find an unwilling participant. Oliver wasn't a monster, but sometimes he had to do monstrous things for survival, and I hated it. I'd been bitten. It hurt, and the paralytic was terrifying, but I wasn't going to volunteer, even to save someone else the dreaded experience. Call me selfish—I called it self-preservation.

I gave him a soft smile of understanding, allowing him to do what his nature demanded, hoping he'd be able to control that need. "I'll be going. I just hope we don't get a call about a dog attack tonight." I sent him a sardonic smile.

"Daisy, I'm more worried about you." Oliver stopped my disappointed retreat with a gentle hand on my arm. "Your father fired a gun a few feet from you and continued aiming in my direction. He claimed he doesn't want your life in danger, but knowing human coordination and eyesight, that was very risky."

"When I was ten years old, he bought me my first microscope. I looked at dirt and bugs for hours. A few months later, I got my own lab coat, and Dad never smiled at me more. When we weren't prepping cultures, Dad was reading industry articles and studies." I pointed at Oliver's wound. "This isn't the Dr. Greg Barrett I've always known. I'm positive he never held a gun before, let alone shot one. He's just not the type."

"That's worse."

"I don't know where he got the gun either. Is it possible after Newt had died, another witch stepped up to play puppeteer?" The idea left a rock in my gut, but Oliver's concern about my dad's out-of-character action was valid.

"I wouldn't be able to tell." Oliver's eyes glowed red for a long moment. The hunger intensified.

"I...I...should be going." Guilt tore through me. We could be having sweet, sweet sex, but instead, he had to run off into the darkness and feed. I shivered at the memory of a vampire feeding on me, but at least Oliver was more refined than his brother.

Knowing how much my dad hated my boyfriend for no reason other than what he was, angered me. Dad wasn't exactly Father-of-the-Year or anything. He had no right to judge. And that he lied to me about Lily to get me to show up in the first place... And that he invited Oliver with the intent of harming him... I should've known he was up to something. "Look, my dad crossed a line that can't be forgiven. After you heal up, we'll figure out this thing together. In the meantime, I'm not going to talk to him again. Okay?"

Oliver gave me a hard stare. "I can never forgive him for what he's done to you or my kind, and I hate that there is such contempt between us, but you can't turn your back on family. Second chances, remember? I'm the one causing this wedge between you. If I weren't here—if you'd never met me—you and Lily and your dad could be a happy family."

I didn't like the sound of that. I shook my head. "No, no, no, you're not doing this. That alternative—the 'what if' you painted—was never possible. If you want to throw blame, it's Newt's for tangling my dad in this mess in the first place. And because of that witch, there will never be a happy family for me—not after what Dad's done, not just to you, but to me, my sister, and my mom. My dad destroyed my family. You're all I have left, and you didn't do anything wrong." Tears threatened to wash over my eyes.

"Daisy—" Oliver's fingers tipped my chin up. "I'm not innocent. He has the right to hate my kind. You don't need to defend me. I've hurt plenty of people."

Okay, yes, he was a vampire, and his bite—the bite necessary for survival—did *hurt*. "But you've never killed anyone, while Dad deliberately tried to." I didn't know why I was comparing them, but I felt the urge to defend Oliver. "I distinctly remember Pierce shot Newt to death, and the basketball player was already dead. You stopped him from attacking me and Megan as a vampire in transition."

Pain behind his eyes broke my heart. "I've killed many. If you want to debate which way the scale tips, it's no contest, truly."

My insides turned to jelly, and I tried pushing away the imagery of his vampire face attacking the throats of terrified people. I added, "For survival, though."

He shook his head. "Turning into a vampire leaves you struggling with extremes of all emotions and senses, like humanity times a hundred, but beyond that disabling life adjustment, the hunger is worse. Way worse. Remember when I told you I regretted that woman who found my family in the cave?"

"Yeah." They'd been turned by a vampire hiding in the cave during the Peshtigo fire, and since they didn't have sun rings, all the vampires, the Rockwells, stayed in the cave for nightfall, but a lone fire survivor, a woman, sought shelter with them, and Oliver's family attacked her.

"After transitioning, a baby vampire needs weeks to adjust to their new senses, and weeks for the emotions, too. But the hunger...that takes much more self-control than some vampires want to bother with. It's easier not to fight. Your dad isn't wrong about what he believes. He's not wrong about wanting to protect you from my kind. But I promise you I'd never hurt you or deliberately place you in harm's way, like he did."

I never knew Dad was capable of such a big, hateful speech, but one thing Dad had said bothered me. "Dad mentioned a truce between you and Pierce. My ex also mentioned it. What happened?" While my relationships tilted, I needed to know if I could trust Pierce Evansson, elusive yet ever-present ex-boyfriend, the elf.

Oliver sighed. "Are you sure you want to know?"

I had the feeling that everything he had to tell me was bad news. I braced myself. Nothing could be worse than what I'd dealt with already. "I do."

Oliver raked a hand through his gelled hair. "In the cave that day, with my worried family huddled around me, I woke up starving. Instinctively, I drank them down faster than they could understand what was happening, but Soren fought me. I did a number on him, and blood splattered. I turned my whole family by accident, my sister Sadie included."

My stomach sank. "Oh, I didn't know. I'm sorry."

"Forty years ago, Evan Logonson was hunting Evangeline Brant, but he found Sadie, and he slaughtered her like an animal."

"Pierce's dad?" Of course, he'd be an elf. The image of the old man running around trying to stake a vampire was just...weird. Pierce had never talked about his father. I hated knowing where this was going, but I couldn't let it drop. "And what did you do about it?"

"Do you want the official story or the truth?"

He was delaying the inevitable. It must be awful. "Truth."

"I drained him while he was on the toilet. I don't apologize for what I did. He deserved it. But Pierce found out, and he'd planned to kill Soren in retaliation. Soren might have issues—a lot of issues—but they exist because of me, and I couldn't live with myself knowing how much pain I caused my own brother. So, I offered a truce before we ran out of family members. As long as neither of us deliberately harms or places in harm's way the other's family, we maintain a precarious truce."

His words triggered a fuzzy memory. "Wait, Pierce's dad didn't die of a heart attack at Abby's wedding?" Supposedly, he was in excellent health for his age, considering he was an attorney at a large, stressful law firm. Pierce had been shady about questions afterward, but then again, dying on the toilet left one craving dignity and privacy. "If you killed him there, how could I not remember you?"

The corners of Oliver's lips lifted. "We met twice that night, actually." Oliver's fingers brushed my temple. "He erased me both times."

My hands curled into fists. "How many times has Pierce messed with my head? What else did I know that was taken from me?"

"Remember that terrible proposal at the park? You broke free from his compulsion then, and you can do it again by eliciting a heightened emotional state. Unfortunately, each episode unlocks only one layer of compulsion. And as you remember, it's not a pleasant process."

"It's a good thing he and I don't have a truce," I ground out through gritted teeth. Now I wanted to strangle Pierce with my own bare hands. I'd pinned a number of bugs for my microscope when I was younger. How much harder could it be?

Oliver chuckled. "If you want to kill the elf, count me in, but don't go all renegade on me. Promise?"

"I promise." I could never take a person's life, of course, but with the pumping anger in my system, the idea was certainly appealing.

Oliver winced again, and his eyes glowed ruby red. That was my cue to get out of here.

"I'm heading out. You take care of that wound." I leaned in and gave him a quick peck on the lips. "I'll see you tomorrow, partner."

Oliver pressed a hand over his wound, and a sad smile hung on his lips. I slipped on my shoes and collected my purse. After one final wave, I rushed down the stairs. Oliver didn't have much time left to feed before the need took over.

After I made myself scarce, Oliver's words repeated in my head. Everything Pierce and I had was a sham. He'd controlled everything about me and blinded me to the real world. I never wanted to see him again, and my life would be that much better for it.

Both Pierce and my dad were dead to me.

When Oliver was healed, he and I were going to wreck his bed, no apologies to Nicole Rockwell or the delivery company who'd trudge the replacement up the stairs. I had a serious case of lady blue balls, and nothing was going to satisfy me but Oliver himself.

For tonight, I was going to settle for another drink.

# 5

# The Secret

**Oliver**

I'D TRIED TO GENTLY remind Daisy that I was a bigger monster than her father could ever hope to be. Instead, she left upset with the elf—so not a total failure, but I needed Daisy to leave. Not because I was losing control—I wasn't capable of such weakness—but I didn't want to burden her with the grave concern on my mind. I could feel the trickling.

In the bathroom, I flipped on the light. The flesh wound was now raw and blistered. Regardless of whether I feasted at all, it should've healed on its own by now. I rinsed and inspected it. Still, it remained angry. In my hundred and eighty years, I'd never been injured with anything that didn't heal within moments, except once.

By 1883, I'd been waiting three years for Evangeline Brant to return to me from whatever soul scarching she'd needed. I finally admitted to myself that who I thought was the love of my life did not reciprocate, and she hadn't forgiven me for turning her. I was a monster, and I couldn't look at myself in the mirror. In a crisis of the existential variety, I'd boarded up the home I built for us and left Wisconsin. I needed a complete change of scenery to recharge my soul, and taking a pilgrimage south toward the warm salty air and breezy palm trees felt like the right move. I never made it that far.

The hunger was an inevitable beast of burden, inescapable and insatiable. It had to be fed. It had to be quieted. To prove to myself I wasn't the monster glaring at me in the mirror, I hunted wild animals. Shamefully, the rabbits were too quick for my despondent spirits, and for the trouble and humiliation, Mother Nature beat me down further.

A forgotten explosive device from the Civil War mutilated my foot and leg with a thunderous bang. Ears ringing, leg hanging on superhuman gristle, I dragged my battered body into a nearby abandoned mineshaft to shelter before sunrise. I propped myself up against the dry, uneven wall, listening to the flutters of wings and the rustle of small animals I'd never catch. If I couldn't pull myself far enough into the shaft, the impending sunrise would be my last, and as a monster—clearly incapable of basic survival—I deserved to be removed from the earth. One less predator for humans to fear and flee. One less pathetic cretin for nature to mock.

I'd managed to avoid the edge of the sun's rays, clearly, as I stood in my remodeled bathroom, courtesy of Nicole's modern taste. If I hadn't, the thick forest blocked any view of the beautiful but deadly sunrise. It would've been a slow, dreadful death. Instead, the excruciating healing process took several starving nights and fitful, restless days.

"Everything okay in here?" Nicole popped into my bedroom. "I heard Daisy rush out."

"In here," I called to my niece.

"Are you decent?"

I chuckled. "You're safe."

When she reached the bathroom doorframe, I turned to show her the puzzling wound. A trickle of blood ran down my arm, and I wiped it clear again. This minor rash from the near-miss, although nothing more than a paper cut to a human, was very concerning. If the doctor had laced the bullet in vervain, it would've hissed and sizzled on impact. This was something else. This was…very worrisome. What did a Civil War landmine and an insignificant modern bullet graze have in common? Only twice in my long existence had an injury given me pause and reminded me that I wasn't immune to death.

Nicole freed a hand towel hanging by the door and dabbed at the wound. It smarted like a sunburn after a hard day's labor in the field. The last time I'd suffered such a minuscule injury was plowing the fields from sunup to sundown with the draft horses. Although having my leg blown to shreds and spending a few agonizing days healing had been unpleasant, the idea of returning to the farm with the drafty cabin, meager food stores, children hiding their hunger, and arduous, endless labor left me shivering with disgust. This wound, and the painful memories it brought back, needed to go.

With a frown, she asked, "Why isn't it healing?"

Good question. Blood pooled on the towel. I took it from her and swiped another trickle, this time pressing harder. What I drew back caused my reflexive and unnecessary breath to catch in my lungs.

"What is it? Why does it look like that?" she asked, worry knitting her brows.

Unable to believe what I saw, I chuckled. My shoulders shook as my chuckle grew to a full laugh and threatened to become hysterical in its absurdity.

Nicole looked at me as if I'd lost my marbles. "You always heal. Something is seriously wrong here, and you're...laughing."

Another trickle of blood slipped down my arm. I swiped it up with a finger and cleaned it on the towel. Where the landmine had patiently awaited some poor schmuck to come strolling along, the modern bullet sought its victim actively—hunting at impressive speeds upon its release—and I'd underestimated it.

I shook my head in utter disbelief. "I should've taken him out when he opened the door."

"Did the elf get you?" Nicole asked. "I've always said, having a truce—"

"It's worse," I interrupted. "That sniveling, whiny human, so easily manipulated by witches, is far more cunning than I gave him credit for. An embarrassingly terrible shot—to my benefit, I suppose. This was more like a game of horseshoes, where 'almost' does count."

"You're not making sense. What did he do?" Nicole shifted her weight, wincing at the pain in her hip.

"Pierce and I found a lab-created serum specifically designed to kill all vampirekind. Daisy had trashed the lab, destroying everything she could find. But the doctor must've saved some, and the bastard shot me with a serum-dipped bullet. It only grazed me, which is why the darkening effects are slower to spread than when Soren was infected." The edges of my damaged flesh had turned black. Tiny veins—capillaries—hardly visible, darkened in a spider-like pattern.

"You've been poisoned?" Nicole clarified, mouth gaping in horror.

"One last laugh for the overprotective yet neglectful father. Figure that one out, because I haven't. No worries, though—the evil vampire boyfriend will soon be toast!" My laughter returned.

I'd fought elves with combat skills the US military would drool over. I'd vanquished vampires far more ancient in years than I, not expecting to stand a chance. And I'd taken down the best of the best witches in the craft. Here, a silly human with a gun, who had zero shooting experience, and no defense, was going to destroy me. Slowly. Painfully. And inevitably.

"Stop calling yourself evil, even if you're being hyperbolic. It's not healthy."

"Healthy? Have you looked at me?" I gestured at the blood dribbling down my arm.

"It doesn't matter what happened. The question is, what are you going to do about it?"

Nicole always centered me, and I appreciated that. I meant what I'd said to Daisy before, pushing her back toward her father. I needed her to be certain of her feelings, because even the worst family members could crawl back under one's skin, receiving all the forgiveness they didn't deserve. But he'd already blown his second chance. "I'm going to kill him."

"Vengeance is not the right focus." Nicole held out her palms as if I were charging out the door right now. "The doctor you want to murder knows more about the serum than you do, right?"

"He deliberately shot me and left me be. I'm not his lab experiment. He won't treat me."

"Then what do you know about it?"

"It's fatal if untreated."

"Perfect." Nicole clapped her hands together as if satisfied with her counsel. "So what's the treatment?"

First, I needed to stop the leaking. I opened the mirrored cabinet. "Is there a first aid kit in this house?" I had never needed one before.

"By your feet. You never know when a human might need patching around here." Nicole sent me a dubious smirk, but I let it go.

I bent, found the kit, and set it on the vanity. "Do you mind?"

Nicole shifted her weight to reach into the zippered pouch. She pulled out a roll of wrap and a square of gauze. "Stitching you up won't do any good, but we need the flow to stop, or at least conceal it. People tend to get weird around fresh, flowing blood." She cleaned up the leaking wound again and fastened a square of gauze to it. She assessed and murmured to herself before adding another square. "Hold here."

I pressed a finger against it while she wrapped a length of bandage around my biceps in several passes. I flexed to be sure it wouldn't tear on me.

"Now that you're patched up temporarily, how are we going to patch you up permanently?"

"Evangeline drank the cure straight from Newt's veins. Soren did the same. If the cure stays in the system, then my brother is my walking cure and a phone call away." I freed the modern tether from my pocket. "I'm glad Daisy convinced me to carry this thing. Now let's hope my brother keeps his on his person, too."

I called Soren, but the line rang and rang. Nicole's face scrunched in worry as the endless rings cycled and ended in a default voicemail. And Daisy thought I was a Neanderthal. "Brother, never there when I need you...or your blood." I tucked my new phone into my back pocket.

"Now what?" Nicole asked softly.

"Don't tell Daisy. She's already worried about me. I couldn't imagine what she'd do if she found out."

"Oliver Rockwell, always keeping his loved ones in the dark for their own safety."

I frowned at her. "What is that supposed to mean?"

Nicole ignored my question. "What's your Plan B?"

"I need the source." I brushed past her, heading to the closet. Nothing was getting done while I was half-naked. "Daisy was smart enough to take a vial of Newt's blood just in case. It's stored at her dad's house. All I need to do is take it." I selected a dark dress shirt from my freshly pressed stack and slipped my arms into it. If I leaked through, it wouldn't be visible. I sighed, and my fingers shook as I tried fastening the buttons.

Nicole swatted my hands away and buttoned my shirt for me with gnarled knuckles that remained calm. "How are you getting past the human's barrier?"

"The doctor already invited me inside, but I've underestimated him once, so I'm taking backup."

"I'm glad you're being reasonable about this." A job well-done, Nicole folded her arms across her chest.

"I'm always reasonable." I tucked in my shirt.

"When you're doing business, you're the trifecta of charming, calculating, and opportunistic. But when you're worried about the people you love, you can be...impulsive. So, I'm relieved you're being careful this time."

I read what I thought she meant. "You're not going with me."

Nicole waved in the air dismissively. "My old bum hip? I wouldn't make it up the stairs without groaning and exposing our position. My days of recon are over. I'll hold down the fort and keep Daisy occupied if she shows."

I leaned over and kissed Nicole on the forehead. "You are the perfect Alfred. Thank you."

"That's because I love you, and I only want the best for my family. Besides, I'm hoping to see a few weddings in my day before it's too late." Nicole winked at me.

She was a sucker for that stuff. I brushed by her, and in my haste, my feet thundered down the stairs. I would've chosen Soren to be my backup, but he was unreachable. Daisy's witch roommates wouldn't help me. In fact, I expected Jamie and

Allison to laugh and slam the door in my face. Again. Enemies remained enemies.

The elf and I had formed a partnership with the joint goal of saving Daisy's life, and I'd dangled the carrot of staking Soren, but that was over. Asking for a personal favor now was a last resort, because I couldn't trust him. Despite reassuring my niece, I'd had a few mixed drinks earlier, so I was well enough to do this on my own. If the idiot doctor tried to pull a gun on me again, my glowing red eyes would be the last thing he saw.

I'd leave behind my Shelby, not wanting to attract extra attention tonight, so I collected the keys to my incognito car, a black Mercedes C-Class Coupe, and headed for the garage. I drove down Shore Drive and slowly rolled past the Barrett household. The windows were dark, and no vehicle sat in the driveway. I tuned into my heightened hearing, and no sounds reached me from inside. Two houses down, I parked at the curb and walked, keeping an eye and ear out for any movement.

I was alone out here. The town was fast asleep.

I crossed the lawn in a blur and stopped at the front door. I peeked through the sidelight for any movement inside, but a privacy curtain obscured my vision. Still, I remained confident the house was empty, or the doctor was asleep. I'd be cured before Daisy ever found out the gravity of her father's gunshot. I gripped the knob and gently turned. Soft creaking pings of metal reached my sensitive ears, and then the knob stopped.

Locked.

According to Daisy and her once-daily meal delivery, he rarely locked the door. The doctor must've been away, which was good news for me. I turned the knob further and broke the tumbler. I pushed on the door, but it stopped.

The deadbolt.

I groaned, having no time for this. I lifted a foot and kicked the door in. With my super speed, I crossed to the kitchen, flung open the fridge door, and shifted the sparse—and partially expired—foods in a frantic search for the vial I couldn't see.

"Where is that damned thing?" I mumbled to myself, shoving over a carton of orange juice.

I continued searching and re–searching every inch, just to be sure. Nothing. Closing the fridge door, I opened the freezer. TV dinners, a few pizzas, and empty ice cube trays. No vial.

Shit.

Blood pounded in my ears, and I glanced around the kitchen for other ideas. The door to the basement. I rushed downstairs, hoping to find a chest freezer, but from one corner to the next, there wasn't one. A beer fridge? Every Wisconsinite had one. I rushed up to the garage, but still came up empty. Well, he wasn't a true cheesehead.

I exhaled a deep breath. Either the vial wasn't here, or Greg had destroyed it.

I called Soren again, but the line just rang. I squeezed the phone in my palm. The cure ran through my brother's veins. Without the elusive Soren Rockwell, I was going to die.

# 6

# The Legacy Revealed

**Daisy**

I PARKED IN MY empty driveway and stared at my dark house, hating that it was so big and lonely. My roommates, Jamie Harris and Allison Kincaid, half-siblings and mutual witches, were usually out. Allison was a bartender at Fully Loaded, and Jamie spent his days at UW Marinette and his evenings as the scandalous party entertainment for women, probably men too. I didn't judge, so long as he paid his rent.

It was one of those scandalous celebrations—a bachelorette party for my cousin Abby—where I'd first met him. No matter how many miles of glistening muscles twitched and shimmied, things between us were never awkward. He was a great entertainer, but I was never attracted to him. We were...friends.

Those were not the people I'd envisioned living in my home. When I bought the four-bedroom house with beige vinyl siding and hideous maroon shutters that I happened to love for all their dated hideousness, I'd hoped to raise a family here someday, after I dug my way out of crippling student loans.

Or met a handsome prince who made them go *poof.*

I expected to fill the rooms with the laughter of children, scrub their creativity off the walls, vacuum pet hair, and mop spills. Even if I didn't want—nor could afford—children anytime soon, I wanted to be ready for when I was ready. Like my parents, I loved my job and had no intention of quitting, but I would be far more attentive and present than they ever were. And when the children gave me a moment's solitude, I planned to hang a swing under the covered front porch. I would rock gently, listening to the morning birds singing, and sip coffee as the sun rose. In this vision, the treasured man beside me, entwining my fingers with his, could be no one but Oliver Rockwell, and he'd regale me with stories of his fascinating and extensive past.

Until the kids woke up.

Grasping that dream was completely delusional. As a human, wrinkles, aching knees, and a popping spine were in my future. But Oliver would remain his strikingly handsome thirty years of age forever. For now, I had him as he was, and our future would be more of the same. No kids, no growing old together, and after a long road that slowly became more frustrating with society's judgment, expectations, and confusion, we'd part. At least I didn't have to worry about being abandoned in a nursing home. I'd lied when I told Oliver I wouldn't worry about our expiration date. Unlike him, I felt the strain of time. Each passing day was one day lost.

I withdrew my keys from the ignition and hugged my purse. With my normal human hearing, I listened to the night. The vampire I loved hunted out there, attacking people with his painful bite and terrifying paralytic, to heal himself from my dad's gunshot. A year ago, I never would've strung together that thought. For Oliver's victim's sake, I should've done more than sit on the couch, dumbfounded.

Dad had never respected me, loved me for who I was. And when he fired the gun at Oliver without hesitation, without regard to my safety or feelings, the betrayal was crushing. As long as Oliver remained in my life, removing Oliver was more important than my well-being. My dad's reputation as a leading scientist was more important than my well-being. Okay, I got the hint. I'd never be my dad's number one. But shooting my boyfriend was truly the last straw.

I had to grip a shred of dignity. Just one—one little piece—so I didn't fall apart.

I climbed out of my car and shut the door. Pressing the button on the fob, the car blinkers flashed to confirm the doors had locked, and I shouldered my purse and tugged my sexy little black dress down, my one and only practical dress. This was not how I wanted the evening to go. I sighed while my heels clattered against the pathway, obnoxiously loud in the silence of the night. I climbed the porch stairs and turned the knob of my front door. It was locked. I groaned, not seeing the point, considering all the coming and going, and that vampires couldn't enter uninvited, but Oliver had insisted and apparently my roommates complied. I flipped through my keyring to find the right one, wishing the porch light had a switch on the outside of the house. A swishing sound behind me stilled my hands.

Oliver wouldn't sneak up on me.

Dad would've called.

Lily would've texted.

Pierce would've announced his presence with the usual, 'You look good, Daisy.'

Soren had been radio-silent since leaving us at the cabin, locked in by daylight.

I turned, hands trembling.

A fast-moving shape pounced on me, tackling me onto the hard porch. The wind in my lungs had been smacked clear out of me, and I winced, trying to suck in a breath. Superhuman strength held me in place, and before I could make a sound, fangs punctured my throat. This wasn't Soren. A woman, disheveled and reeking of a dank basement, gripped me with fingers of steel. I had seconds before the paralytic took effect, so I shoved at her, but all that did was tear my skin deeper.

Out of nowhere, my attacker screamed in surprise and pain, and she reeled back on her own with a hand to her temple. I applied pressure to the wound on my throat, the silver chain with my vervain and black nightshade locket under my thumb. I finally caught a breath. My attacker wore mismatched, ill-fitting clothing. Her hair was wild, and that face—that angry, snarling face—I would never forget.

Evangeline Brant. Since regaining her freedom, she looked and smelled less civil than I'd expected.

I took a step back, as if that would place a protective shield between us. Her glare raked over me and landed on my necklace. "Where did you get that?"

My hand moved to protectively cover the necklace Oliver had gifted me, and my hand slipped in warm, trickling blood. She'd punctured me, and as my heart pounded in my chest, the bleeding continued to worsen, but at least she didn't get to my carotid. I needed to calm down and think rationally. I had to get inside where she hadn't been invited. To do that, I had to delay the short-tempered ex-lab-rat, who probably hated my dad more than I did.

"I'm in your world. You don't think I'd have vervain?" I tried to smirk, but fear and anxiety pulsed through me, and my face twisted with pain. As Evangeline slowly recovered from the burn of the allergen, my fingers slipped along the keys, trying to decipher the correct one.

I got it.

"That doesn't answer my question," she said and spat my blood over the railing. She wiped her mouth with the back of her hand.

I sidled toward the door as inconspicuously as I could and slipped the key into the lock, speaking over the sound of the metal inserting. "Oliver gave it to me a little while ago." I turned the key as gently as I could. "Why?"

Evangeline's face morphed into a horrifying picture of monstrous fury. She lunged at me again, knocking me over once more, and I gasped as my spine smacked the porch and the air ripped from my lungs. I struggled to pull in a breath. My keys remained dangling in the doorknob.

A lot of good that would do me now.

Evangeline leaned over me, assessing me like some curious predator surprised by its prey. I tried shoving her off, but her strength was...well, superhuman. Because of my necklace, she wouldn't bite again, but after watching Oliver snap the basketball player's neck as easily as twisting the cap off a bottle of water, I had to act fast.

The necklace had hurt her. It was all I had to fight with, but I couldn't risk taking it off. I picked up the locket and pressed it against her chest. She screamed at the hissing burn of her flesh, and she recoiled away. With a tiny window of opportunity, I scrambled to my feet and rushed to the door. Trying to bury my panic and calm my hands, I turned the knob, and I flung myself inside.

I landed on my carpet with the door wide open behind me. I panted, adrenaline and relief washing through me.

Evangeline pounded on the mystical barrier of the threshold like a wild beast, snarling in fury.

I was safe. Climbing to my feet, I plucked my keys from the knob.

"That's my necklace," Evangeline said. "Oliver gave it to me. It's mine, and I want it back!" Her fists silently banged on the invisible force.

I tilted my head to the side, curious about why she'd want something that harmed her. Deadpan, I repeated, "It's vervain."

Evangeline scoffed. "Humans, so stupid. It's amazing you've survived as a species as long as you have. If we hadn't shown the necessary restraint to maintain our food supply, you'd be extinct. It's a *locket*," she enunciated the word as if that would explain it. "With a pair of gloves, I can open it and empty it."

I lifted the locket in my hand. It was the only reason I stood safely inside my house and not dead on my porch. No way was I giving up the only defense I had. "Sorry, but no."

Her lips curled into a dark smile. "The sentimental value alone is worth more than your life."

Sentimental value? I'd thought they were ancient history, and I didn't want to think about what had happened between them, but the way she was acting, I wondered just how ancient it was.

Safely out of her reach, my confidence returned to full strength. "That's the least convincing argument possible. You've spent a long time locked up. I'll try to explain in a way only a stupid human can. Next time, try asking nicely or offering to pay for it. There's a saying about catching flies with honey. You should look into it."

Evangeline cackled, not in a funny kind of way, more like I'm-about-to-enjoy-tearing-out-your-insides kind of way. "What I want goes beyond my necklace. That's a consolation prize, but mine nonetheless."

"Then what do you want?" If I could toss her a cookie and she'd leave, I'd be all for it.

"You have no idea who you're messing with. Come out here, and I'll show you." She curled a finger at me, urging me closer.

I shook my head. I was nobody's snack tonight. "My answer is no. Stay away from me." I slammed the door shut in her face and pressed my back against it. I exhaled a long, shaky breath.

Oliver had told me I wouldn't want to meet his ex. Hoo, boy, was he right. She was worse than I had imagined, reminding me of Soren when he was under Newt's control. But Newt was dead. So, this Evangeline was the real Evangeline. What did Oliver ever see in her?

I shivered and dragged my hands along my dress, smoothing the wrinkles, and my fingers caught on a tear. Just great. My one and only little black dress was ruined.

"That was a close one." Allison approached from around the corner, removing headphones from her ears. Woodwind instruments reached my tired ears. Ten minutes ago would've been awesome, but my problems weren't her problems.

I lifted the damaged fabric. "Vampire tried to eat me, but she tore my dress."

"She would've torn far more than that if you'd given her the chance."

"No kidding." I pointed to my neck.

"You got lucky." Allison kneeled by the tear in my dress and inspected it. "This I can fix, if you want."

I never saw Allison with a sewing machine. Maybe she knew a tailor, a tailor that accepted VISA? "Sure. That'd be great."

"Hold still." Allison held her palms facing my body, right over the frayed fabric. Her hands glowed, and I shifted, genuinely startled. Quickly, she said, "Don't move."

I stared at her wide-eyed and held my breath.

The torn edges knitted themselves back together as if the damage had never happened. When she finished, her hands lowered, the glow dissipated, and I inspected her work. Not a sign anywhere that the dress had been ruined. "How did you do that?"

"Magic." Allison stood.

The last time she'd done a spell, or whatever, it was to keep vampires and elves from entering my house—regardless of an invitation. That had required candles, chants, herbs, and a whole show. "Where's the circle of chanting?"

"This is a higher level of magic, attainable after mastering the basics and learning control. This also happens to be an easy spell too, but before you ask, it doesn't work on wounds. I've tried."

That was my next question. "Bummer." I went to the kitchen and found a clean hand towel. I pressed it to my neck wound and drew it back. Only a few blotches of blood.

Allison followed me and looked at the blood. "You'll live."

Having the ability to fix things—like my leaky sink—without a hammer would be convenient, since contractors emptied the bank account and DIY strained my back. "Thanks, doc. How did you learn that spell? It seems mighty useful."

"A witch's grimoire, handed down through the generations, and a whole lot of trial and error, but don't worry. I fixed the drywall in my room."

"What was wrong with the drywall?"

"Nothing. There's nothing wrong." Allison said quickly to suppress my concern.

I frowned for a second before curiosity brought me back to our conversation. A grimoire, huh? Aunt Lisa had left me an ancient book I couldn't understand. Could it be one of those? Only one way to find out. "Come with me."

I brought Allison upstairs to my bedroom, tossed the towel in my hamper, and kneeled at my hiding place.

"Where did you get this?" Allison asked. She pointed at the drawing on my wall. Oliver's antique charcoal portrait of three smiling women dated 1870.

I collected the fragile book and carried it over. "That was in my Aunt Lisa's belongings."

Allison beamed. "Do you know who these women are?"

I shook my head. I never had the chance to ask Oliver yet.

My roommate pointed to each woman, from left to right. "Rose Watson, Edith Johnson, and Henrietta Daisy Barrett."

I blinked. "*My* ancestor? That's Henrietta Barrett?" I looked into her eyes. I couldn't see the resemblance, but there was something in those eyes that called to me. I loved the drawing because it was Oliver's, and now that I knew my ancestor was staring back at me, I treasured it even more. Remembering Oliver's hallway of smiling portraits, he likely drew them from afar, lost in his loneliness.

"She's yours. Right next to mine, Edith Johnson."

I remembered what Oliver had told me and tried to make the connection. "They're the three witch friends who died in the Peshtigo fire. Who's the last one, Rose Watson?"

Allison sighed. "Oliver's mother."

I blinked again, stunned. "Are you sure?"

"I know my history. Yes, I'm sure."

I remembered Oliver telling me his mother was a witch who'd created spells for healthy crops and placed the spells in rings. During the Peshtigo fire, his family had escaped into the cave, where they'd met the rogue vampire who turned Oliver, and afterward, his mother had run off to her sacred space for the rings, but she'd never returned. He'd never told me her name. Rose Watson.

"Is this the book?" Allison asked, pointing at the thick tome in my hands.

"Yeah," I said absently, holding the book out to her, still staring at the drawing. A thought swirled in my head, but I couldn't quite grasp it.

Allison turned the book over in her hands, marvel widening the smile on her face. She opened the book. "Oh, this is definitely a grimoire." She turned pages. "There's stuff in here that's truly powerful. Just... Wow."

"My aunt willed it to me before she died. I know nothing else about it."

"Our ancestors were best friends. I don't believe in fate, but maybe there's a reason I'm your roommate. We have some studying to do to see what you're made of."

I deciphered her meaning, flabbergasted. "Are you telling me I'm a witch?"

"Not yet, you're not. But we can work on that." Allison sent me a friendly smile.

For the first time since I was aware of the hidden world, I felt comfort knowing my roommates were witches. They wouldn't attack me, eat me, or violate my head. They were capable of devious spells, as Mr. Reed was proof of that, but good and bad existed in all forms, and these people here and now were firmly on the good side. So yeah, I'd learn to sling some weird words and smelly herbs if it meant invisible magic forces could fix the leak under the kitchen sink. Seemed like a harmless hobby to me.

And if I could defend my home or myself against vampires like Evangeline, well, what else could I say?

"I'd appreciate your help."

# 7

# The Deal

**Oliver**

THROUGHOUT THE DECADES, SOREN had repeatedly succumbed to his inherent and voracious need to feed, and afterward he'd retreat into hiding to wallow in self-loathing. Every cycle hurt me as much as him, because his pain was my fault, and he rightfully hated me. But this last time, Newt had forced him into a bout of recklessness to return Evangeline to the witch's clutches. I was grateful to hear it, having feared my brother had lost himself on another murderous rampage, leaving him incapable of reason. I needed to reason with him now—I needed that rare compassion he'd shown when he'd given me my ring back.

Since Soren was now ring-free, there were only so many places he could go before the sun barbecued him. I rolled the Shelby to a stop on the gravel driveway of the cabin where Daisy and I had been trapped—near our family's cemetery. I directed my sharp senses toward the interior. A vampire lurked inside, and I was eternally grateful for my brother's predictability. With a grin of relief, I entered the unlocked door on swift and silent feet, and darkness swallowed me. Only hints of light broke through the blankets tacked over the windows, so I left the front door open and allowed my eyes a second to adjust.

The moose and bear theme remained, a proudly displayed shrine to mass-produced discount retail. The folding table and chairs were collapsed flat and leaning against the wall. With an extra layer of dust, not only had no one else been around, but my brother wasn't much of a housekeeper. The only reason he and I could enter without resistance was that the ownership of the property had been transferred on death to an LLC.

On the floor in the darkened corner, my brother slumbered on the dusty mattress. Since vampires didn't require respiration, he appeared to the untrained eye to be dead. A human stumbling upon him would've panicked and then become food. A Venus flytrap, in a way. Not classy, but effective, if he weren't in the middle of the woods near a cemetery that time had long since forgotten.

I shook his shoulder to wake him. Soren's vice-like grip snapped around my wrist. He popped open his eyes, but his face shifted into disappointment when he saw my handsome mug. In my weakened condition, if he wanted to toss me out of this cabin, he could.

Or steal my ring back.

"I hoped for a lost hiker. How did you find me?" Soren released me and climbed to his feet and stretched.

"I've known you for over a hundred years, my brother. I can always find you." This also happened to be the cabin Soren ran toward when he caused Daisy's family to crash on the highway. Lots of memories here, none of them pleasant.

Soren eyed the cast of sunlight spilling onto the floorboards from the front door. "I did enough harm for one decade. Leave me alone. And close the door."

Like Daisy's fruitless attempts at her family's acceptance, I too desired that connection. "I have more bedrooms than living family. My house is clean and fully stocked with liquor and, of course, tastefully decorated. Yet you choose to live in squalor." I swiped a line of dust and showed it to him.

Soren brushed himself off and shook out his long, messy hair. A cloud of dust erupted. "The dirt was the point, so your highness would leave me be, unless it was an emergency." Soren smirked, reminding me of when I'd been ringless and burning up. "So, let me spell it out for you. If you came to insult me, be prepared to kiss my fist."

Soren was still in his self-loathing phase. In my position as the eldest brother, the family expected me to maintain a level of stability, pride, and strength, and I'd done that all these years—long after our family had splintered and been lost to time. The provider in me was so thoroughly instilled that asking a favor of my younger brother was shameful, and the words I needed to utter were painful to my psyche. When I finally pushed the courage to my tongue, I spit them out a little too fast. "I have no desire to fight. On the contrary, I need your help."

My brother frowned and folded his arms across his chest. "I saw your stack of missed calls and the text. You get a gold star for making it to the twenty-first century. You wrote, and

I quote, *I have a matter of utmost urgency to discuss with you face to face.* FYI, people don't text like that. So, who's dying now?"

I knew my brother didn't mean that literally, but I wanted him to eat a few words, so I painfully shrugged out of my suit jacket. Seeing there was nowhere acceptable to rest it, I flung it over my shoulder and began the arduous process of unbuttoning my dark dress shirt. Certain movements were beginning to hurt, and dexterity was getting difficult. I also had enough dignity to refrain from asking Soren to unbutton me.

"I've seen enough of you to last a lifetime. Really, this isn't necessary."

"I wouldn't show you if I didn't think it was." I shook off my shirt, exposing the dressing on my biceps. It was soaked in blood. Beyond the bandage cover, the inky black veins stretched their claws up my flesh.

Soren's face turned ashen in genuine horror, and his mouth popped open. He'd suffered the same affliction, but Daisy had saved him. "I...I didn't..." He raked a hand through his hair, more distraught than I expected. "Awe, shit. How? Who did this?"

"The good doctor Greg Barrett isn't as innocent as I thought. He coated a bullet with the serum, and a skin graze was enough to infect me with its poison." I slipped my shirt into place and shrugged into my suit jacket, feeling the return of a small semblance of myself, but I'd skipped one step.

"Aren't you going to button up?" Soren asked, brow raised.

I gave him a pressed-lip grimace.

Soren swiftly fastened my buttons without me asking. "Daisy took a vial of the cure from the lab. Why didn't you—?"

"Why would the doctor keep the cure when he intended to infect me with the serum? Anyway, his house was the first place I checked. I should've figured he'd have destroyed it," I said, glad Soren cared enough to brainstorm.

"Then what's the next move?"

I pointedly stared at his throat. "I think the answer is right here."

Soren frowned at the intimate request. "You think the cure still runs in my veins?"

"That's the idea—it ran in Newt's for you and Evangeline."

Soren gave me a hard stare. *Here it comes.* Nothing in life was ever free. "If I do this, we're straight, right?"

In 1880, Soren had drained Evangeline to the point of death, intent on killing her to teach me a lesson about the consequences of humans and vampires being together. His attempt at a lesson had failed, since he never gave us the chance to discover if his hypothesis had been correct.

Over the decades, Soren had wreaked havoc on various small towns and disappeared. I tried to intervene when I felt the urge to pull our family back together, but time and again, my efforts had failed. Now he wanted a clean slate, as if this one favor surpassed all the damage he'd done.

I met his stare. Faced with my demise, Soren didn't hate me. He needed forgiveness for the one brutal act that destroyed my life—and that mattered more than the one brutal act I committed that destroyed his life. In his own twisted way, Soren was forgiving me for turning him, but he wanted my forgiveness in return.

Or, faced with my own demise, I was yearning for a deeper meaning that wasn't there. "When you tried to destroy Daisy, I truly believed killing you was the only answer."

Soren waited silently for my verdict.

"You fall off the rails every so often and do terrible things, but this last time wasn't your fault, so I haven't lost hope you can be redeemed."

Soren shook his head, fighting back tears.

"Daisy forgave you for attacking her when she handed you the cure. When you gave back my ring and told me to go after her, I forgave you for everything you did to her."

He dabbed at his lower eyelid.

"But as far as Evangeline?" Forgiveness for my life. Sounded easy. But the only way to keep Daisy safe from Soren's twisted humans-and-vampires-didn't-mix rule was to be certain he understood the gravity of that mistake. This way, Daisy would remain human, as we both agreed we wanted. This decision, for Daisy's own protection, could cause her immense grief, but with fallible human memory, she'd eventually forget. "What you did to her—to me—changed the course of my life and hers. And so you understand how important it is never to be repeated, I can't ever forgive you."

Soren's eyes pinked with pressing emotion as he processed the weight of my words. It killed me to see my brother completely rejected when he was already at his lowest, so on the other matters eating away at him, I added, "As far as everything else, I consider us square. Can you live with that?"

He blinked back the tears shimmering on his lids. "Are you refusing my apology to force me to heal you so I'll earn your forgiveness?"

Asking if 'we're straight' wasn't much of an apology, but I had to admit, I hadn't thought of that. "I wouldn't blackmail you with eternal guilt, but if you don't help me, you'll never have the chance to find out."

Soren cleared his throat and held out his arm. "Fine. Take the wrist."

With relief, I brought my brother's wrist to my mouth. A quick puncture with my fangs sent the healing liquid through my body. To destroy the serum coursing through me wouldn't require much blood—about a lab vial's worth. I drank what I needed and released him. My brother tucked his hands into his pants, assessing me with caution.

I closed my eyes and focused on the sensations flooding my body. Warmth charged my muscles. Energy permeated my every cell. My brain ignited with fireworks of clarity. Vampire blood wasn't as nourishing as human blood, since it had already been processed, but it was still a powerful source.

"Feel anything?"

The stinging pain in my arm wasn't lessening. "Not yet. How long until you felt the healing?" I shucked out of my suit jacket and struggled with the buttons. Impatiently, I tore the sleeve to check the progress, and my stomach sank.

Soren leaned in close, inspecting the wound. Glumly, he met my worried gaze. "Did you take enough?"

"I took plenty." The veins were just as black as before. I raked a hand through my gelled hair.

After Soren's loud and clear lesson, I'd vowed to stay away from humans. Then I met Daisy. I didn't choose to love her—it just happened, like a magnetic force impossible to resist. And I'd do anything to protect her. I'd do anything to be with her. If Soren had declined to cure me, I would've taken it by force. For her, I would've done it without a hint of guilt. In the back of my mind, I knew that one day time would take her from me. Until then, I was prepared to enjoy decades together and live the rest of my life pining for the love that I'd lost. I was used to grieving.

But at the rate the poison spread, I had maybe a day to live. I'd never considered for a moment that Daisy would outlive me. She would suffer through the loss and bear the pain alone. This wasn't how things were supposed to go. This couldn't be how it ended. I'd lived too long and survived too much, including a damned landmine turning my leg to bone shards and gristle. There was no way I died like this—sick, weakened, poisoned by a human—hallucinating and vomiting like an infirm elderly human.

Leaving Daisy vulnerable, unprotected.

A firm grip on my healthy arm slowed my panicking thoughts. My brother gazed into my eyes with a level of seriousness I hadn't seen in years. "Does Daisy know?"

Without a shred of doubt, I knew my brother's blood was the answer. "She didn't need to. You were supposed to be my cure."

"Then you can go to her, tell her what happened. Apologize for keeping her in the dark, say your goodbyes, and shed copious amounts of tears together."

I sensed an 'or' in there. I waited. The silence was excruciating.

"Or, we don't give up. There's another cure out there somewhere. We just have to find it."

For the first time in almost two centuries, I felt the weight of time, and without concrete answers, I didn't have enough to spare. Panic rose once more. "The cure ran through Newt's veins, but his corpse is useless now. Daisy had destroyed the cure in the lab, and the vial she'd taken from Newt is missing. I'd bet anything the doctor destroyed it the minute he left her sight. I don't see how this brand-new vampire weapon has a happy ending for me."

Soren stepped into my personal space, anger twisting his features. "You're Oliver goddamn Rockwell. You have more money than I could spend, a life of luxury I could only dream of, and the love of a good woman. You've defeated witches and elves, and vampires twice your age. Are you really going to let a stupid, feeble human take you down like this?"

Too bad the cure wasn't flattery. "It almost sounds like you care, brother."

Soren reeled back and slugged me in the face. Now I had momentary relief from the pain in my arm. "I can hate you and love you at the same time. Of course I care, you asshole."

I covered my new bruise and checked for bleeding. There were a few streaks. "I love you too, dick."

"Then let's figure this out."

Having my brother at my side and confidently in control, we were unstoppable. Soren was capable of nearly anything. With a surge of energy, the next step came to me. There was only one place that made sense. "We have to get to the lab. See what else the doctor has cooking behind closed doors."

Soren brightened. "Put your fancy clothes back on. It's time for some redecorating."

I shrugged back into my suit jacket with a minor wince at the increasing discomfort and followed Soren to the doorway, where he quickly hissed at the light hitting his arm.

"Or we wait until dark. I've got a deck of cards."

# 8

# Power Within

**Daisy**

"Close your eyes," Allison said, holding my hands over a ring of flickering candles. "Repeat after me."

In celebration of my newfound interest, Jamie decided to skip the waffles and treat me and Allison to a real meal. When he was properly motivated, he was a decent cook. A pot of water burbled on the stove, and Jamie prepared dinner with an apron on, which read, *I only smoke the good stuff*, while whistling to himself with earbuds jammed in his ears. A knife rhythmically collided with a wooden chopping board. There was a little dancing, and it was a little distracting from the spell at hand. But I couldn't help but smile.

I hated to think it, but I missed this normalcy. I didn't have to wonder what mind games the elf was playing, and I didn't have to wonder if a vampire thought I was an hors d'oeuvre or the main course. Even Soren could be safe or a deranged killer, and I wouldn't know until it was too late. I couldn't trust their motivation, except Evangeline. She was transparent—firmly in the avoid category.

Like Jamie, Oliver was an excellent cook, but Oliver couldn't eat. Whenever Oliver and I were together when I ate, he'd watch me. It was awkward, but something he used to do. However, I couldn't stomach watching him eat. A shiver climbed down my spine. No freaking way would I volunteer to watch him munch on a person. I could hardly stand him draining a blood bag into a glass—blood bags meant to save human lives, not feed someone who was designed to kill humans.

These thoughts weren't healthy.

For a while, I had been content to stick my head in the proverbial sand, but this—having friends around to eat a meal and engage in a shared interest—was the complete opposite of what I'd grown up with. Lily was my closest living relative, but for the last several months, she might as well have been a ghost, and her absence hurt. I missed my mom and all her imperfections terribly, but she was never coming back. And Dad, well, he was a whole bag of cats I didn't want to release. My nostalgia for my family was an illusion. We were never a big, cozy, happy family. Something like...this.

Jamie spun in place and bobbed his head, dancing to the tunes channeled into his ears, and I cracked a smile. This was what I always imagined a happy family would be like, and it left me with the warm-and-fuzzies, just good food and good company. Best friends, like our ancestors had been. Hopefully, we'd part ways someday as old people, not burning in a raging inferno...

Nah, this wasn't the 1870s. People were far more civilized now.

I couldn't be more appreciative that Jamie and his half-sister were teaching me to defend my home and myself—bonus points if I could do minor home repairs too. In the living room, butt firmly planted on the carpet, I tried to remember the words. Allison was a patient teacher, and this was fun, a distraction from the necessary feeding Oliver was doing in the darkness.

Head, see sand.

"Daisy, focus," Allison chided.

I chanted the foreign phrases she'd taught me. After a pause, I opened my eyes. "Did it work?"

The tiny green army soldier on the coffee table next to us stood resolute, armed, and ready to fire plastic rounds at the giant invaders—firmly where Allison had left him. Of course, it didn't work.

"I can't do this. I'm not a witch." We were trying to knock him over—an offensive move to buy myself time to flee next time I was cornered by someone of the Evangeline variety, but so far, no dice.

"Have you ever walked into a room and the light was on after you swore you turned it off? Or you set something down and returned for it, but it moved just a little, enough to think you were going crazy? How about any time you almost knocked something over, but you caught it right before it spilled?"

I rolled my eyes. "That's good reflexes and absent-mindedness."

"That's dormant power. Both of our ancestors were witches. Your aunt left you her witch paraphernalia, passed down through the Barrett family line. Your genes haven't activated yet, but we'll keep trying, so when they do, you'll be ready."

I couldn't believe I was a dormant witch on my father's side. Men rarely harnessed the power of witchcraft, but it flowed through their bloodline as a recessive gene, and no one knew for certain if I had it or not. Oliver didn't like witches all that much, but after his tales of the witches hunting vampires almost two centuries ago, and my experience with Mr. Reed, I didn't blame him. But I could change his perceptions, show him not all witches hated vampires. Besides, once I was strong enough to stay by his side, then no one could tear us apart—cough, Pierce, cough—ever again. I could do this. For Oliver, I could become strong enough, so he didn't have to worry.

So he wouldn't have to take a bullet and be out there feeding now instead of in my arms.

"Let's try again. Repeat after me," Allison said.

I listened to her pronunciation and chanted along with her, holding hands with my eyes closed. I focused on what effect I wanted—to knock the tiny green army guy over. After three repetitions of the command, metal clinking from the kitchen distracted me. I opened my eyes, expecting failure again.

Over Allison's shoulder, the army guy stood resolute with his gun in the air in unwavering challenge. My tiny adversary had won again. I squinted at it.

"You did it," Allison said, breathlessly.

"What do you mean? He's still standing there, taunting me with his menacing eyes and tiny green gun."

"I put him right here." Her finger stabbed the table. "He moved two inches."

I didn't believe her. "Next time, we'll mark the spot with an X."

"I'm serious. You moved him." She beamed.

I couldn't remember the exact location where I'd placed my adversary before the spell, so I couldn't refute her claim. If she were right, I didn't feel any different. No warm throb of power surged through me or anything fun like that. I held up my hands as if I were palming an invisible ball. "Am I supposed to feel different?"

"Probably not until your power grows. It takes time and practice. Rome wasn't built in a day. Let's try again."

"One second." I got up and found the empty noodle box in the kitchen recycle bin and tore off a corner. I set it on the coffee table and placed my adversary on top of it. "There's my X." I returned to the proper position and collected Allison's hands in mine. This time, I led the chant, confidently pronouncing the words correctly. Another clank of metal pulled my focus away, and I frowned. Jamie was too distracting while I tried to work the spell.

Blocking out his noise, I started over, completing three repetitions. Allison and I eagerly assessed my progress. The little green army guy was knocked over, two inches from the scrap of cardboard. I raised an eyebrow. "You didn't do that, did you?"

"Of course not. That was all you." Allison smiled reassuringly.

I was still skeptical. From Jamie's position in the kitchen, draining the pot of boiling noodles, he couldn't have done it physically. "Neither of you is messing with me?"

"I didn't do anything but let you channel my magic. That was seriously all you." Allison wouldn't benefit from lying to me, and if she had, I'd figure it out pretty quickly. Jamie's focus was on his music and dinner prep. He wasn't even replying to me. So it was true? Really true?

"I really did it?" A foreign feeling—pride—lifted my spirits, and I leaped to my feet. The book slipped off my lap. It knocked into and tipped over the burning candles. "Oh, shit!"

Allison immediately rescued the fragile, antique, and flammable grimoire, and I spun in place, trying to find something to save my carpeting. On the couch, I pulled a throw blanket free and patted out the smolders. Panting with excitement and the surge of adrenaline from almost burning down my house, I sat back and ran a hand over the baby hairs falling in my face. Still, I couldn't stop smiling. "I did it. I actually did it."

"And almost torched the house. I need a place to live, so be careful." Allison sent me a crooked smile while she closed the book and set it on the coffee table. She collected the smoking candles and stacked them safely away.

"I'll have to check my homeowner's policy to see if accidental fire by witchcraft is covered. You know, for next time."

Jamie shouted from the kitchen, "Fire's covered, but leave out the source. If the fire marshal can't figure it out, then you're in luck." Someone had experience.

Allison gestured to his ear, and Jamie removed the earbuds. "Oh, sorry," he said quieter.

"Well, that's comforting." With a big grin on my face, I grabbed my phone from my pocket. I wanted to tell Oliver what I could do. He'd be so excited I was on the path to becoming a badass...or at least a strong, independent woman capable of not dying at the fangs of Evangeline. I opened the app, tapped his name, and stopped.

If I told him, would he be proud or would he discourage me?

Allison got up and stacked all our supplies back into her witchcraft chest. Jamie collected plates from the overhead kitchen cabinet. These two were proud, but I didn't think Oliver would be.

I texted him, *I hope your night is going well. I'll see you at work. Love you.*

I waited for a response, but the little bubble in the corner told me he hadn't read my message.

9

# The Break-In

**Oliver**

As much as I appreciated our little understanding, I couldn't sit in the hunter's cabin, playing Euchre with Soren while waiting for twilight. So I'd parked the Shelby close to the front door and covered him in ample heavy blankets from the cabin—Daisy's idea. He'd only complained for a few minutes about the smell, but considering his domicile preference, I told him it should be a familiar comfort.

Soren wasn't amused, but he'd run and dove inside the car with only a minor hissing of his flesh. Since he'd refused a ride in the trunk, Soren had to remain slouched and covered for the duration of the ride, but it worked. Unfortunately, we were a little too efficient in arriving at the lab. Parked in Pharmaceutical Development, Inc.'s parking lot, I played games on my new phone while Soren stayed smashed uncomfortably on the floorboard of the backseat, waiting for sunset. His phone battery was too low to allow him gameplay, and my old Shelby didn't have a charging port. He was bored. Surprisingly, I found myself entertained with word puzzles, and it was Daisy's thoughtfulness which helped pass the time and grant me patience with my brother.

"Sriracha or spicy brown mustard?" he asked.

I grumbled, "Mustard."

Soren made a noise of disagreement. "Burger or brat?"

I dragged my finger along the scrambled letters to form a word for the puzzle. "We can't eat human food. What's the point of this?"

"I'm trying to remember which foods were better, and what they tasted like. I've forgotten." The car rocked with Soren's shifting.

"It makes no difference. You'll never taste them again." Becoming vampires left us unable to process human food. If we tried, we would vomit, and the flavor both ways made it unpleasant and senseless to try. Wistful nostalgia was all we had, and it was pointless to dwell on. But Soren's inane game helped me keep my mind busy.

"Is the sun down yet?" Soren asked.

Keeping my eyes on the game, I said, "Nope."

Soren groaned. "Did you even look?"

"Don't need to." I had one word left in the puzzle, and my repeated attempts to submit my choice only left it shimmying with rejection. "*Shit* is a word, you stupid—"

"Oliver?" Soren said, deadpan.

"What?" I barked at him.

"Scrabble says shit's not a word."

I grumbled some more and closed the app. The last of the sun's rays dipped beneath the horizon. "Look at that. Time to go."

"Finally." Soren yanked the heavy blanket off his head, leaving his hair a mess.

My phone chimed with a text again, and I read it. Yesterday, Daisy wanted to know how the night was going. Now she was worried because I hadn't contacted her all day. I wasn't about to admit I was dying over a text, and I didn't want to lie to her. So, I tapped out a piece of the truth to calm her fears. *'I'm with Soren. I'll see you soon.'*

"Daisy again? You didn't tell her anything, did you?" Soren asked accusingly.

"The cure is within these walls. After I'm all patched up, I'm going straight to her, and she wouldn't have to concern herself over me."

"It's clear she's already worried."

"Then let's get this done," I said and got out of the Shelby. I straightened my suit and checked my sleeve for dripping blood. I should've brought spare bandages, but my dark fabric should be concealing enough for a human's dull senses.

Soren followed me across the sparse parking lot of PDI in Green Bay, where four stories of humans tirelessly discovered treatments for human ailments. The upper floors, where the work was admirable, were a beacon of hope with a sleek glass exterior. But we headed to Dr. Greg Barrett's research lab in the basement, encased in gray stone, trendy but effectively secure and private. The hidden lab was an atrocity of grisly, inhumane treatment of vampires in the name of 'science'.

Humans needed rescuing from illness, not fangs.

After closing, the foot traffic was light, but compulsion remained a necessary skill. Unfortunately, it didn't have an area-of-effect range. When humans panicked and sounded alarms, compelling them one at a time to calm down and not remember anything took precious time.

So, just like when Pierce and I had broken into the lab to rescue Soren and found Daisy held hostage, I retraced our stealthy steps. With my brother on my heels, I pushed through the side entrance, a locked security door, which even in my compromised state was no match for my strength.

The night security guard, who'd received accolades for a job well-done that he couldn't remember, sat in the surveillance room surrounded by glowing screens. I knocked on the glass, and when the rotund, uniformed man answered the door with bushy eyebrows raised in surprise, I gazed into his eyes. "No one is here. Nothing is wrong. You won't remember us or anything out of the ordinary."

He absently nodded, shaking his jowls, and I gestured for Soren to follow me. At the lab's door, I peered through the narrow window. As expected, it was closed for the evening. The lab rested in darkness, and LEDs on a wall panel blinked and changed colors, monitoring the conditions of the equipment and refrigerator. No sound reached my sensitive ears. Perfect conditions for a break-in.

"Ready?" I asked.

Soren rubbed his hands together. "Let's do this."

I ripped open the door and headed to the refrigerator. Racks of dozens of test tubes filled with blood lined every shelf. They'd been busy. I opened the glass door and removed a tray. I lifted a vial free and read the label on the side. It was gibberish to me. "How am I supposed to know which one to drink?"

Soren carried a handful of racks and cautiously set them on the counter. "Drink them all."

I was desperate, not reckless. "Greg made the weapon here. Who's saying none of these are the next generation?"

Soren's mind blanked with the implications. "Shit." After a beat processing that information, he slipped a tube out and read. "I spent a lot of time in here. Maybe something rubbed off."

I continued emptying the refrigerator, stacking racks on the counter, and waiting for the brilliance of Soren Rockwell to pull through for me.

"This one…" he started.

"Hand it over," I said impatiently. The burn was spreading, climbing, taking.

"This one…I can't even pronounce in my head. I have no idea what this is." Soren selected another, brows furrowing. More and more, he rushed, seeking something familiar on the labels. My brother sighed deeply in defeat. "Negative. Now what?"

"Find a box or crate. We're taking them all. If any are weapons, we're destroying them. Whichever one is the cure, goes down my gullet."

"What makes you think anyone will decipher these labels for us?"

I tapped my temples. "Dr. Barrett won't have a choice." And if he wore vervain, I would relish tearing it off his flesh.

"He spiked Daisy's water bottles with vervain. I'd assume he drinks it, too."

I should've thought of that. I blamed it on the poison. "Then we tie him until it clears his system."

Soren rubbed his arm uncomfortably. "You don't have that kind of time."

I gritted my teeth, hating that Soren was right. "Then I'll force it from his system faster."

"Bleed him out?" Soren guessed.

"Yep. So, get something to transport these and let's get out of here." I continued stacking full racks on the counter.

"Good plan." Soren crossed to the wall of plain, unmarked doors, likely supply closets, to find something suitable. My gaze settled on the door Pierce and I had ducked behind, where we'd discovered Evangeline had been a prisoner and a test subject. Thankfully, she'd escaped. No one deserved that kind of life. Now she was out there somewhere, running free. Until a string of bodies appeared in the area, I had to believe she was coping—far away from my home. If she was happy with her new life, that was all that mattered to me. It was the least she deserved.

I piled the last of the test tubes carefully on the counter. Soren returned, tossing a box next to my hand, and I assessed its strength. I didn't want my life to depend on the quality of cardboard construction, but it seemed sturdy enough. I stacked the racks inside while Soren flung open drawers.

"What are you looking for in there?"

"Screwdriver, keys, knife, I don't know. Something strong or sharp." Soren fished around in another drawer, a metallic rattle reaching my ears. He lifted out a hammer and chuckled. "The most useful tool in the world." Soren disappeared through the door where Evangeline had been held captive, as if he intended to destroy the holding chains Newt had installed.

One less vampire prison cell was fine by me.

Newton Reed was a despicable witch, the worst kind, who relished the suffering and murder of vampires. But his hatred wasn't entirely his fault. All witches had an innate pull, a desire they couldn't control, to kill all vampires. The older they were, or the more they trained, the better they could control it. Newt didn't want to. Since I was still vertical after a few encounters, Allison clearly had some self-control.

If Daisy activated her gene, she and I would be over. She'd stop at nothing to kill me. Gaining self-control took so much time—years—*if* she could beat the instinct at all. Time wasn't a factor, as I was immortal and willing to wait, but having your loved one always on the edge of murdering you wasn't how I pictured a loving relationship. Daisy had been worried about us only having the next sixty years. I've been worried about the next sixty days. Her witch gene used to keep me up at night, but right now, my punch card was about to clock out for the last time, and all those old worries seemed so pointless now. I didn't even have sixty hours left.

A crash of chains came from the indistinct room, and moments later, Soren returned. He flung the hammer aside.

"What was that about?" I asked.

"Making amends. Let's go." Soren lifted the box off the counter.

I frowned at his unnecessary chivalry. "I can carry the vials."

"Your arm looks like a python coiling around it, squeezing the life from you, from limb to chest. I'd rather you didn't drop them."

"You don't want to see me dead?" I asked playfully.

Soren scoffed. "Not today. And if you're going to die, it'll be by my own hand, not some crazed evil human doctor. No offense to your girlfriend."

"Daisy's angry with him. She understands." But Daisy was the forgiving type. I didn't know how long her anger would last. I would never forgive Dr. Greg Barrett after this, even if he cured me, but hopefully Daisy forgave me for killing him.

Unless I died first.

"Good. Let's go."

# IO

# He Put His Hands on Me

**Daisy**

I DIDN'T WANT TO think about my boyfriend dealing with whatever drama Soren had brought back into his life, but at least Oliver had to be healed by now. To keep my mind off blood-drinking vampires and homicidal ex-girlfriends on the loose, I'd agreed to go to a private party with Allison at Fully Loaded. I was surprised she wanted to spend her time off at work, but she and I hadn't gone out in a long while, and I missed our girl nights.

Thumping music vibrated my eardrums, and bodies in minimal clothes gyrated. Beer, sweat, and perfume filled the air. Green laser lights shifted around the tight space, and the neon green accents in the bar glowed. Not only was the design choice sleek and modern, but it was a means of increased visibility in the darkness. Neat trick.

Allison leaned into my ear. "I'll get us drinks."

I gave her the thumbs up, and while she squeezed her way to the bar, I was surrounded by long hair, curled into luscious waves, and tight asses with heels. There was a serious lack of men tonight. Well, that just meant Allison and I could have a great time without unwanted interruptions.

The music dimmed, and the DJ spoke, "Welcome to ladies' night. Tonight, I order you to have a raving good time. Here to spice things up is our very own Jamie Harris."

*Wait, what?*

The crowd went wild, and I pushed my way into the side room for what must've been a misunderstanding. Nope, my roommate climbed the stage, and women filled the space where pool tables had been. I pressed my palm to my forehead, needing to look away but...unable. An elbow nudged me hard, and I turned to see a beer in my face.

I took the drink from Allison. "Did you know about this?"

"Not at all." She chugged her drink with a look of horror on her face as she and I watched her half-brother gyrate on the stage.

Laser lights reflected off his bare skin, and another piece of clothing peeled off, twirled over his head, and flew into the crowd. The ladies went wild. When he was a stranger to me, I thoroughly enjoyed his show with my cousin Abby. Slick muscles and sharp thrusts of his hips had been titillating, and I'd reacted just as the crowd did. But now that Jamie and I were long-standing roommates, it was...weird. "Wait, is he oiled?"

Allison sighed, or I think she did, over the noise. "And glittered. Let's not watch, for my sake."

"Agreed."

We pushed our way back to the main room, and Allison finished her drink. I took the opportunity to make mine disappear as well. Allison took my cup and offered to get refills, and I graciously accepted. I scanned the crowd for familiar faces, who also avoided the show. One big head above all others stood out, literally. Pierce Evansson danced with a trio of lovely women. I was happy for him. The more attention he gave others, the less he gave me. He spun with them, and his eyes caught mine, as if he could feel me watching.

Great.

The DJ switched tracks to a slow song, and the ladies in the side room squealed with excitement. A few surrounding Pierce pointed to the side room and made their way over, abandoning my ex. Pierce clawed his way toward me, fending off hungry and disappointed hands along the way.

A dopey smile filled his face. "You look good, Daisy." I internally groaned. "I didn't expect to see you here. Trouble in paradise?"

My fingers reached for the locket around my throat, my protective layer against compulsion. "You're the one who doesn't belong here, but your trolling ladies' night is none of my business."

Pierce leaned into my ear. "Dance with me."

"No." I turned away, but he pulled my arms around him. He couldn't compel me, but I was no match for his strength. I didn't love Pierce. I never did, and his insistence on being in my life was frustrating. Avoiding Pierce's gaze, I caught the women's faces around us. Several were jealous. I'd love to volunteer them for the position.

"I'm sorry for everything I put you through," Pierce said, and he sounded honest. The sooner he spat out what he needed to, the sooner he'd let me go. "By keeping you from my world, I only did what I thought was in your best interest. And your dad—"

I wasn't ready to face my dad's painful betrayal of Oliver and my family. "No. Don't even mention him," I cut Pierce off.

"I understand. He hopes..." I sent him a glare and Pierce corrected, "I hope we can put those troubles behind us and start over. I can make you the best waffles ever, none of that junk from a box."

Even though I'd prepared filling and cheap casseroles for Dad—or I used to—I happened to like the junk from a box. Jamie was the Master Toaster of the house, and a pretty decent cook who didn't deserve to be insulted, but I didn't interrupt Pierce this time.

"I always imagined something small and quiet at a hotel courtyard or something. You in a gorgeous gown, all hip-hugging with a veil that drapes down your back."

"Wait." I pushed Pierce back to arm's length. "We are not a thing. Nothing's changed. Don't even ask what I think you want to ask."

Pierce frowned and brushed the hair off my neck, as if she'd tried to compel me already but it wasn't working. His eyes settled on Evangeline's fangy kiss. "What's this?"

I pushed his hand away. "It's nothing." Because I'd escaped that vampire myself, and I was fine.

"I can heal it with no trace left behind." Pierce glanced around as if looking for potential witnesses.

I didn't want permanent scarring to remind me of Oliver's ex forever. Part of me was curious about how it worked, and I'd never seen these so-called wings of his either. I couldn't picture it. The last time he'd put his hands on me, I'd blamed him for drugging me and doing nefarious things, but now I knew the truth. He'd healed me from the damage that otherwise would've taken a long time to recover from. I nodded approval for my ex to put his hands on me once more.

Pierce pressed a hand against my throat and pinched his eyes shut in concentration. A blast of warmth hit my skin, like opening a hot oven to pull out a sheet of cookies. Sweat broke out on my chest and back, and I was about five seconds from shaking the hem of my shirt to cool off when he released me.

Pierce smiled warmly. "All fixed."

Slightly disappointed that I didn't get to see any wings, I touched the spot and felt nothing but smooth skin. World's best paramedic, all right, but there had to be a catch. "What happens now? Any side effects? Wooziness? A need to...I don't know...feed?"

"Not for this size wound." Pierce beamed proudly.

"Thanks," I said, wanting to rush to the restroom and see for myself, but a tapping on my shoulder held me in place.

"Hey," Allison said, interrupting. "Bottom's up." She handed me a drink, and I gladly took it. Allison pressed against the small of my back, leading me away. "If you don't mind, Pierce, I'm claiming this dance."

In our wake, he was quickly swallowed by the sea of women eager to put their hands on him. My elf ex-boyfriend pressed his lips together, disappointed. I'd rejected him, but he'd done me a solid favor anyway. A pang of guilt passed through me until I remembered all the times he'd violated me with his mind-control, which I still hadn't gotten to the bottom of.

I slammed down my drink and smiled at my wonderful roommate for the rescue. "Is Jamie's show over yet?"

"He's collecting his glittery, oily bills. Why?" Allison took my empty and gestured to the bartender on duty for a refill.

I shook my head. "I've had enough."

She followed my eyes to Pierce. "He's such a buzzkill. Let's get out of here."

"Agreed."

Allison disposed of our cups on the way out the door. I needed fresh air.

## Daisy

I FELL ONTO MY couch, smelling of sweat and beer with traces of Pierce residue on me, and I stared forlornly at my phone. I was beginning to think Oliver and Soren were in trouble. But they'd been alive for almost two centuries, and if anyone could take care of themselves, they could.

Still, what were they doing? My mind immediately went to a brother-bonding feed. I could never hunt and attack people, but I imagined myself as a vampire at the park, starving. Who would I find? Teenagers, the epitome of hygiene. I grimaced. Innocent children—who were far too trusting. No way in hell. Adults who didn't shower frequently enough, or those who wore too much perfume. Ugh. The idea of touching another human's skin when I wasn't fighting to save their life gave me the shivers, and having to use my mouth made my stomach flip. No wonder Oliver preferred the bags.

If we were an old married couple, I'd be stuck at home, listening to the television with muscle cream on my back, a sleeping mask over my eyes, and me feet in a cheap massage bath, while Oliver would be out zipping around with superhuman speed, biting people for survival, and returning home in his fine suit, looking as amazing as he was today. What would he do after I was gone? Would he find someone else to warm his bed, share his secrets, love him? Would he do it when my body no longer could?

These were dangerous, depressing thoughts, and I needed to lay off the beer until I could reconcile his infinite life span while, relatively, mine was short. Too short.

I dropped my phone onto my thigh and sighed.

"No response yet, huh?" Allison said, setting a drink down in front of me. "Have a whiskey sour. Despite the name, it's quite uplifting. Besides, we should celebrate your victory over the green army guy, and we ditched Pierce."

Allison was always great at cheering me up. "For that, I'll have one more." I lifted the glass to my lips and sipped. I liked it, but I still hadn't decided on my favorite.

Jamie sat on the other side of me on the couch, sinking the cushion under his weight. He hadn't showered yet, but he'd placed a towel beneath himself. I still obsessively watched the cushions for contact with his glittery oil. Jamie had a trough of beer in his hand. "So, 'welcome to the club' is in order for the newest witch in the household." He grinned and chugged several generous swallows.

I didn't want praise, and after my excitement had long passed, I doubted I had any real effect. "I wouldn't say I'm a witch because I knocked over a two-inch piece of plastic, which, by the way, didn't have a sturdy base. A breeze is just as likely to deserve the credit."

"Don't be so hard on yourself," Allison said, folding her legs in front of her. "Your aunt passed down the book from your family line. It's who you are, and with enough practice, the sky's the limit on your power. Our great-great-great-grandmother Edith Johnson survived a fire just to make sure future generations of warriors were left to fight the vampires and keep humans alive."

And she'd left an incredible legacy behind. I'd grown up trying to meet my dad's strict expectations of becoming a doctor, and I'd failed time and again. My sister had been unfairly given lower standards, but I thought all that was normal—family expectations and a healthy dose of competition. Then, a cascade of crushing deaths revealed I was part of this hidden world all along. Now I had new expectations to fail—my roommates'.

I wasn't smart enough to become a medical researcher, and now I had the pressure of becoming a witch tasked with keeping humans alive. If there were less organic chemistry involved…

I chugged down my whiskey sour and glanced at the little green army guy. My windows were drafty, and for all I knew, Allison herself knocked the army guy over just to motivate me. My roommate's high-pressure words repeated in my head, and I blinked. "Did you say *warriors*?"

A grin lifted Jamie's lips. "Witches are the protectors of humans, who are at a great disadvantage over elves and vampires. You know vampires suck people dry for food, and you're aware of how awful that experience is. If the public found out, there would be pitchforks and a revolt. It's happened before."

I hated playing devil's advocate, but I was curious about this seemingly unnecessary balance. "Dumb question. If you don't like vampires at all, why don't you kill them all and be done with it?"

"It's a numbers game. Humans outnumber all vampires, witches, and elves combined. It's not even close. If the secret were revealed, eventually the pitchforks would win. So we keep their existence secret, but if they get out of line or if we're having a bad day, we take them out at any obscure opportunity."

I *saved* people. I didn't kill people—fangs or no fangs. Everyone deserved a second chance. The universe was playing a cruel joke. "Can I opt out of the second half of that deal?"

Jamie chuckled. "You wouldn't want to."

"And don't forget the elves. They're so much worse," Allison said.

Snarls flashed through my mind—Evangeline's and Soren's while under an evil witch's control. They had been the epitome of danger. Toss in a sprinkle of immortality, homicidal tendencies, and a total loss of humanity. They were literal walking nightmares. I knew almost nothing about elves, and now I was morbidly curious—mostly about the elf who put his hands on me and wanted to marry me apparently every time he saw me. "How could they be worse?"

Allison shifted position to face me. "Now that you're out of Pierce's control—"

I had to stop her there. "Control? You guys are witch warriors tasked with protecting people. If elves are so bad, and you knew he was compelling me, why you didn't do anything about it?"

Allison and Jamie shared a look.

"What?" I demanded.

Allison said, "He tried to compel you for a long time. It worked only during a narrow window. I suspect when the spiked water bottles ran out and when you started wearing that." She pointed to my gift from Oliver. I listened to her words, mulling them over, trying to understand what she was telling me.

My stomach twisted. "Are you saying I was choosing to be with him?"

"He's cute. And there's some charm there sometimes," Allison said sheepishly. "But if we would've warned you before you knew about all this, would you have believed us?"

I was more angry with myself. Through gritted teeth, I said, "Tell me what I'd almost signed up for."

"Forced procreation," Allison said slowly. "When the children reach the age of five, they are taken away to be raised by the elf clan, and the mothers' memories are wiped. All traces of the child's existence are erased, including the mother's physical changes: stretch marks, sagging skin, c-section scars. Elves can heal that away."

Surely I heard wrong. "What?"

Jamie took over. "There are no female elves left in the world. They substitute human women, but only male offspring result, so the cycle continues. For the survival of their species, they keep their secret and compel the mothers to forget their children."

I remembered the shockingly painful truth Pierce had admitted after we returned from the gruesome hostage situation at the lab. Now strong enough to tell my roommates without crying, I said, "And elves can't love, so they don't care about the pain they inflict. They only erase it for their own protection."

Allison said, "Correct."

Still, there was a loophole. "But if a human is emotionally charged enough, they can break the elf's compulsion. What then?"

"With no trace of the child, or physical reminders of the child, the mother tends to...struggle...mentally." Allison sipped from her drink and broke eye contact.

I couldn't imagine being the only one to remember my own child. That was cruel, and that was what Pierce wanted for me, what my dad pushed me toward. I wanted children in this house. Even if I'd settled for the one who could give them to me, he would've stolen them and magically gaslighted the shit out of me. My hands turned into fists. Fury surged through the alcohol in my swimmy brain. "But it takes a village. What happens to the neighbors, daycare workers, relatives?"

"Elves compel the mothers into certain services and, when necessary, come out in teams to compel any witnesses," Allison said.

"Daisy," Jamie's hand rested on my arm. "We understand how upsetting this is. We did what we could without influencing your decisions, and we told you the truth in pieces because it's a lot to swallow."

I dated a loyal, handsome blond with an uncanny ability to heal patients. We hadn't been a match in the bedroom, and he never seemed to truly 'get' me, but that didn't mean I didn't respect him. If my roommates had told me Pierce Evansson was a mythological creature intent on mating and abandoning me, oh, and stealing my child, I would've laughed. And after I'd regained my composure, I would've asked if they needed mental health services. My roommates did everything right, and they really cared about how I was feeling throughout this whole learning curve.

"I get *why* you protect people from elves, and I get why people need protection against vampires," I said, calming down. "But why do elves feud with vampires?"

"It's a matter of their survival," Jamie said. "Vampires feed on humans—elves' procreation source, and unless an elf heals away the taint of the vampire's bite, the victim is rendered unable to carry an elf baby to term."

My hand went to my throat. Soren had bitten me, but Pierce had shown up to heal me immediately after while I'd been unconscious. Evangeline had bitten me, and he healed me tonight. Pierce couldn't love me. He didn't care about me at all. The elf only wanted to protect his future offspring—the real reason why Pierce was a paramedic—for easy access to the public after vampire attacks. "I think I'm going to be ill."

"Here," Allison said, holding a bottle of whiskey. "This helps."

I drank until I didn't remember the rest of the night.

# II

# Interrogation

## Oliver

I ADORED THE RAW beauty of horsepower, and ignoring the throbbing pain spreading from my grazed arm across my chest and back, I'd never needed to use it more than now. Instead, I drove like a stereotypical grandmother, focusing hard to stay rational. Soren hugged the box of fragile vials, and my urgency couldn't compromise the integrity of the cure itself. Soren refrained from commenting on my leisurely driving, which was unusual but appreciated.

I pulled my Shelby to the curb in front of Dr. Greg Barrett's upper-middle class home, resting on a quiet road between the bustling city center and the local branch of the University of Wisconsin. The backyard privately abutted the Bay of Green Bay. Depending on the time of day, this location was peaceful and quiet, like now. Still, I didn't need a student jogging by to catch an eyeful or record a video on their phone.

Open curtains revealed the doctor reading alone by lamplight. When dear old Dr. Barrett shot me, I'd received an invitation inside his family home, but Soren hadn't. We approached the door, and my brother waited patiently on the porch, trapped behind the mystical barrier at the threshold, arms carrying the critical box full of vials.

"What if someone asks me what I'm doing? I'm not a package thief." Soren shifted his weight, carefully hugging my life in his arms.

"Tell them you're selling Girl Scout cookies."

"Then they'll want some."

"At this hour? Soren, compel them." I swept into the house on silent feet and sped around the living room, closing the curtains before the doctor even felt my presence.

Greg pushed thick glasses up his nose and turned a page on the stapled pack of papers in his lap. I lurked behind him, waiting for the homicidal geriatric to notice the change in his surroundings, while an anxious pen wiggled back and forth between his fingers. I fought the immense urge to re-home that pen into his throat. But if I killed him, I was dead too.

I leaned over his shoulder to see what was so fascinating that he hadn't noticed the curtains closing, when my eye caught on the white wires dangling from his ears. I tore one free from his ear canal—not so gently.

The doctor startled, dropping the papers, and he craned his neck.

Before he could say a word, I gave him a fair warning. "Be very careful of what you do and say, understand?"

Greg nodded, eyes widened in both terror and shock. Words failed to pour out, but his gaze sought the wound on my arm. His mouth popped open and closed like a fish out of water. And finally, he spoke. "How...? How...are you still alive? I—I shot you! You should be dead. How is this possible?"

I circled around to face him. With just the two of us and no witnesses but my brother, I descended my fangs to threaten him. "Give Soren an invitation."

Dr. Greg Barrett sized me up further, and the fear melted into a smirk, stupidly deciding I wasn't a threat to him. His gaze settled on my neck. "If you kill me, Daisy will hate you forever. And I'm guessing, based on those inky track marks reaching above your collar, you won't be around much longer, so I recommend you use your time wisely with her. Not me."

"You make a strong point, doc. But killing you sounds fun, and my brother can compel her to forget your murder. Although if you would've spoken with her lately, I don't think she'd be that upset."

The smirk slid away, and I enjoyed the taunt. I couldn't kill him—not yet, anyway.

"Invite my brother inside."

"If you're going to kill me anyway, why should I bother?" The doctor asked, trying and failing to hide his fear.

I gritted my teeth, wanting to rip him limb from limb like a roasted turkey at Thanksgiving. And since I didn't eat human food, I'd carry his parts over to a hungry mutt and relish in the dog's enjoyment of an unexpected feast. Instead, I trembled with restraint. "You know about vampires—the painful puncture, the paralysis, the draining of your blood until your heart pumps in a panic, and then you pass out. It's quick, sometimes clean, and not as scary as what I'll do to you.

Like your old buddy Newt, I happen to have a master's degree and decades of experience in torture."

As a demonstration, I gripped Greg by the throat and lifted him clear off his plush recliner. His face flushed red with strain and lack of oxygen. A tiny pleasure surged through me, temporarily easing my own throbbing pain. "I'm not going to tell you again."

Greg blinked rapidly and tried to move his head. I supposed he meant to agree to the deal, so I loosened my grip on his airway and lowered his feet to the floor. He folded over and coughed and gasped uncontrollably.

I gave him a few beats for the fit to end, but I didn't have all night. "Doctor, someone is waiting for their invitation."

Greg Barrett waved at the door and croaked, "Soren, come in."

My brother delivered the box of vials to the coffee table and set it down carefully.

After the doctor regained his composure, he asked, "What's this?"

"Pick out the cure, and we'll walk away," I said. "If not, well, I foresee you choosing to light yourself on fire to destroy your own nerves."

The doctor nodded, sweat beading on his forehead. He lifted out trays of vials, eyes widening. "Did you take everything from my lab?"

"Every last one," I said, and a stab of pain radiated down my thigh.

"But these must stay refrigerated," he said, aghast at the risk to his life's work.

"Doctor," I said, capturing his attention and activating my compulsion. "Choose the cure and only the cure now."

Greg nodded and dug deep into the box. He slipped one vial free from a rack and handed it to me. "This will do it."

I didn't trust him one bit. "Doctor," I repeated, reactivating my ability on him. "Do fifty jumping jacks."

"Fifty? I'm too old for that." His face shifted as he realized his mistake.

I shouldn't have been surprised, but after all the mud I'd been dragged through, I was hoping for a clean stretch of road. Instead, a crumbled bridge over an endless dark abyss awaited me, and the reach to the other side grew further away by the second. I returned the vial to him. "Take a drink."

"What?" Greg said, aghast. "I can't."

"If it's not poison, you'll be fine—grossed out, but fine."

Greg accepted the vial and paused, considering. He threw the vial, shattering it over the television, and blood dribbled down the wall like the gruesome gunshot scene he'd wanted from me. "If I drink it, I'll vomit. The human body can't tolerate ingesting blood, so that tells you nothing."

"Soren," I said in a warning tone.

"Don't kill him," Soren replied lightly.

Sometimes...my patience was tested beyond its limits. "How long have you been ingesting vervain?"

Greg sneered. "Months. You don't have time to wait me out."

No, kidding. "Then I'll simply have to speed up the process." I pulled the doctor's arm and twisted it, exposing his wrist, and I dug into his flesh with a sharp fingernail.

"Wait!" The terror on Greg's face returned, and he tried to pull free, but his human strength was no match for me, even in my weakened state. "When Newt died, he took the only cure with him. Everything in that box is a different version of the weapon."

I exhaled as an old habit to center my anger. Somehow, I already knew that. I nodded to my brother, who silently understood my message. He lifted the box and tipped it over onto the carpet. Glass shattered, blood splattered, and the doctor yelled in horror. One vial didn't break, so Soren took it upon himself to stomp on it.

Finding no further use for Greg, I released him, and the doctor dropped to his knees by the mess. If I waited around long enough, I expected the doctor to break down in sobs over his loss. Daisy had been right. He really cared more about his work than his own daughter. Greg didn't deserve to live, but I couldn't take that from her. I had to be satisfied with destroying the only thing he loved.

I tipped my head toward the door, gesturing to Soren my intent to leave. My brother followed on my heels. Outside, the calm night swallowed us. Water from the bay lapped at the shoreline, and a bicyclist rode by with blinking safety lights. The city was at peace, but I was dying. After a hundred and eighty-some years, I never imagined it ending like this.

"Now what?" Soren asked grimly.

"I have to tell Daisy goodbye, a conversation I planned sixty years into the future." Her breakdown would devastate me, but I'd kept this news from her long enough. I wished only for a Hail Mary pass—Soren had spent months as Newt's personal slave. "Unless you know of someone else who carries the cure in their veins."

Soren kept pace as we approached my Shelby. "Actually, it's a long shot, but what do you have to lose?"

I lifted an eyebrow. "I'm listening."

"Evangeline."

Since Soren's blood didn't work, I was skeptical of Evangeline's. But I had nothing to lose by trying. Facing my ex-girlfriend was the last thing on my bucket list, but I would do anything to live, to stay by Daisy's side, and to keep her safe from her conniving father and the evil elf. "Where is she?"

Soren and Newt had worked closely together with Evangeline as the witch's subject, so if anyone knew where she wanted to go or what she was after, it was Soren.

"She's here."

## Oliver

SOME THINGS IN LIFE had to be done alone. Facing the woman I'd wronged all those decades ago was one of them, especially since I needed a favor, and my brother had killed her once and returned her to the lab for further torture. I parked in front of the address Soren had given me. Considering the depravity Evangeline had lived in for years, I wasn't surprised she'd chosen well.

I climbed out of my Shelby with a searing pinch in my thigh, hoping I didn't collapse under my own weight, and I closed the door with the wrong arm. I gritted my teeth against the sharp pain. As the poison progressed, the pain became a dull throbbing ache with pokes and stabs, twitching my muscles, and my body temperature rose. At first it was great, since I naturally ran cooler, but any higher and I was going to perspire, and that wasn't attractive to anyone, unless they were tussling the sheets with supple skin in their mouths.

The two–story home was something straight out of a bland builder's magazine—an identical neighborhood with slight differences in options. This one had a wooden rowboat next to a lamp as a landscaping feature. Surrounding it and sprinkled around the perimeter was red gravel with baby shrubs dotting the length of the house. There were no vehicles on the concrete driveway, but the three-car garage likely had some parked inside. A single light in a downstairs window glowed on the front lawn.

I strolled up the porch and knocked politely before reaching out with my heightened senses. A vampire's presence registered inside, and I braced myself for anything as the door opened. My jaw dropped. Evangeline Brant cleaned up well—hair tamed into silky straight strands cascading over her shoulders, a low-cut blouse she must've nabbed from the homeowners, and a pair of slim jeans hugging her shape that had been hidden by the layers of our time.

A hand rested on her hip. "You're catching flies."

I closed my mouth. "Evangeline, you look..." I trailed off, lost for words. She was no longer a disheveled lab rat. Nor was she a lost girl stifled by her Puritan parents and draped in the drab clothing of village life in the 1870s Wisconsin. She was simply stunning, and even more so when her lips curved into a satisfied smile.

"Come inside." She flicked her index finger at me, urging me to follow.

I reached a hand to test the barrier, but there wasn't one. I frowned. "Did you kill the humans who live here?"

She shrugged. "They had what I needed. We came to a mutual understanding. Sit down and let me pour you a drink. These humans have such a fabulous selection. Scotch?"

Still stunned by the transformation, I followed her inside, and with disbelief and self-loathing, I peeled my eyes from her. I missed Daisy. It should be Daisy's fine ass shimmying in front of me, but instead, I was here to beg a scorned woman to save my life. I wasn't confident she'd agree, and then that flattering outfit of hers would get ruined. Such a shame.

"Tequila, if they have it. Neat, please."

"Coming right up." She approached a small bar, more modern and of less quality than my own, and she poured us drinks, her back facing me. Rocks rattled in one glass. I focused on the sleek furnishings, a place that screamed of a household free of pets and children. Glass accents left the room spacious and airy, and the couch was a light gray, contrasting pleasantly with the dark cool tones of the hardwood flooring. Trendy, modern, nice but cheap. Mass manufactured, the sign of our times.

Evangeline carried a pair of glasses and handed one to me. I sipped. Not terrible, considering their taste in furniture.

"Tell me why you tracked down my little sanctuary all by your lonesome." Evangeline sipped from her glass, and a sensual lift of her lips made my skin crawl. She wasn't the woman I'd wanted all those years ago, but then I'd changed too.

"You know I don't ask for favors lightly."

Her brow lifted in amusement, and she smiled seductively. "Oh, do continue."

I unbuttoned the top buttons of my shirt, revealing the blackened veins crawling up my throat.

"No," she said angrily. She set her empty glass on the coffee table and rose, staring at the gruesome poison circulating through my body.

I stood up and fastened the buttons back in place, not dissuaded by her refusal.

"No, this isn't how you die. No way. The doctor did this, didn't he? That bastard." She pointed rigidly at me, accusatory. "How could you gallivant all over town with his daughter—*human* daughter—knowing that evil doctor wants to kill us all?"

"In my defense—" I started, intending to finish with, 'You were human when we met, and my involvement with Daisy predated our knowledge of her dad's work.' But I didn't think either of those would help my case.

Evangeline cut me off. "I almost say it serves you right, but no, I can't let this happen. That doctor isn't going to win. Come with me."

Eagerly, I swallowed the last of my tequila, not wanting it to go to waste, and dropped the glass next to hers. I followed

Evangeline down a darkened corridor, through a door, and down carpeted stairs into the basement. It was finished like normal living quarters, but the windows were much smaller and the carpet cheaper. The mounted television and leather recliners made me believe this was a human's 'man cave'. I always wondered about the appeal. Having designed and built my own house, having an entertainment area separate from the social spaces seemed pointless, which was why I had the bar built in the center of the first floor—easy hosting.

"Right through here." Evangeline gestured through a door she'd opened, and I walked in ahead of her, ready for the cure.

Trust was such a fickle thing. One moment I thought I knew the woman I'd wanted to marry all those years ago, and the next, she took a baseball bat to the back of my head. There was no forgiving her for it, but I supposed after everything I did to her, I deserved it.

My vision turned black, and my consciousness took a dirt nap. I didn't have time for this.

# 12
# The Confrontation

**Oliver**

THE RHYTHMIC POUNDING OF a figurative hammer on my head woke me. To prevent my skull from splitting, I lifted a weakened arm, and as I pressed a palm to my temple, the weight of the effort was almost unbearable. Then I realized the rattle of chains accompanied my movements. I opened my aching eyes and found myself in darkness. The room didn't have comfortable furnishings, like the rest of the basement. The floor was cold, hard, and barren. Iron rings had been mounted in the concrete wall above my head. I feebly tugged at the bindings attached to my wrists. I wasn't strong enough to escape.

I was all for kink, but this had me judging the shit out of these humans.

With my arms raised by chains, I just barely reached two tired fingers to drag my shirt sleeve away from the wrist, and the spidered veins told me I was still dying. Evangeline had declined my request. I tilted my head back against the cold concrete and winced at the lovely reminder the baseball bat had left. I shouldn't have been surprised. The Evangeline I knew died the night Soren had drained her. I didn't suppose her years in captivity helped her personality any.

My eyelids slid closed in exhaustion from the pain. I wanted relief. I needed to feed. My body was on fire, and only the chill of the concrete stopped me from becoming my own personal fountain of sweat. My head sagged forward. I couldn't muster the energy to be angry at myself.

"You're finally awake," Evangeline said.

I tipped my head back up. "Hardly."

She squatted in front of me. The smirk was back. "By now, I assume you know why I brought you here."

Even with brain damage, I could guess vengeance. I shifted my wrists to rattle the chains. "This is iron. Did you have someone else in mind when you set this up?"

"I didn't put these in. The wacko humans did."

I managed a self-satisfied smile. "But you didn't coat them in vervain."

Evangeline chuckled. "You still have a sense of humor. Imagine that."

I had nothing to escape with but my rapidly fading wit. Perhaps I could plead with the remaining sliver of humanity buried somewhere deep in the recesses of her fancy blouse. "I don't know what you want me to say. Am I surprised? No. Am I disappointed? Absolutely."

A flicker passed across her features. "I disappointed you? I thought you were the man of my dreams. A strong, hardworking, sexy-as-hell farmer with a big, tight-knit family. Even my father approved, which said a lot."

And none of that stung. She wasn't very good at twisting the knife. "Plans rarely go the way we want." Or never, in my case.

"Plans...?" she repeated in a tone of disbelief. "You and your brother were monsters in sheep's clothing. And stupid me for not having figured it out until it was too late. Soren Rockwell attacked me and left me for dead."

"And I never forgave him." It was the truth.

Evangeline rose and placed her hands on her hips. "What he did was unforgiveable, but you—do you want a 'thank you', a pat on the back? You're the one who killed me. You're the one who made me like this, and then you abandoned me."

A weight settled on my shoulders. It was all true, except she'd left me. Evangeline was the reason I would never turn another human again. "Nothing I could ever say would be enough to properly convey my deepest apologies, but you must understand, I am truly sorry."

"Rather than let me die and take the deserved fallout in the village you both deserved, you turned me into a monster to keep your secret. As if I'd do you such a favor, you coward."

It didn't happen often, but I hated when Soren was right. "It's not cowardly to save the woman you love," I said, sadness dragging me down. Evangeline scoffed. "I never would've turned you without your permission, but I didn't have that choice. I couldn't watch you die."

"You could've healed me," she countered.

And there was the twist of the knife. Bravo. "I believed our love could survive the change, that you'd eventually come to accept the new you and continue loving me. I selfishly wanted us to be together because I was too weak to let you go."

While I poured my heart out with decades of regret, Evangeline only stared daggers at me. "You should've let me die."

Those were words of self-hatred. Regret. "I would've taught you to control your urges and how to feed without detection."

Evangeline tensed. "You know fresh vampires are out of control, yet you didn't have the patience for me to learn."

"You murdered dozens of people on a rampage, threatening to expose us. We had that discussion, and you took off for Europe, never giving me a chance."

"And after figuring myself out, I came back for you. But instead of open arms, you killed me again—or thought you had."

Generally, I was an efficient killer, but Evangeline was slippery. Forty years ago, I'd received word vampire Evangeline had returned to town looking for me. To prevent another pile of bodies from becoming public, I'd confronted her, and I honestly thought I had killed her.

"I couldn't risk a repeat of 1880." The bodies. The screaming. The pitchforks and angry mob. I still had nightmares on occasion.

Evangeline slapped me across the cheek.

Oww. I pulled in my lower lip to ease the sting, but it didn't help. "Even if I'd walked away, Pierce's dad was hunting you, but Logonson killed Sadie instead."

"I heard about you doing the elf, but you avenged Sadie. I don't see how that's supposed to be a defense. That night, your stake was off just enough to take me down but not out. It wasn't the physical damage that hurt. PDI took me. I'd been trapped in that cell getting poked, prodded, scraped, and injected for forty years—because you are a terrible killer. Because you couldn't finish what you started. Because you rejected me again." Evangeline held back tears, and the guilt was crushing. "Even worse, in all those decades, you never rescued me. I bet you never thought of rescuing me."

"I didn't know."

Evangeline kicked my leg. I almost couldn't feel it anymore. "I suppose my torture can be to your benefit, though, so it's not a total loss. With a whole lot of nothing to occupy me between their experiments, I learned a lot. For instance, the cure remains active long enough to neutralize the poison, and then it's gone. Since Newt was never infected, the cure floated in his system a little longer. You're welcome."

There was never any hope.

"And now that you've destroyed my life, I'm going to destroy yours."

The veins all over my body had turned inky during my baseball-bat-induced slumber, and now my flesh began to blacken like soot. "You might want to hurry up."

"I know the pain that's still coming for you. The sharp stabs, the constricting dull ache, the sweats, the hallucinations. I'm going to watch you die slowly, and when your corpse begins to stain the floor, I'm taking out Soren, but don't worry. I won't have the patience to drag out his death. After that, I'm reclaiming my necklace. I'll drink your replacement human dry, so at least her life won't be a total waste, and she won't have to live with regrets."

Tears of defeat streamed down my cheeks. I couldn't do a damned thing to stop my malevolent ex-girlfriend. I hoped Soren sniffed out Evangeline's plot before she killed him and that he had sense enough to protect Daisy. I'd failed to save the woman I loved from the darkness of my past.

"Don't go anywhere. I'll be right back." Evangeline stepped out of the room.

But I couldn't give up until the end. I tipped my head back against the cold concrete and sucked in a deep breath. Giving my all, I clenched my upper body to rip the chains from the walls, but engaging the muscles felt like I'd been thrown into a fire. Raging heat tore through me like a field of dry grass. Sweat dripped down my forehead. I roared through the pain and pulled.

The iron strained under the force. Metal squeaked. But nothing was giving. I sagged, and my face pinched with the agonizing burn.

"There you are! I've been looking everywhere for you." Daisy's voice.

I snapped up my heavy head. My love, with fear and panic on her beautiful features, rushed to my side and gripped my face in her hands. To my burning flesh, she felt like ice—relief. She kissed my lips with a fervor only our separation could bring about. My dreary state left me unable to feel her soft lips, and she pulled away far too soon. Big brown eyes searched my battered face.

"I've never been more grateful for your beautiful face than right now." I managed a weak smile.

"Save your energy. I'm getting you out of here." Daisy reached for my wrists.

My love was no match for the angry vampire lurking in this house, and I couldn't defend Daisy against her. "You'll never get me out of here, and Evangeline's close. Save yourself. Find Soren if you must. But go, Daisy. You have to go."

"I didn't even try." Daisy grabbed the heavy chains and braced her feet against the wall, tugging with all her might.

Nothing happened.

"It's no use," I told her.

"Don't give up on me yet. I have new tricks." Daisy pulled a knife from her back pocket. "Hold still."

That wasn't going to help, but I didn't have the energy to argue.

"But please do scream when it hurts." Evangeline's voice so close turned my blood colder than usual.

I blinked. My ex stood where Daisy had been, with a serrated steak knife in her hand and a quirk of amusement on her lips.

Frantically, I searched for Daisy. "What did you do to her? Daisy! Daisy, run!"

Evangeline's sinister smile curdled my dead heart. "Hallucinations starting? Well, then I better be quick about this." She kneeled by my side and dragged the tip of the blade along my shirt, teasing.

The poison coursing through my veins was incurable, but for as long as I survived Evangeline's torture, then she couldn't harm those I loved. All I had to do was stay conscious until the poison inevitably took me. The phone in my pocket rang, a hollow plea I couldn't answer.

Evangeline punctured my chest with the blade.

I gritted my teeth and grunted.

"Louder, please," she ordered with a melodious tune.

I hoped for the hallucinations to return while Evangeline carved my soul to pieces.

I screamed at the next stab.

# 13

# Gather the Team

**Daisy**

I begrudgingly rolled out of bed, hair a tangled mess around my face, head pounding with a hangover. I'd only slept a few hours, terribly at that. I finger-combed the snarls hanging in my eyes and picked up my phone off the end table. All my calls to Oliver were unanswered, and only one text had been read. Since his last response told me he and Soren were together, I'd tried his brother too, but he hadn't answered either. I dressed in jeans and a T-shirt and went downstairs.

Jamie was making waffles and eggs in the kitchen, half dressed, but covered with his apron and thankfully free of oil and glitter. He grabbed a knife from the wooden knife block in the cabinet. It was weird Allison insisted the knives stay in the cabinet when there were no children around, but I never pressed the issue. "Good morning, sunshine. Do you want some?"

Food was the last thing on my mind. I poured a glass of water and downed a pair of painkillers. "You were dancing in a packed club a few hours ago. How did you wake up so bubbly?"

Jamie dragged eggs around the pan. "The trick is not to imbibe the refreshments...and not to go to bed. It's easier to stay up for a morning class and crash later than function on less than four hours of sleep."

"I'll keep that in mind for next time." I checked my phone again, now clearer headed, and inspected the bars of service. That wasn't the issue either. "Have you heard from Oliver?"

Jamie dropped waffles into the toaster. "Why would I?"

"Did he drop by while I was comatose?"

Jamie turned to face me, finally catching my concern. "What's wrong?"

Everything. "He's not answering his phone."

"An ancient vampire hasn't figured out technology. I'm not surprised. If you're worried, go to his house. I bet you'll find him sound asleep in his fancy-pants bed."

"How do you know his bed is 'fancy pants'? Been there recently?"

The toaster popped, and Jamie lifted the scorching hot waffles onto plates. "A rich guy always has a fancy bed. It's in the rulebook for picking up women. Expensive clothes, check. Sexy car, check. Big fancy house, check. Naturally, he has the bed to go with the whole package. I bet he has mirrors mounted on the ceiling."

I frowned. Oliver did not. "Whatever. I know he's not asleep. Something is wrong, and I need your help to find him."

Jamie paused, and seriousness crossed his face. He considered for a few beats and said, "You're talking about a spell."

"Is there one? Something to locate a person, I mean." It sure beat driving all over town and knocking on doors.

"Are you sure that's necessary?"

"I've tried everything I know." Which, admittedly, wasn't much. Oliver had gone out to feed, so his gunshot wound would heal. Since he'd been strictly a bag-guy, I'd been concerned about his ability to control the need. Next I knew, Soren was with him, which made me feel a little better, but neither brother was answering the phone.

Jamie paused and assessed my rapidly growing concern. "Okay then. Locator spell it is."

A grin crossed my face. "Thank you, thank you, thank you so much. What can I do to help?"

"I'll need something personal of his."

"No problem." I slipped the anti-vampire and anti-elf locket over my head and handed it to him.

"This will work. While I set up, can you man the eggs?"

I accepted the spatula while dutifully supervising the toaster. Jamie dragged a chest of witchcraft supplies into the living room. He set up a circle of candles and placed a map of the tri-city area in the center. The toaster popped, and I set the steaming discs of starchy goodness on plates. I turned off the burner and shifted the pan of eggs to cool before joining my roommate.

Jamie placed my necklace in the center of the map and sprinkled some herbs over it. We held hands, and he chanted, focusing on the map. After picking up the incantation, I repeated with him. The herbs lifted into the air and danced like leaves blowing in a cyclone of wind. Candlelight flickered dramatically in the same invisible storm. At once, the candles extinguished, and the herbs settled in a circle over a spot not far away in Menominee.

Jamie stopped his chanting and pointed. "He's right there."

That was a solid middle-class neighborhood across the bridge in Michigan. What would he be doing there? "Are you sure?"

"The spell is always right."

I collected my necklace and dropped it over my head. "I'm going. Are you coming with?"

"Me?" Jamie flinched with surprise and cast a forlorn glance at the cooling breakfast. "Well, yeah, I suppose I could, but I have a class soon. I'll drive."

Jamie grabbed a pair of dry waffles and ate them like a sandwich as we both headed outside for his SUV. Dawn sent a dim blanket of warm light over the landscape, and the sun would laze over the horizon in another few minutes. I was wide awake with nerves and worry. Something or someone had to be holding him. There was no other explanation for his ignoring my messages or not coming here to see me.

I counted on Jamie's witchy defenses to help. I climbed onto the passenger side, heart pounding in anticipation, and cringed at the overpowering cologne. "What's that smell?"

Jamie turned to me, puzzled, and I followed his gaze. All his show props and costumes were in the back. "What smell?" he asked defensively.

"You should wash that stuff more often."

"Are you volunteering your machine with all my glitter and oil?" I shook my head. "All right then."

I cracked a window as my roommate started the vehicle and took a left turn—in the wrong direction.

"The house is that way." I pointed in the opposite direction.

"I'm bringing a friend, you know, just in case."

"Okay," I said hesitantly. I didn't know what to think of that.

Jamie pulled to the curb outside Fully Loaded, and I smiled in relief. As if I had any reason to doubt Jamie's intentions. He sent a text, and moments later, Allison pushed through the front door with a cheery smile on her face. She climbed into the back seat. "Welcome back from the dead, Daisy. I bet that was one awful hangover. What's with the valet service?"

Jamie tipped his face into the rearview mirror. "We're hunting a missing vampire."

I frowned.

My roommate backpedaled, "*Finding*. I don't mean hunting literally, of course. Oliver's your man, so he's our friend by association."

"I appreciate that," I said, not realizing how much hearing those words meant. They were true friends, and I could count on them.

"What are we expecting to find?" Allison asked.

"Last I knew, Oliver had to feed. Since he normally avoids live humans, I'm guessing he may have...lost a bit of...control. And Soren must've locked him up until it passes." I shivered at the thought. My mind had jumped to the worst—a whole lot of bodies Soren was helping to hide. "I should've heard something from one of them by now."

Jamie drove us over the Hattie Street bridge, and we wove through sleepy city streets. At this hour, the traffic was light, but people were stirring for their morning routines. Hopefully, we could solve the mystery without anyone getting hurt—or noticed by the public.

At the house indicated by the magical herbs, Jamie parked at the curb behind another vehicle—one I would never forget. Nerves skittered down my spine.

"Doesn't look like anyone's here," Allison said. The entire neighborhood was quiet. The house in question was dark.

"He's here. He has to be. That's his car." Oliver's Shelby rested in front of us.

"Daisy, are you sure you want to do this?" Jamie asked. "You said he claimed he was with Soren."

I didn't understand their hesitation. It was almost like they wanted to talk me out of finding him, but I could handle the shock of a vampire in the throes of bloodlust. "Of course, why?"

Allison touched my shoulder. "If Oliver's inside...with someone else," she said slowly, "and he used his brother as an alibi, are you sure you want to see what's going on in there?"

I stiffened at the heart-wrenching thought. I hadn't considered Oliver could be cheating. But if he really wanted to hide a side piece, he could've compelled me to forget her whenever I questioned his whereabouts. I couldn't believe that. Not my Oliver.

Before I could string a coherent denial, Jamie said, "Well, prepare yourself for the chance they both fell off the wagon, and that means you might see an orgy in there or a mass feeding session—either one is messy and gruesome, and certainly not for the feint of heart."

My lips curled in disgust, but I refused to accept that possibility. "I'm going in. Come with or not. Your choice."

"I'm coming," Allison said. "Regardless of what you see, I'll be by your side."

I was relieved Allison agreed, if for no other reason than a shoulder to cry on.

"I'm in. Never know what the bloodsuckers are up to."

I darted Jamie a look.

"Relax. Oliver and Soren are off limits, but if anyone else attacks me or Alli, they're fair game."

"Fine." I climbed out of the SUV and quietly closed the door behind me. My roommates followed on my heels, and we all kept watch as I approached the front door. Since Oliver was here, I didn't expect to find any homeowners, so I turned the knob and pushed my way inside.

"Hello?" I whispered.

The glow of the coming dawn lit a dim path into the living room, but the rest of the home's interior was shrouded in darkness. I grabbed my phone out of my pocket and lit up the screen. My battery was too low to run the flashlight. I'd forgotten to charge it last night in my drunken, glitter-and-Pierce-infested stupor. "I don't hear anything, but I need a light."

Allison touched my shoulder, and I startled reflexively.

"Sorry. Repeat after me." Allison chanted softly, and I repeated her words, focusing on the dormant power within as she'd taught me. I funneled my fear into my palms. After several rounds of chants, I opened my eyes, expecting a soft flicker of light, just a tease like the little green army guy who may or may not have fallen over. Instead, a soft light, less than a nightlight, glowed from my palm, as if I'd held a flashlight beneath it. It wasn't enough to function by, but it was proof Allison was right about me, about my ancestral line.

I was a witch.

A witch in hibernation, but still. The realization hit me like a sack of bricks. What would it feel like to have all my power at my disposal? The thought of what I could do...someday...lit a second proverbial fire in my chest. "Holy shit!" I whisper-yelled.

Allison lit her own palms, glowing bright enough to light the whole reachable first floor. Show off. She smiled in her own firelight. "I don't mean to say, 'I told you so,' but I told you so."

"Yeah, yeah," I agreed dismissively. "Let's find Oliver."

"Light the way, ladies," Jamie said.

"Hello?" I called. "Anyone here?"

My roommates spread out on either side of me, likely looking for the primary bedroom, while I headed for the most likely place I expected to find him: the basement. I opened and closed doors, making my way toward the kitchen, searching for the right one. Finally, I opened a door leading to a stairwell down. With my dim palm, I squinted to find my footing.

Since no one had answered my call, I stayed silent, wanting to retain any element of surprise I might still have. I stepped carefully down the carpeted stairs. Across the finished basement, a door was ajar. My footsteps were muffled by the carpeting, and I pulled it open slowly.

I reached for the light switch and flicked it on.

My heart jumped into my throat.

# 14
# Bite Me

**Daisy**

In all my time as an EMT, walking into people's homes to aid a person in distress, I'd seen many strange things. From a shoveled pathway through stacks of newspapers going back decades, to half-eaten takeout containers discarded randomly all over, to creatively placed swings and a shameless shrine of sex toys—some that clearly hadn't been washed since their last use. I never judged.

People came in all shapes and sizes, and more recently, with different teeth and magical abilities. I treated every patient with respect, even when getting kicked or spit on or introduced to new colorful language. The finished basement of this normal family home apparently ended at this ajar doorway, and now I was judging. I judged hard.

This could've been a secret BDSM room under construction, but the small concrete-encased room had nothing fun inside, only a pair of rusty iron rings mounted to the wall. The haphazard scrape marks from the sloppy mounting job told me this room wasn't for kink. No, this was a torture chamber assembled in a hurry.

With a glance at the singular occupant, my breath caught in my throat, and blood swished through my ears. Sitting limply against the wall, legs stretched before him and arms raised by the force of the chains, Oliver was bleeding, dark shirt clinging and glistening with his own blood. Beneath him, a puddle of blood stained the floor. Even worse, his hands were blackened—he'd been burned?

While I'd enjoyed ladies' night with my roommates, Oliver had been here, suffering immense torture. When my calls and texts went unanswered, I should've acted sooner. I should've listened to my instincts. His pain was my fault, and I didn't even know if he was alive.

I couldn't think like that. I was an EMT, trained for situations like this. Quick actions and rote processes would save his life. Oliver was like any other patient...sort of.

I rushed to his side and collapsed next to him, and just as quickly as I composed myself professionally, all my training went out the window. I cradled his face in my palms. "Oliver?"

His beautiful pale eyes were closed. I pressed fingers against his throat for a pulse. It was weak. Too weak.

"No, no, no. Oliver? Oliver!" I tapped his cheeks, trying to rouse him. I didn't have any medical supplies.

"What's going on?" Allison stood in the doorway, posture on the magical defensive. "Oh."

Oliver's eyelids fluttered open. "Evangeline, I know it's you. You can't fool me again." His voice was hoarse, as if he'd been screaming for hours.

"Oliver, it's me." I blinked back tears of relief while cursing whatever his psychotic ex-girlfriend had done to him.

His head rolled on his shoulders, and he focused on my face. "So realistic this time. I'll take what I can get before it's too late, but I know...I know it's you."

What was he talking about? "Oliver, it's me. Is Evangeline here? Is there anyone else in the house?" We hadn't seen anyone, but that didn't mean there weren't more of these torture rooms.

"Only you and me, silly." Oliver looked down at himself. "But I regret...never having bought the dry cleaners on Carney Avenue. Could've saved a fortune." His speech was slow and punctuated by pained breaths. He was out of it, as if he'd been drugged. It was so unsettling.

A sense of humor was a good sign, and a wet laugh escaped my lips. "I'm going to get you out of here." I curled myself under his arm, but a metallic rattle sank my stomach. The damned chains. I followed the links up through the rings and down to the floor behind him. Padlocked. "Where's the key?"

"I'm grateful...the hallucinations are giving me...the best gift I could ask for...you rescuing me on repeat. One last consolation I don't deserve. That's all I ever wanted for you—to be happy, but also safe. You're strong and capable of keeping yourself safe. I believe that now."

I couldn't imagine the amount of torture necessary to bring a formidable vampire into a state of delirium. "Oliver, I'm really here. I need the key to the lock. Please."

A slight lift of his lips had me worried. "You've really been here...four times already. Each time...gives me great hope…and crushing sadness. Let me bask in the hope a little while longer." His face pinched and his breath caught, a sign of terrible pain.

How was I going to get through to him? I leaned in close and pressed my lips to his. I released and repositioned, trying to coax him to kiss me back. He gasped and finally kissed me back.

"Daisy? It's you?" Clear, bright eyes stared back at me. "I felt you."

I smiled. "I guess hallucinations really do come true."

Oliver chuckled and winced in pain.

"I need the key to get you out of here."

"I wasn't…awake…to see where she placed it," Oliver said. "If I had full strength, I'd rip them…off the wall with the ease of a fly's wings. But Evangeline planned for that." His fingers swept along his chest, and his eyelids fluttered closed.

I looked over my shoulder, and Jamie stood alongside his sister, both wearing grim sets to their mouths, as if for a second, they pitied Oliver's plight. "Jamie, Alli, do you guys have a spell to break the lock?"

Allison rested a heavy hand on my shoulder. "We're too late. There's nothing we can do for him. Let's get out of here."

I rose and spun on her. Allison and I had worked side by side at Fully Loaded. She'd cheered me on when I enrolled in EMS school. Jamie was like a brother to me. I'd cut him a break on the rent a few times when gigs weren't flowing for him, and we shared sports and drinks on lazy weekends. And now, my best friends, my roommates, with whom I shared my life for years, turned their backs on me when I needed them most. "Can't you see he's been stabbed and burned? I'm not leaving him here for Evangeline to continue torturing. Help me!"

Jamie shook his head. "As witches, it's against our nature to save a vampire. Someday you'll understand, more than you know."

"Then why did you come with me?" I shouted. Tears sprang to my eyes. I couldn't believe this.

Jamie squared his shoulders and tipped his head up. "To make sure the job was done." After a moment for the words to sink in, he turned away, and Allison followed him out.

My mouth gaped. When Jamie had told me the tale of witches burning vampires and easily accepting the collateral damage of human lives, I thought his dismissiveness was due to distance and time. But here he was, fully capable of such cruelty himself. My fists shook at my sides.

"Daisy," Oliver whispered, recapturing my attention.

Pleading with them wouldn't solve the problem. I had to think, focus. He was my priority. I could deal with my roommates later. My hands supported his weak neck. "I'm going to get you out of here."

"It's too late. You need to...go with them." His hands covered mine. They were cold.

"There's no such thing as too late for a vampire." I inspected him more closely. His dress shirt was sliced and diced like he'd been thrown through a blender's blades. Blood smears covered his chest. I tore open his destroyed shirt and fell backward with a gasp.

The blackened flesh wasn't a burn. The black spidery streaks were familiar—the same as Soren's when he'd been poisoned by my dad's vampire weapon.

"Oh, but there is," Oliver countered softly.

My hands trembled, but this time, in total fear. "The gunshot—my dad infected you with the serum, and you didn't tell me? How could you have kept this a secret? We could've figured this out together. We're partners."

Oliver's heavy eyelids opened. "I thought I could find the cure...so you wouldn't have...to worry. There's nothing left to be done. You must go. Protect yourself against Pierce and Evangeline. Your dad. Those witches." Oliver's voice broke. "You have to protect yourself. I'm sorry I couldn't."

Oliver was a strong, bullheaded man who relished his power and strength, who always had a smile for me when I struggled. He was the one I could always count on to be strong and know what to do, but those were terrifying words of defeat and resignation. Luckily for him, I wasn't giving up.

"Don't give up on me. I'm getting you out of here." I released his beautiful face and gripped one of the chains. Using my full body weight, I yanked on the metal links, straining against the immovable iron and the thick padlock. Again and again I pulled, breath panting with exertion. I spun and searched the room for a tool, something for leverage, but there was nothing. On my way down here, I'd found carpeted floors, a television, and a pair of leather recliners. Nothing of use.

A fork or a spoon was a waste of time, but I didn't check the garage. "Be right back."

## Daisy

I RETRACED MY STEPS and headed for the hulking attached garage, on alert in case Evangeline decided to reappear. In the garage, I conjured my minuscule palm light and glanced around. No vehicles. It was almost as if the owners had moved out and had taken damn near everything. A yard rake wouldn't help. Negative on the garden shovel. No hammer. No drill, but the diameter of the ring mounts was smaller than the dimensions of the links. It wouldn't have helped either. Even if I found a crowbar or a damn chainsaw, I knew it wouldn't be enough to free Oliver.

The hardware store didn't open for several more hours. I headed back to Oliver empty-handed, just as defeated as him, trying to stay on my feet and not collapse along the way. Inside the torture chamber, Oliver didn't look up at me. I dropped to my knees and stared at my useless hands. Blood pumped through my veins, carrying a surge of adrenaline, but even my strength had its limits. I was only human. I didn't have any way of freeing him. My fingers were scraped and dirty from my useless attempts. Pricks of blood lifted on the scrapes.

My eyes widened.

I had the perfect tool right in front of me. Human blood. My blood. There was only one thing I could do—the scariest thing imaginable—give myself over to a hungry vampire. I didn't know if he could maintain control in his weakened condition. Remembering the nightmarish attack from Soren in front of my own house and Evangeline's foiled attempt, I never wanted another vampire's teeth anywhere near me, especially one suffering from bloodlust. But if I didn't offer myself to Oliver right now, he was going to die. Pushing aside the fear of being paralyzed and helpless against an apex predator, I removed my necklace and pressed my wrist against his lips. "Drink."

Oliver's eyelids fluttered open and closed.

I refused to believe I was too late. "Don't give up on me now. Drink and break the chains."

Oliver didn't move. The scrapes weren't enough to trigger his urge to feed. My lip quivered. With a shaky exhale, I used my own fingernails to dig into my wrist and expose a larger welling line of blood. I pressed the wounded flesh to his mouth.

Oliver shifted as if his instincts overrode his mind, and his fangs descended, puncturing my skin. My face pinched as searing pain radiated up my arm, and I tried to calm my breathing as the terrifying paralytic took over. One by one, I lost control of my muscles, and I couldn't hold myself upright. I tipped over onto the cold, hard floor, but Oliver's mouth held my wrist to his lips. He drank and drank, dragging more blood from me by the second.

My heart sped up, the warning sign of too much taken, but I couldn't stop him. I couldn't plead with him to stop. I watched as my love drained my life, unable to move, but seized with pain.

Oliver's eyes opened wide, and he released my arm with a satisfied sigh. My arm tumbled onto his lap.

"Daisy," he said breathlessly, worry creasing his brow. He craned his neck, seeking the source of his confinement. Chains rattled with his frustration. Gritting his teeth, he mustered his renewed strength and broke the chains free from the wall with a metallic screech. But it wasn't at all like plucking a fly's wings. He collapsed next to me from the effort, the inky veins having reached his throat. "...so sorry."

I'd never been more frustrated in my life watching a patient—my love—die before my eyes, and I was helpless to do anything. My roommates weren't fond of vampires, obviously, but after all this time, why couldn't they give Oliver a pass? He'd never hurt either of them. I'd trusted Allison and Jamie with my home. I trusted them as friends, but they only brought me here to make sure Oliver would die, and I could never forgive that. In fact, when all this was settled, I was giving them a formal 30-day notice to vacate the hell out of my house. Regardless of my inability to afford my mortgage without their rent payments, I'd rather be homeless than forgive their betrayal. I didn't know who to trust anymore, and that feeling left a pit in my stomach.

Tingles on my wrist slowly climbed my arm. The paralysis was wearing off, but it was painfully slow. I had to get Oliver out of here, but neither of us could move. I focused on the unnecessary but appreciated rise and fall of his chest as reassurance while I waited. For a moment, I wish I had vampire strength. We wouldn't be here right now if I could've broken him free without compromising myself.

I tried to curl my fingers into his fine suit fabric, and I surprised myself with a firm grip. My arms were working. With an unpleasant stiffness, I climbed to my knees and lifted his shredded shirt. All the bloody marks were healed—Evangeline's damage—but now I could see the extent of the poison. Dark veins had fully covered his chest, and the blackening of his flesh was now spreading. We were running out of time.

I tilted Oliver's face upright, and my thumb rubbed along the scruff of his jaw. He was unconscious. "Oliver, wake up. Wake up. Can you hear me? I need you to get up."

He was still too weak to move, and he weighed far too much for me. I had no one to help me, and no equipment to assist. Dragging him by the ankles seemed too risky in his condition, if I could manage it at all. Once again, vampire strength would've been handy. I could flip him over my shoulder and walk out. Alas, that was never going to be an option.

When he woke up, he was going to complain about his ruined suit. He had been joking, but after all the skirmishes he found himself in, he should seriously consider buying the dry cleaners.

*Think, Daisy, think!* I had to try something, anything. I dropped my necklace back over my head. Rather than drag him crudely by the ankles, I lifted him by the underarms and turned him around. I dragged him out while his head lolled on his shoulders. Across the cold concrete floor, I pulled, and I took a break to reposition my hands every few feet because of his weight and no good grip. Agonizingly slowly, we passed over the carpet and up the stairs, where I was more careful, since I wouldn't have the energy to restart after a tumble down the stairs.

Sweat broke out on my back and chest. My arms trembled with the Herculean effort. But we were almost there. "Hang on, Oliver. We're almost free."

He slid easily over the hardwood floor, and I stopped at the front door sill. The sun had risen to wake the world. That meant Evangeline was safely out of the way, unless—I checked Oliver's hand for his ring, and it was surprisingly there.

Finally, a break.

I gripped his underarms, and with a deep inhale, I pulled him across the porch and down the steps. His feet bounced, and I lost one of his shoes. He'd forgive me.

Oliver's car waited at the curb. With a smile of relief, I settled him at the passenger door, dug in his pockets, and grabbed the keys to the candy apple red Shelby. I unlocked and opened both doors. From the driver's side, I leaned across and dragged him into the seat. Panting, moved back over and positioned him well enough so I could close his door. Dizzy from blood loss and way too much exercise, I stumbled back around to the driver's seat and dropped in.

I pushed wild, sweaty hair out of my face and beamed. Little, weak, human me saved Oliver. I actually did it. Tomorrow, I was going to feel every awkward, overused muscle, and I looked forward to it. With keys in hand, I froze.

I couldn't drive stick.

I was so close. So damn close. Even if I could figure out how the hell to use three pedals, I'd grind gears—getting us nowhere and ruining his prized car. Snorting back a sniffle of defeat, I slipped my phone out of my pocket and rolled through my contacts. My dad was off-limits. He'd stand here and laugh, proud of the damage he'd inflicted, and probably shoot him again for kicks. My roommates—I didn't understand why they couldn't choose to help, but after they'd abandoned us, Jamie and Allison wouldn't help now. That left Pierce Evansson, ex-boyfriend, elf, a mind-flaying betrayer of trust, who also hated Oliver. But they had a truce, and I had no one else.

My fingers touched my healed throat. Pierce didn't have to heal away Evangeline's attempt to drain me. But he did anyway, even knowing I wouldn't be a participant in his elf breeding plan, and I was still grateful. I tapped his name on my screen, and the line rang.

"Daisy?" The confusion in his voice was fully warranted.

"I need help," I said softly, trying to hold back tears. "Oliver's dying from the vampire weapon, and I can't drive a stick."

"Those two things don't make sense."

"Just come here and drive us to Dad's, please." My dad had the only vial of the cure, so there was nowhere else to take him.

"Oliver's with you?"

I confirmed and gave him the address.

"I'll be there in five. Hang tight."

I hung up, and my arm fell to my lap. Oliver leaned in an awkward position.

"You're going to have the worst crick in your neck tomorrow." I smiled, and tears rushed to my eyes.

Assuming he lived that long.

# 15
# Betrayal

**Daisy**

Out of nowhere, the elf appeared at the driver's side window, startling the shit out of me. It was weird that he could fly undetected while still looking like a normal human. And it was quite impressive he and his kind could keep their ability secret with modern technology canvassing the sky. Although I wondered how much compulsion had been used over the centuries. Rather than badger him with criticizing questions, I had to remember Piece offered to help, and I needed it.

I climbed out of the driver's seat and handed him the keys. "I appreciate your coming."

I slipped into the back seat and scooted over, directly behind Oliver, while Pierce took my place. I didn't like his being so close to Oliver, especially while completely vulnerable, but I had no choice but to trust him. It wasn't like I could get a cab or summon a rideshare.

My ex stroked the steering wheel with envy, which surprised me, considering he drove a late-model SUV. With no heavy obligations on his paramedic's income, if he wanted nicer things, he could have whatever he wanted.

Actually, uh, no. He couldn't have me. I shivered at the thought.

Pierce glared at Oliver's unconscious body next to him, as if debating whether to take advantage of the situation and dispatch my love for good. To nix that idea, I focused his attention. "Let's get going. He doesn't have much time."

Pierce started up the car. "I'm glad Oliver got the shit kicked out of him."

I frowned, about to tell him how much I seriously regretted calling him. But he added, "I've always wanted to drive this ostentatious machine of excessive power and fortitude. With a vampire driving it, I'm honestly bewildered how it's remained in one piece." His hand caressed the dashboard, and he glanced at me in the rearview mirror. "Don't tell him I complimented his car, though. I don't need that going to his big head."

"Thank you for doing this." It felt weird to thank my ex. "It really means a lot."

Pierce shifted into gear, and his feet worked the series of three pedals like second nature. We peeled away from the curb, and I gripped the seat back in front of me. At the stop sign, I leaned forward between the seats and buckled Oliver in, and I darted Pierce an annoyed look.

Piece laughed dismissively, and I scowled at his carelessness.

"Hold on, Daisy." Pierce's lips lifted deviously as he cranked the wheel and spun out, engine roaring and tires squealing.

As irritated as I was at his inconsiderate driving, I understood Oliver's car ignited a universal excitement, so I refrained from complaining. I rested my hand on Oliver's shoulder, giving him soothing strokes of encouragement to keep fighting, but he made no indication he was conscious at all.

Pierce steered the antique muscle car across the Hattie Street bridge back into Wisconsin. The dam's overflows were open, and the dark river roared with turbulence, not unlike the kind inside this car. Taking a left on Riverside Avenue, we drove across town. Dad lived on West Bay Shore.

The urge to feel out Pierce's intentions in accepting my request overwhelmed me. "I know you two don't always get along, but I hope there's no bad blood between us."

"You and me?" Pierce said, brows rising. "Daisy, anytime you need me, I'll be there for you. I hope you know that by now. Your fangy fiend here and I have a truce, so I'm not going to hurt him, but I want you to brace yourself in case we don't succeed here—I mean the weapon was designed to kill, and it's proven to be effective." Pierce glanced at me through the rearview mirror as we took another corner. "Why? Is there something you want to talk about?"

Pierce's reassurances didn't hold much weight. "People who I thought were my friends turned on me. With our history, I hope if you intend to be next, you'd be willing to give me an honest heads-up."

"Sorry, Daisy," he said simply, not affirming or denying he had any nefarious plans.

We pulled to the curb outside Dad's house on the shore. With one last reassuring squeeze of Oliver's shoulder, I scooted over and urged Pierce to move so I could climb out. Lazily, he did. He followed as I ran up the porch, pushed through the unlocked door, and headed straight to the fridge. Throwing open the door with a rattle of condiments, I looked right where I saw Dad had left the vial of Newt's blood.

It wasn't here.

I shifted food and drinks around, searching for the cure that would save Oliver's life. The *only* thing that would save his life.

Footsteps approached behind me.

I spun, panic squeezing my chest. "It was right here. Where is it?"

Pierce pressed a hand against the fridge door and closed it. Not a flicker of tell appeared on his face. "It's not here."

"What do you mean? Where is it? Did Dad take it back to the lab to make more? I need it! Oliver needs it now!"

"What's all the noise down here?" Dad climbed down the stairs and entered the kitchen. His thick glasses perched on his long nose, and he wore a matching pajama set with a robe over it . I didn't wake him, but he had apparently slept in. In his calm state, perhaps he'd be more inclined to help rather than make this worse.

"The cure. Where's the cure?" My voice rose almost to yelling, but I didn't care. "I need that vial now, Dad! Where is it?"

Dad shared a glance with Pierce, who nodded. Dad nodded in return and failed to suppress a tiny lift of his lips.

"What?" I asked, frustrated at their silent conversation. I hated that they were so close. Pierce was more like a son to him than Lily and I were his daughters. I gritted my teeth, trying not to tear my hair out. "What's going on?"

Dad approached me. "Kitten, there's something you need to know."

A sharp, choking sting at my neck had me turning around. I touched my bare throat, and I heard the sizzle. Pierce held my vervain and black nightshade locket in his meaty, iron fist. Alarm bells rang in my head, but I needed that cure. Nothing else mattered. "What are you doing?"

Pierce tucked the necklace into his jeans pocket. "You were right. Take solace in knowing that."

"Right about what?" I asked, frustrated that Pierce always seemed to speak in code.

"After you verified the only cure was safely in this fridge, not five minutes passed before I destroyed it. I should've given you a heads-up, but that would only have led to a longer argument."

My mouth gaped open. I shifted my speechless shock from Pierce to Dad. He didn't appear to care at all. I shouldn't have been surprised, considering Dad wanted Oliver dead, but the complete lack of concern for what I wanted stung. I fought back tears. "How could you?"

Pierce said flatly, "Elves are a superior race to humans. Vampires are a scourge. Soon, the hierarchy of our society will be clear to you."

I stared at a stranger, angry at the audacity. Fighting against a wave of tears threatening to show how weak I was, I ordered through gritted teeth, "Give my necklace back."

"No," he said, eyes glowing green as a golf course on a summer's clear day.

"Give that back." I reached into his pocket, avoiding eye contact. It was the only thing that protected me from what he planned to do to me. "Dad, help me. He wants to get inside my head again. Stop him. Reason with him. Please." I clawed at Pierce's pocket, but he was too big and too strong—a blond, meaty wall of muscle. I was no match even on my best day. He swatted my hand, and I lost balance, reeling back.

"Daisy, Pierce knows what's best for you," Dad said. His tone was a horrifying mixture of total calm, slight affection, and honest belief.

"What?" I frowned with disgust and took a step back. Without the vial, there was no hope for Oliver. Without the necklace, there was no hope for me, and I wouldn't be by his side when he died. Tears filled my eyes.

Dad reached out, but I shrugged away from his touch. "Vampires are murderers, leeches on society that care nothing for the humans they feed on, hurt, and kill. They will manipulate you into doing whatever they want and toss you aside when they're done. You've seen the discarded, innocent bodies left behind by them. Oliver has you under his thrall, but Pierce will fix that right up, and then you'll see the truth for yourself."

"Dad?" I begged, pleading to the paternal instincts that had to be locked away somewhere deep in the recesses of his confused and warped mind. He calmly stood and didn't intervene as Pierce approached me, eyes glowing.

Eyes shut tight, I shook my head, refusing to believe this was it. Oliver was dying alone in his car, and rather than allow me to stay by his side while he passed, Pierce was going to wipe him from my head.

Again.

I turned and ran, but a vice-like grip on my arm stopped me in my tracks, and a solid hand painfully gripped my jaw, forcing me to face Pierce's manipulative, glowing eyes, but I closed mine.

I needed something—a weapon. What had Jamie told me about elves? They're allergic to iron and iron alloys...like *stainless steel*. Silverware in the drawer. "Wait!" I shouted. "How about we all sit down and talk? I can make sandwiches. Are you hungry?" If I could get my hands on a butter knife or a spoon, I could get free.

No one answered.

"Coffee then?" I asked. The pot rested near the drawer.

"Enough. That's enough. You win, Daisy. Here you go." I heard the rattle of my necklace being removed from his pocket.

I stupidly opened my eyes, and Pierce captured my attention for a split second, but that was all he needed to worm his way into the recesses of my mind. "Daisy, you will stop fighting and come home with me."

A calming sensation relaxed all the muscles in my body, forcing me to give up the fight. Pierce released me with a smirk. I still had my memories, and the anguish of Oliver helplessly dying tore into me like sharpened claws puncturing my chest and tearing through flesh to rip out my broken heart. I wanted to scream. Instead, I brushed away spilled tears and calmly asked, "Why didn't you erase Oliver from my memories?"

Pierce folded his arms over his thick chest like a warden about to give the orders to reprimand a prisoner. "You deserve to remember his death and feel all the wretchedness that goes along with pointless love."

"You want me to suffer?" My chest squeezed, and my vision sparkled. I couldn't breathe.

"I prefer to call it a consequence of your weakness."

"Love is not weakness. Dad?" I pleaded, holding back sobs.

My dad poured coffee grounds into the pot and pushed the filter basket door closed, apathetic to the horrors behind him. Dad turned to face me. "As I said, kitten, Pierce has your best interest in mind, but how he goes about your memories is none of my business."

Pierce said, "I'll be right back." He dipped out the front door, likely to do something to the love of my life. Such a cruel action against a good, dying man should be beneath a person who declared superiority over the world.

"Did Pierce get inside your head?" I asked Dad, needing a reason, an excuse, for my father's disregard for my life.

The coffeepot burbled behind him. "Never needed to. He and I have always been on the same page. But you've always been stubborn and a little behind the curve. So, we pushed you harder to see the fine print before your eyes. Since Pierce's compulsion was necessary again, we aren't there yet, but don't worry, kitten, you'll be on our side soon enough."

"Did he compel you to say that?"

Dad smiled and poured a cup. "You want one?"

In utter disbelief, I dropped onto a stool at the kitchen island and rested my head down on my arms. I couldn't fight even though every fiber of my body wanted to rush out the door, collect Oliver, and cure him somehow. Instead, he would die alone, and I didn't get to say goodbye.

I cried, frustrated with my impotence, abandoned by my father, and betrayed yet again by someone I'd trusted. "You don't know anything about what I want."

# 16
# Facing the End

**Oliver**

DR. GREG BARRETT'S POISON blackened my skin, and blinding pain crept along my body, as if Evangeline had indulged in steak-knife stabs every few minutes. I had no muscle control, and not a sound of agony breached lips. Since I only breathed to speak, for all intents and purposes, I looked dead. With hell tearing through me, I wished I were dead.

The vampire feeding process terrified Daisy, so I knew how hard it was for her to offer me a vein. I'd experienced it only once when the mysterious vampire in the cave turned me, but the memory was fleeting these days. So, no, because of her strength, because of our love, I didn't wish I were dead, but it was coming for me, regardless.

Sweat rolled down my forehead, and my trashed suit clung to me with both dried blood and even more sweat. I hadn't felt this disgusting since my leg had been turned to hamburger, and I'd dragged myself into the shade of the abandoned mineshaft. Oh, how I yearned for my bathroom's four showerheads. Nicole's remodeling had been genius. I was content to dwell in my home the way I'd designed and built it, but since I gave my niece carte blanche to do as she judged for guests, she threw in a bathroom remodel for me, and I loved it. A sinking feeling in my gut told me I'd never get to experience the waterfalls of luxury washing away the trauma any longer.

And in my near-paralyzed state, I couldn't inspect the progress of the dying tissue. Had I moved beyond the hallucinations yet, the final stage before death? Dying wasn't pretty or clean. It never preserved the dignity of the one chosen to be next, so why would it make an exception for me? Now I understood what Soren had gone through at the lab, but his dose had been higher and more immediate, directly to the bloodstream. Was his poisoning better because the stages of suffering were faster to pass and faster to end? Or was it better for me, because I had time to reflect? I missed my brother. He'd screwed up more times than I could count, but I still loved him. I only hoped he wouldn't fly off the rails and devolve into another path of endless destruction and self-loathing.

There was nothing I could do to prevent it, and no one else could help him if such a course repeated itself. I attempted a sigh, but I didn't think it worked. I opened my eyes to check, and I sighed again. No, nothing moved.

It was dark out, and I wasn't in my car. I must've lost consciousness. I was leaning against the base of a thick pine tree, right on the bay. Gentle waves lapped at the shore, and green and red lights of passing boats coasted along the horizon. By the increasing paleness of the sky, dawn would be here soon. How long had I been out for?

Nearby footsteps were alarming, but I couldn't do anything about them.

Pierce approached and squatted down beside me. "Still alive? You're one tough bastard, I'll give you that."

*"I never liked you, elf,"* I said, but the featherbag didn't flinch. He must not be able to hear me. In that case, I added, *"We vampires might feed on humans to survive, but we also love them. I love them. Daisy is the light of my life, and I couldn't survive a day without her. But you treat humans as cattle to serve your own purpose. You hurt them, and you never respect them. I don't regret killing your father. The smarmy attorney had it coming, whether he was elfkind or not. I have a long line of enemies, but I never expected an elf and a retirement-aged human to best me. Perhaps that was the secret to your victory. In leaving my guard down, I was shortsighted. But you win, elf. This time, you win. Do me a favor and keep Daisy safe. Leave her mind free. Can you do that much?"*

"Since you'll be dead soon, I'm going to leave you with a parting gift, old friend." His tone was gentle. I could almost call it friendly.

But his term of endearment only left me wondering if he regretted the end of our long-held rivalry. If I had a choice in the matter, I'd stay by Daisy's side and keep the rivalry, but hey, Pierce wasn't asking for votes here. If he came a little closer, I could take a nip and then voice my opinion, but I had a sinking feeling he didn't actually want it. No, this unusual friendliness was Pierce's own version of handling a goodbye, his own form of closure. If I could speak, this would go much differently.

Probably hurt a lot more, if that were possible.

"You'll keep your sun ring and watch the last sunrise of your life. When the serum takes you, I'll return and remove the ring from your gray, shriveled finger and then sweep your ashes into the water with the side of my shoe. There will be one less pest walking during the daytime, and when I destroy that abomination, I'll be preventing another from taking your place. Sometimes progress is slow, but anything forward still counts."

*"And there's my old Pierce."* I used to like him—past tense. Elves were all alike, even the ones where I thought a modicum of trust was possible, but I was wrong. My scalp slipped against the rough bark of the tree. Pierce gripped my hair and dragged my head upright to straighten me out. To be sure I was going to stay put, he shoved my head against the tree a few times.

Thanks, asshole.

"Now you won't fall over and miss the view. And don't worry about Daisy. She's in my expert hands now. Did you really think a necklace would keep me from her? Not even you, Mr. Oliver Rockwell, rich douche extraordinaire, could keep me away. All you did was delay the inevitable, but I still won. Not you. Me. A human and a vampire?" Pierce snorted derisively.

"Soren's only redeeming quality—he's not delusional." Pierce continued his monologuing, much to my dismay. "Your brother understood the ranks of society. But a vamp's still a vamp." He released my head and brushed his hands clean, as if I were filthy. Well, I actually was a little filthy.

Pierce looked me over from patent leather shoes that had seen better days to my gelled hair tossed about by his own hand. His wandering eyes lingered on my shredded chest. "You're going to miss the wedding. I regret that I won't get to see your heart breaking as she gives me her vows, however temporary they are. And after I take our sons away, I would've almost considered dropping her off on your doorstep. Oh, well." Pierce stood and straightened his jeans. With a final look of pity, he turned away.

Pierce stopped. "And I'm still considering whether I want to keep that Shelby of yours. I'd get far more enjoyment out of it than you did, but I don't need it causing Daisy to break her compulsion. It sure is an ostentatious toy, just like you. Enjoy your last sunrise, vamp."

Fire burned through my veins, and not just the poison. Rage coursed through my system, temporarily numbing the pain of the poison. If I had the strength, I would've torn his head clean from his shoulders. The further he walked from me, the closer he got to Daisy. The rage grew. Over my long years, I'd been in many hairy situations, making myself well acquainted with the depravity of the worst kind, but in this civilized era, Pierce won the trophy. And I couldn't do anything to stop him. I couldn't save Daisy from a horrible fate I wouldn't wish on my worst enemy.

I focused my hatred into my arms, willing them to move. I didn't have time to sit here. There was an elf that needed killing, and no one was happier to do it than me. Gritting my teeth against the surging pain, I glared at my hands. *Move, damn it. Move!*

Nothing happened.

Where was Soren when I needed him most?

# 17
# Trapped

**Daisy**

I'D BEEN INSIDE PIERCE EVANSSON's modest home many times while we'd dated, but never once had I considered moving in. It wasn't my home, and I'd never felt a desire to take our relationship to the next level, so I'd kept my independence—no matter how much my dad seemed to like Pierce. His marriage proposal in the park had caught me completely off-guard, because I could never picture us together in old age.

Or at any age.

Now I strolled inside Pierce's house, but rather than an emptiness where I didn't belong, all I could see were happy memories—when I'd caught Oliver about to pummel him, and I'd tackled Oliver to save him from the sunlight. An intimate moment where I was on top of him, about to kiss him, regardless of the audience. When I was in Oliver's arms, there was only me and him.

I would give anything to go back to that time. As painful as many of my memories were, I was grateful Pierce let me keep them. When I couldn't face my new reality, I had somewhere I could hide—my own happy place in Oliver's arms, in his bed, or sipping coffee on the balcony overlooking the river. My home would always be with him. Pierce could never take that away from me, as long as he believed he was punishing me. A sad smile lifted my lips, but it quickly fell again.

My own dad, my closest family member, tossed me into Pierce's arms like I was a burden to be disposed of, or a piece of property to be sold. No matter how many times I told him I wanted Oliver, my dad could never see Oliver for the man I knew he was. Dad would never change. Was it worth explaining it again and again until I was blue in the face? My only solace was in believing Pierce got into his head, too. He denied having his beliefs tampered with, but I couldn't believe Dad wanted me to suffer. That he'd used Mom and me as bargaining chips. That he'd shooed Lily away from us, destroying our dysfunctional family for good.

My mother was dead, and my sister vanished into the wind. My roommates sided with Dad and Pierce. Was there something I couldn't see? Were they all right, and I was wrong? The strongest urge to elbow Pierce in the gut and run like a track star to save Oliver left me on edge. Pierce's compulsion kept it tightly under wraps—kept me tightly wound. What was worse—not being able to fight, or knowing I wanted to, but not having control over my own body?

I hugged myself as Pierce closed the front door behind us, and the coming dawn cut off. He flicked on a switch, and eerie light stung my eyes.

"I'll make some coffee." Pierce brushed past me, not giving me a second glance.

"No, thanks." Having caffeine surging through my system, begging for the sweet release of a fight, was nothing short of torture. Pierce had caused me enough pain already. I tried to block out what elves did to women, what he planned to do to me. I'd never sleep wondering if that was the night he'd crawl into my bed.

Would he compel me to like it? I shivered.

Pierce emptied his pockets into the basket in the kitchen. "It's been a long night. I'll take the couch. You can have the bedroom. There're blackout shades in there."

I never wanted to set foot in his bedroom. "I'll take the couch."

"You sure?" He approached and stroked my upper arms.

I wanted to leap away as if his touch was poison, but I couldn't. My skin crawled like ants under his touch, and I fought a telltale grimace. He knew I didn't want to be here, but since I couldn't escape, I didn't want to make this worse for myself. "Yeah, I'm sure. I'm definitely sure. You go ahead."

"No problem. Suit yourself." Pierce shrugged and made his way further into the house, disappearing into another room and shutting the door.

I wanted to run so badly my legs ached, and my chest constricted. Alone, my head turned toward the kitchen. I could arm myself with stainless steel silverware, but when the moment arrived, would I be capable of defending myself? Normally I would without hesitation, but Pierce's compulsion meant I couldn't fight, and if he knew what I was up to, I feared he'd make my captivity worse.

Like delete Oliver.

I had to be smarter than that. Since Pierce liked to cook, he had a wide range of herbs in the cabinet, but I didn't have any witchcraft supplies, and my magic was as strong as wet toilet paper. Would it do me any good to try a spell only to get caught?

In five years, if I looked back at this moment, would I have regretted not trying? I took a step toward the kitchen, but Pierce's bedroom door opened, heavy footsteps giving his approach away. I stopped and slipped onto the couch quickly and quietly, and I punched a throw pillow to pretend I was only adjusting my position.

Pierce wore a white T-shirt and pajama pants. I already knew everything under those clothes, and I had no intention of returning there ever again. "I can see you're still upset."

*No shit, Sherlock.* I didn't confirm the obvious to him.

"This is going to be an adjustment for both of us, and I can see you need a friendly face right now. Why don't you call Lily? She could help you through this."

I refused to meet Pierce's eyes in case he planned to mess with me even more, but that wasn't a half-bad idea. I shook my head anyway and lied, "She doesn't know about you or Dad, and it would take too long to bring her up to speed. And I certainly don't need her in harm's way, either. She's all I have left."

"Just a suggestion. Take it or leave it." Pierce returned to the bedroom and closed the door. The creak of a mattress frame told me he'd gone to bed.

After he'd bought my fibs, I texted Lily anyway. *'I hope you're safe. Things aren't good here. Dad's gone off the rails. Oliver is'*— I paused, unwilling to write the truth of that thought. I decided to make it a happier message— *'sick. He's very sick. I miss you. I love you. I would really like to see you.'*

I stared at the message, hoping for a sign that she was alive on the other end of the phone. I waited and waited. I shifted position on the couch, knowing I'd get no sleep during the daytime.

There was no beep of a tiny avatar telling me she'd read it, no bouncing dots telling me a reply was coming.

Nothing.

I texted her again, *'In case you see this in the future, whatever I might say about how happy I am, it's a lie. I'm trapped with Pierce, and I'm miserable.'*

There. If Pierce compelled me to be happy, at least Lily knew the truth.

If she ever saw the message.

## Oliver

RARELY DID A MAN savor a beautiful sight when facing down death. Rays of light bathed the early morning sky in purples and pinks. Popcorn puffs of clouds were orange. Ripples from a gentle breeze sent the colors dancing on the mirrored surface of the bay, and birds flew along the lakeshore and rested on exposed sandbars, calling to each other with a sweet melody. I'd forgotten the tranquility of a sunrise on the bay, one I hadn't stopped to appreciate in ages, and one I would've appreciated more without the fires of hell crackling along my body. My skin crawled with needles the size of pencils, jabbing me everywhere over and over.

The rage at Pierce's devilish plans for Daisy had worn off. I'd tried for what felt like hours to do something, but all I did was exhaust myself further. I'd accepted the elf had won.

The hand that I'd attempted and failed to move wore Daisy's sun ring. My ring. She didn't have to give it to me, and I wouldn't have compelled it from her, but she chose to. She loved me, and despite my history with Evangeline, I never loved anyone else but Daisy. Now I would never get the chance to tell Daisy properly, every day for the rest of her life. To explain to her that although I couldn't give her everything she wanted, I would try. I would spend every breath of every day treating her like she deserved. Daisy was my queen. She *was*...my queen.

Against the burning in my limbs and the water streaming down my cheeks, I'd fought to the end. Now I fought one last time with every remaining ounce of strength I could muster. I shifted one hand over to the other. I exhaled in rapid breaths of relief that I'd done it, and a fresh barrage of pain sparkled across my vision. My useless legs trembled with the exhausted supply of adrenaline, and I gasped, tensing muscles against the next wave of pain.

The sun would crest the horizon at any moment, and I would receive Pierce's final gift—an escape from the torturous pain. Rather than leaving him a body to desecrate, I would leave him ash. Holding my breath and funneling one last burst of energy, I shifted my fingers and pulled off my sun ring. A tingle of the coming sun hit my burning flesh. If I hadn't known what to expect, I wouldn't have noticed the difference.

I breathed a sigh of contentment. Soon it would be over, and someday I might meet Daisy again on the Other Side, if the rumors were true. Tears pricked my eyes, and I blinked them away, focusing on my calming breaths and the flutters of the birds' wings as they played in the shallow waters.

"I've been looking all over for you," Soren said, appearing from behind the tree and silhouetted against the coming dawn. "You weren't at the house where I'd sent you. You didn't answer your phone. When daytime hit, I could do anything, but now, here I find you in the doctor's backyard enjoying the view. Next time people are worried, answer the damn phone."

I couldn't move, and when I tried, my features pinched in agony against the roaring inferno beneath my blistered and blackened flesh. I was done. Overcooked. Burned to a crisp. I wouldn't bother trying to respond anymore.

Soren crouched over me, taking in my current state. "You look like shit. For not being a real word, it sure is handy."

A pained chuckle only sounded in my head.

Soren kneeled beside me and collected my hands. He frowned. My brother frantically shifted his weight, checking under himself, and he painfully shoved my hands around. "Where is it? What did you do with the sun ring? Did Pierce take it, or did you give up?" He didn't look at me. He kept searching in the grass. "Damn it, Oliver. Almost two hundred years and how many times have you saved my ass from self-destruction? I'm not giving up on you."

Soren found the ring on the grass next to my thigh, and he pushed it back up my finger. The searing of the daylight instantly stopped, but Soren must've been feeling it.

"I can't believe you were willing to give up like that, but since I'm not choosing the way of the barbecue, let's go." Soren scooped me up and flung me over his shoulder. The sun's rays steamed his skin, stinging my eyes, and he moved with vampire speed to his car. Soren opened the passenger side of his Prius and settled me inside, much more gently than Daisy had attempted, but I didn't blame her. I was proud that she'd tried and succeeded.

After starting the silent engine, Soren rolled us down the street. Rolled...away from my Shelby. If by some miracle I would be cured, I had to detail my car to remove the elf residue.

We needed more horsepower to make it to shelter before the sunrise. Sensing the urgency along with me, Soren sped up, taking corners faster than the suspension appreciated, and with moments to spare and gritted teeth, he drove the car into my garage at the bed-and-breakfast. With unusual thoughtfulness, he collected me again and brought me into my house and deposited me on a bar stool. My face smacked down on the bar, but Soren left me like that. In a flash, he rushed to the basement and back, returning with bags of blood in his arms.

"It's not great, but it's better than nothing, and you're in no condition to go hunting."

He was right, but unlike him, I didn't mind the bags. Soren popped open a port and punctured the seal with a fang and grimaced. He shoved the line between my lips and squeezed, filling my mouth with strengthening blood. I would've groaned in sweet pleasure if I weren't still dying. I drank pint after pint until I could move my limbs. They still seared with the burning poison, but now I wasn't an invalid.

My tongue loosened, too. "There's no use saving me, Soren. All you did was prolong my suffering."

Soren stepped behind my bar and set a pair of glasses on the wood. "After you and Daisy saved me from certain death and the grip of a witch, I did some soul searching."

"Did you find it?" Chatting helped distract me from the pain, and I appreciated a formal goodbye from my brother.

"Hardy-har. Good thing you didn't lose your sense of humor. Look, I live with many regrets and more guilt than any one man can reasonably handle, but I still stand. I have a lot to make up for, but I can't start if you're dead."

Touching.

"How did you end up in Barrett's backyard?" Soren poured me a shot of tequila.

"Pierce left me out there to die." With aching, stiff joints, I tossed it back in one swallow. The heat didn't help the burning in my body, but it did ease the pain. I gestured for more. Much more.

"I promise you this: if you're going to die, it'll be by my side, not alone in some human's backyard, rotting like old compost." Sadness touched my brother's eyes as he filled the glasses again. No snarky comment, no retraction, no flick of his features, giving away his traitorous thoughts. This was the second time I realized my brother genuinely cared. The first—when he'd given me back my sun ring—had not been a fluke. I didn't believe in coincidences.

My chest squeezed, and tears pressed against my eyes. *My brother cares.* Swallowing the thick lump in my throat, I said, "I knew what I was getting into when I opened my heart to Daisy, which was a short lifespan, and then I discovered she's a dormant witch. When she activates, I'll lose her even sooner. My grief is natural, but this," I gestured at myself, "this isn't. My dying before her isn't natural. She doesn't need the pain of grieving me."

"So you're ready to keep fighting?" Soren asked, giving a pointed glance at my sparkly ring in stark contrast to the dull coal of my finger.

"In the last several weeks, I've spent more time contemplating my mortality than I have in my entire life. Then again, why would I? I couldn't die at the hands of time, and I'm not a supporter of idle, baseless activities. The doctor's poison had me thinking plenty about what I really wanted and never accomplished in life."

"The portfolio of commercial properties, a fancy car, several bank accounts fat enough most people couldn't wrap their brains around the number of zeroes, and a retail-store's-worth of designer suits isn't enough?" Soren joked.

None of that stuff mattered at all. "Can't take it with you."

"But you don't *want* to die," he said as if concerned for my mental health.

Most of my body was covered in blackened necrotic flesh, and growing by the minute, I smelled like I was rotting alive. Every drag of breath to speak was like igniting flames inside my lungs. I'd never been this low in my life, and his concern was valid. "I want Daisy in my arms as a vampire like me, bloodbonded for all eternity, but you can see by my lovely, charred complexion, I'll never get that wish, and she doesn't want to become like us, anyway. So do me a favor, brother," I said and swallowed another shot.

"Anything." Tears rimmed his eyes, and he didn't hide them.

"Keep Daisy safe. Make sure she lives long enough to be a smiling, wrinkly old lady and dies warm in her bed, surrounded by people who love her. I want her to be happy. Can you do that for me?"

Soren tilted his head. "Even if she cooks my ass as a witch?"

I gave him a sad smile.

"Speaking of the woman, why isn't she here?"

I knew Pierce would erase me from Daisy's head—again—so she wouldn't suffer my loss, and her life would return to its previous course, as if I'd never met her. But if my brother could save her from the fate elves demanded and fulfill the promise he'd made, I'd do whatever I could to help. "Follow the elf."

Soren slammed an empty glass on the wood, frowning, and all-too-familiar anger boiled under his skin. "Pierce has her again? Elves are disgusting. I'll get her away from his creepy mitts, I promise. You stay right here. Don't go dying on me now."

I mustered a wet chuckle and slipped off my sun ring. I held it out to him. "You're on the clock."

Without hesitation, Soren placed it on his finger and moved to the back door.

"Soren?" I called.

He stopped, waiting.

"Thank you."

Soren smiled, tears glistening in his eyes, and he disappeared into the early morning light. I hoped he wouldn't waste too much time enjoying the sun. The clock was not in my favor, but drinking helped with the pain and mobility, so I poured myself a line of blood-mixed shots, spilling dribbles of tequila as I moved from one glass to the next. When finished, I tried to set the bottle down just right, but I dropped it. The tequila tipped over and glugged all over the bar. The bottle rolled and fell. What a waste.

"What's that noise?" Nicole rounded the corner with a limp, and she gasped. "Oliver? Is that you?"

I waved fingers at her and grimaced at the pain. She approached, and her hand rested on my shoulder for support, and I flinched.

"You look like someone shoveled you out of a coal pile. What happened?"

"Daisy's dad." I gave her a smile to comfort her, but she wasn't fooled.

My niece settled on the stool next to me and lifted a shot glass to my lips, and I drank. "I'm going to pop a cap in his ass."

I spurted a laugh, and every muscle in my body spasmed with pain. "Ow, ow, ow. Thanks for that."

"I mean it," she said, lifting another shot, dignity be damned—she was family. "His serum really did a number on you. It's...scary, honestly. To bring such an inhuman beast down to a nursing home geriatric is...quite impressive, but the doctor is less than scum for it."

"In his defense, my kind eats his."

"You need strength to fight this. Drink from me. I've been dairy-free for a long while, just in case."

A sweet gesture, but she was old and frail. It wouldn't do me enough good for how much it would harm her, but if I explained that, she'd only push harder. I loved that stubbornness. "That only delays the inevitable."

"Then turn me so I can avenge you." Nicole's hard eyes meant she was serious. "I've lived a long time, watching people I care about get hurt or killed while I sit on the sidelines, a weak human with this stupid hip, incapable of doing anything meaningful. Give me this. Let me do this for you."

I lowered a hand onto her forearm. "You're grieving. It's okay to lash out." I sent her a gentle smile. "But do you really want to live for centuries with a bum hip?"

Nicole shook her head and smiled. "My whole life you've been by my side or off in the shadows, but I could always count on you, my one constant. How did Daisy take the news?"

"I'm sure she's completely fine."

Nicole squeezed my forearm, concern and disbelief knitting her brows. "Don't tell me it was the elf again."

"Pierce Evansson," I confirmed.

My niece growled in frustration. "Those damned elves. I wish vampires fed on them, you know, to thin the herd."

I chuckled, but I hated that this could be our last conversation. "Nicole, thank you for everything—keeping this place running and helping me behind the scenes." I grabbed her hand and gazed into her spitfire eyes. "I don't know what I would've done without you. I love you."

Tears shimmered on her lids, and she pressed her lips thin, holding back emotion. "Don't you do that. Don't you say goodbye now. You've lived nearly two centuries, but you're going to let some human's scratch kill you? Don't give up. Don't you dare."

"I've tried everything."

"There's always a way. I'm sure someone will figure this out before it's too late." Nicole stood up and kissed the top of my head before mussing my hair. "I love you, too." She limped away, and when she closed the door behind her, my vampire hearing picked up her quiet sobs.

I also loved her stoic, if misplaced, optimism in the face of despair. I slammed down the remaining shots on the bar, regretting the loss of my tequila bottle, and debating if I wanted to spend the energy to get another one off the shelf. I couldn't feel the burn as the liquid filled my body and numbed my brain.

*Soren, make it back on time.*

# 18

# Crippling Truth

**Daisy**

Pierce's lumpy couch was an abomination, and I'd never slept worse in my life. Everything that had happened repeated in my haunted mind, taunting me into an action that I couldn't take. I'd checked my phone every few minutes, hoping for a sign Lily had read my messages. What would she think of me right now? Was I a strong fighter, doing what I could to survive, or a quitter? On Dad's orders, Lily had run away to hide from all this chaos. Was that surviving or quitting?

Pierce had left the house to run errands or something. I wasn't listening. I'd just smiled thinly and waited for him to leave, and my prison cell was a little bit better without him in it. Pierce had compelled me not to fight him. He hadn't defined 'fight'.

Alone in the kitchen, I sighed. I didn't have any spell books or magical supplies, and after my witch roommates had left Oliver to die in that suburban hellhole torture chamber, I wouldn't ask them for assistance. No matter my situation, I could never forgive them. To keep my mind from wandering toward Oliver and his suffering—was he even still alive?—I blasted music on Pierce's household surround sound system, and it pumped a rhythm through the walls.

I sang along, terribly off-key, trying to drum up a semblance of myself while I opened and closed cabinets, seeking a trove of herbs the cooking-enthusiast elf had to have. In the back corner next to the stove, a rack was filled with more choices than I was aware of, and they were alphabetized. I didn't know what to think of that. I retrieved herbs I remembered seeing listed in my aunt's grimoire, and I poured a circle of salt on the kitchen table.

I'd succeeded with the little green army guy, and I managed to ignite a glow in my palm. Neither of those actions was useful, but I had to try something, or I'd lose my mind in here. I chuckled. My mind had already been lost. I was imprisoned by Pierce. I didn't have a plan to avoid forced procreation, besides a swift kick in the proverbial family jewels, but I couldn't fight him. How else could I delay that nightmare? He'd proposed to me during an unfortunate picnic in the park not long ago, and he'd alluded to trying again at the club during ladies' night when Jamie had been dancing. He really, really wanted to marry me. Perhaps I could postpone his urges by claiming a need for marriage first, and a very elaborate, very expensive wedding on a special date somewhere in the future.

Pierce wasn't stupid enough to fall for that ruse, but he was also proud enough to accept it.

In a different cabinet, I found a large mixing bowl, and I placed it in the center of the salt ring. Into the bowl, I sprinkled a few choice herbs. After practicing with Allison, I'd learned enough phrases to be confident I could improvise something, although I didn't expect it to work, but if I didn't try, I was going to tear my hair out.

I collected a lighter from his junk drawer, and I flicked on the flame. I chanted the words Allison and I had used to push the little green army guy over, planning to direct the energy to push Pierce's compulsion out of my head. Well, I thought it was a smart idea.

I lowered the flame to the herbs and continued chanting. When the tiny fire touched the dry mixture, a splitting headache tore through me. I dropped the lighter. The flame vanished, and I collapsed to the floor. My jaw opened wide, trying to release the squeezing pressure on my skull, but it was no use. I pissed off the figurative compulsion gods. They were smart enough to see my true intentions.

"Okay, okay," I groaned. "I won't do it again."

But the pain continued. I climbed to my feet and swept the bowl and salt ring to the floor. The dry ingredients spilled with a thump and rattle, and a dust of herbs floated into the air. I coughed.

The pain softened. I glared at the mess I now had to clean up before Pierce returned. A big part of me wanted to leave it there, a clear message of my disapproval, disgust, and future disobedience. But I was terrified Pierce would erase Oliver one last time, just for his own convenience.

A pounding on the front door caught my ear over the booming of the music and the ringing in my head. It was mid-afternoon, and I wasn't expecting guests. But it wasn't like Pierce communicated his schedule and plans with me—and if he had, oops, I hadn't been listening.

I turned off the tunes and braced myself for my father coming to apologize. I snorted to myself. Never going to happen. I opened the door, expecting door-to-door sales of some sort. I wouldn't turn down cookies.

My brows popped at the glum, disheveled vampire before me. "Soren? But how…?" I glanced at his hand. My sun ring, which Oliver had proudly worn, was sparkling on Soren's finger. Pressure grew in my chest. I felt like I couldn't breathe. "He's not… You didn't…? Oh, God, please no…" My hand covered my mouth, and I fell to my knees. "Tell me he's not dead. Tell me you didn't take that ring from his body." I sniffled, trying to focus my thoughts before I turned into the world's most annoying wailing banshee.

"He's still alive."

I couldn't believe what I heard. I whispered, "What?"

Soren dropped to his knees in front of me, blocked from entering by the mystical force field. "I'll be honest with you. He's not going to live much longer, but I'm here to save you from this deplorable fate and take you to him."

The words were like music to my ears, beautiful but incapable of fixing the problem. "Pierce compelled me. I can't leave, and I can't fight."

A gentle smile lifted his lips, and a hand reached out and touched me. I gasped. His…his hand passed the barrier. "That's what I'm here for."

"What? How?" I sniffled.

"Elf's house. You must not consider this your home to seal it against vampire entry."

He got that right.

Soren stood, and he helped me to my feet. At one point, Soren was compelled to do an evil witch's bidding, leaving him a monster in the true sense of the word. Since he'd regained control of himself, I trusted him. Soren stepped inside and looked around as if searching for something.

I backed up to give him space to do whatever he needed. "From experience, you can't whisk me out. The pain is excruciating. So, what's the plan?"

Soren faced me, arms crossed over his chest, lips grim. "Daisy, Newt had sent me here on the hunt. I wasn't planning on being chased. While evading my hunter, I'd darted across Highway 41 that early morning last May."

I didn't want to believe what I thought he was telling me.

"I'm the one who caused your car crash. I killed your aunt, your uncle, and your cousin Abby. I had a job to do, and I didn't care about collateral damage. It's kind of my default setting."

I backed up a step. My hand covered my gaping mouth.

Soren smiled wistfully. "I heard Abby's wedding was lovely. You know, the part with the elf in the bathroom? I wish I would've been there."

"What are you doing?" The horrible things coming from his mouth were so uncharacteristic now.

"I'm telling you the truth. I'm giving you what everyone's been keeping from you." Soren stepped forward. "Secrets that shielded you from the agonizing truth."

"Why now? Why are you telling me these things now? What do you want from me?" A suffocating blanket draped over me, and I struggled to pull in a breath. My fist pressed against the constriction, willing the air back into my lungs. Soren had left me to die that morning, and his cavalier attitude about it was like a stab to the heart. I trusted him.

"I didn't check on you or your family because I didn't care. I was laser-focused on the job. My target was Stacey Barrett. She made me a lovely meal before I gave her a mercifully quick snap. She didn't even scream." Soren chuckled. "By design, the venom stops that. You would know, wouldn't you? I've attacked you before." Soren smirked and stepped closer, fingers reaching out for my throat. "Yes, I remember your taste."

I backed away further, avoiding his touch, trembling all over. My knees were weak, threatening to drop me to the floor.

He growled, "I want my prey to be afraid. The blood tastes better that way."

My stomach churned, and I refused to accept what he'd said. "Dad told me Newt killed my mother."

"You think that witch ever got his hands dirty? I was Newt's weapon, and I never hesitated."

I panted. My head swam. "You murdered my mother? *You?* After everything I did for you, you kept that from me?"

I'd saved his life when he was infected with the vampire serum. I didn't have to give him the cure, but I believed in second chances. Right now, regret crept into my heart. I never should've saved a monster, and Soren was the textbook definition—a vile, disgusting monster who treated people like disposable food. Dad was right all along. Vampires deserved to die. They couldn't be civilized. My fists curled. "You took my mother from me for a snack?"

"I was ordered to kill her. I didn't want to waste her, so in a way, you should thank me for being so considerate. Stacey's blood was exquisite, a warm blend of type A." He kissed his pinched fingertips as if he was a proud chef. He leaned in close to me and inhaled deeply. "Just like you are. Oh, I smell something delicious."

Soren gripped my wrist—the one I'd deliberately hidden from Pierce. The one I'd offered to Oliver when he'd been in the torture chamber. The puncture wounds were still there. Not healed. "Someone imbibed recently. Well, call me jealous. Care to offer or shall I take? Is it more fun for you to be forced? It is for me."

His smarmy grin sent anger curling in my gut. I drew the surge through me and into my hands as I'd been taught. With an ear-piercing scream, I thrust my fists forward as if I could force him away with sheer will alone.

Soren fell over, and I kneeled over him and punched him in the eye. I gripped his hair in my fist and pulled. I punched his shoulders and pounded on his chest. Tears streamed down my cheeks as I whaled on him, a feeble attempt to punish him for stealing my mother from me and enjoying it, for coming here and threatening me, for showing me that not everyone deserved a second chance.

He shattered the very core of my beliefs.

As I continued to beat him senselessly, a tightening pressure squeezed my head, like the world's worst migraine, and incapable of continuing my barrage of punches, I fell over and curled into a ball. My face pinched as a sharp stab repeated in my head, like dozens of knives, searing, sparking, blinding pain. I couldn't breathe. I couldn't see. I pressed my hands against my temples, holding my breath against the pain. Vampires couldn't do magic. What was this?

As suddenly as it assaulted me, it lessened, throbbing instead of stabbing, and the tightness in my chest reduced. I inhaled rapid breaths and slowed my system's overload with a series of deep inhales and exhales. I uncurled and sat up, quickly scooting back from Soren, who sat comfortably on the couch, watching me. "Feeling better?"

Soren hadn't stopped me from attacking him. He let me. I rubbed my arms and stood on shaky legs with a frown. My compulsion to stay here was gone. I no longer *needed* to stay. I no longer *needed* to refrain from fighting. He helped me break Pierce's compulsion, just like Oliver had during the dreadful picnic proposal. I glared at him, confused about whether I should be upset or grateful.

"You're welcome." Soren stood with an apologetic smile, and he held out his hand in invitation to assist me. "Let's get out of here. Oliver's waiting for you."

I hesitated. "Was any of that true?"

Soren sent me a hollow expression. "Oliver doesn't have much time. We need to go now."

I nodded. Oliver was the most important person in my life. Whatever Soren had done in the past was something we could work through later. Oliver didn't have a later. I reached for the vampire's palm, but with lightning speed, he flew from sight and crashed on the other side of the living room. Soren landed with a hard thump on the floor.

Pierce.

The bulky elf turned on me, his calm face giving me nothing about what festered beneath the surface, as usual. "You still haven't learned to stay away from vampires. I'm going to take care of you next, after I take out the trash."

Soren fished in his pocket and threw the keys at me. "Go. Run. Now!"

I caught them, and Soren stood up to use his vampire speed to escape, but elves were fast too. Pierce captured Soren by the throat. "She's slower and easier to catch. I've been meaning to kill you for a long time."

"Pierce, no. You can't do this. He didn't do anything to you. Let him go," I ordered while stepping toward the door.

"Daisy, run!" Soren said roughly through Pierce's grip.

I hesitated, with tears filling my eyelids, and with one last look at Soren's desperate face, I ran for his car. The vampire was strong, far stronger than me, and he could handle Pierce. I had to get to Oliver before it was too late.

In the driver's seat, I picked through the keys, and sunlight glinted a flash of red. Oliver's sun ring. Soren had attached it to the keys. I glanced back at the house, swallowing back a sob, while I started the quiet engine. Both brothers were about to die, and I had no idea what to do about it. I had to see Oliver before it was too late and trust the younger Rockwell could figure out something.

All Pierce had to do was throw him out onto the porch, and Soren would burn to ash in seconds. I couldn't think of that. I drove down the road, speeding to the bed-and-breakfast with my heart bleeding.

# 19

# A Miracle

**Daisy**

I sprang through the front door of my love's lavish home. "Oliver? Oliver!" With no answer, I ran through the foyer to the bar, his favorite place, and I stopped short. Oliver sprawled on the floor, staring vacantly at the ceiling. His face was half black. The other half was covered with black veins.

I collapsed at his side and checked for a pulse. He was alive, but hardly. My trembling fingers fussed with Soren's keys to unfasten the sun ring, and I pushed it up onto his charred finger. I touched the blackened skin, not sure what to expect, but it wasn't hot. It felt just as soft as healthy skin, but nothing good was happening beneath the surface.

"Oliver? Can you hear me?" My plea broke with a sob. Was I too late? I needed a shoulder to cry on, and unfortunately, that would no longer be Allison's. I tugged my phone from my pocket and texted Lily an emergency S.O.S. *'Lily, please. I need you. Come to the bed-and-breakfast on Riverside. Oliver's sick. He doesn't have much time left. I really need you.'*

I stared at the screen, willing her to finally see and respond. But as usual, nothing.

I rubbed my thumb along his scruffy jaw, and I brushed hair off his forehead, but his eyelids didn't twitch with the soft tickles. My chin quivered as I fought a fresh wave of tears. I opened his dress shirt, fearing the worst. All traces of the infection in the veins were gone, replaced with blackened skin covering his whole body. It had spread too far. Oliver needed strength to fight this for however long he had left. "Hang in there. Don't you leave me until I get to say goodbye."

He didn't respond either.

A sob escaped my lips, and I ran downstairs to his stash of blood and retrieved an armful of chilled bags from the bottom of the fridge. His supply was low. Carrying as many as I could, I returned to his side and popped the port on the first one and poked through the seal with a key. I pushed the port between his lips and squeezed. Instinct had him swallowing, and I smiled with relief as I fed him bag after bag. Any strength I could get into him would slow the progression.

I leaned my head down on his chest and listened. The slow heartbeats comforted me. I gripped his limp hand in mine firmly, waiting for him to press back. A tiny urge told me to kill him, to put him out of this agony, but I couldn't do it. I was too selfish and too stubborn to give up. I sat upright and smoothed his suit. Releasing his lifeless hand, I buttoned his sport coat and brushed off lint. I finger-combed his hair and told myself I wasn't fixing him up as if he were already dead.

He wasn't dead. I wanted to pound my fists against his chest, but I couldn't hurt him more.

"We never had enough time. There would never be enough." I stroked his jaw. "Nothing in life is fair, I know, but after everyone I'd already lost, saying goodbye to you, my love, seems excessively cruel." I sniffled. "Remember when I said you can't hate your family, only what they've done? Well, my dad did this to you, to me, and he was *happy* about it. I hate him. It's true. I hate what he did, and I hate him. I don't believe everyone deserves a second chance anymore, but you do. You can't leave me. I won't accept it. I can't. You can't leave me!" I gripped his hand in mine again and squeezed.

If I had the strength, I'd pick him up and set him on the couch, a soft resting place. But I couldn't, so Oliver lay on the hardwood floor and an uncomfortable angle, as if he'd fallen off the stool.

A knock at the door turned my head, and the most wonderful face—dark blue eyes framed by brown curls and a nervous, melancholy smile—appeared, and I gasped.

"Lily!" I got up and ran to her, nearly knocking her over with my enthusiastic hug.

"How's Oliver?" she asked quietly.

I didn't want to tell her the cold, hard truth. "How did you get here so fast?"

"I've been staying in town." Her eyes glanced over my shoulder, and her lips thinned. "He doesn't look good."

I wished Lily could brainstorm an idea I hadn't tried, but introducing her to vampires during an emergency wasn't likely to go over well. At a minimum, it would take too long. "He's dying, and there's nothing I can do about it."

Lily released me and approached Oliver, who still rested on the floor. She glared at the empty bags of blood. *Oops, I forgot to shove those away before rushing to her side.* Lily stepped back from him. "He's a vampire? Oliver is a vampire? All this time, you've been dating a *vampire*?"

I held out my hands in desperation to calm her. "I can explain everything, I swear. He's not going to hurt you, not that it matters, because he's dying. Dad shot him." I paused, considering her string of questions. "How do you know about vampires?"

My sister fidgeted uncomfortably. She looked out the front door as if planning to run.

I couldn't let that happen. "Lily, talk to me. No one is going to hurt you, I promise. What do you know about all this?"

Lily faced me. "Dad told me to leave to protect myself."

"I heard," I muttered, not that I still held a grudge.

"Are you sure you want me to help him?" she asked, pointing to Oliver.

I frowned. "How can you ask that? I love him. I would do anything for him."

Lily rested a hand on my shoulder. "For you, I'll do this, but you can't tell anyone, and I mean *anyone*." Lily gazed at Oliver's unconscious body with compassion. "Promise me now."

"I promise. I'll promise you anything if you can help him. Is there another cure?" I asked. Hope weaseled back into my heart. I didn't care if it was destined to be destroyed all over again. I grasped onto Lily's every word with pure, blind hope.

"There is." Lily kneeled beside Oliver and used her car keys to scratch her wrist.

I didn't ask, and I didn't interrupt, because I was simply grateful for anyone helping.

My sister pressed her damaged wrist to Oliver's mouth. He didn't move. Lily pressed her skin harder against his mouth, but still he didn't react. She pulled back and scratched harder.

"What's going on?" I asked.

"He's not drinking." She pressed the blood-soaked skin back to his mouth.

"I just fed him several bags of blood. Maybe he's not hungry?"

"My blood is the cure."

I sank to my knees next to her. "What?"

Lily focused on Oliver. She squeezed her blood into his mouth. It dribbled onto his lips. "Hold his mouth open."

I pushed at his jaw to give Lily's blood access. She dripped it into his mouth, right onto his tongue, but Oliver still didn't move. Just when I didn't think any more tears were left, more streamed down my cheeks. "We're too late."

"Not yet," Lily said.

I sobbed while holding his mouth. Lily pulled away and scratched harder at her own wrist. She pressed the wound against his lips. "C'mon, drink, damn it."

Lily shared a glance with me, and I didn't know how to read it. We were so close.

"Oliver," I said with a begging tone. "The cure is in your mouth. Drink. For me, please drink." I needlessly raked my fingers through his hair and smiled through my tears.

He didn't move.

I checked for a pulse, and it was so faint, I had to focus hard to feel anything at his throat. "Don't give up now. Take the cure. Come back to me."

Lily pulled away and wiped her wrist. Her eyes were rimmed in red, fighting back her own tears. "I think I'm too late. I'm so sorry."

"No! No. No, no. This isn't... This isn't happening." I leaned over Oliver and pounded my fists on his chest in frustration. "You can't leave me now. Come back. Swallow the cure. It's right there!" All my desperation and anger unleashed in a torrent of weak punches.

Oliver gasped and blinked.

I sniffled and swiped tears from my eyes to see. "Oliver?"

His eyes shifted to me. "More." His voice was raspy, pained, dry.

I sent a silent plea to Lily, and she replaced her wrist at his mouth. Oliver bit down and drank hungrily. The char on his arm receded. The blackened veins hidden beneath the char faded next, rapidly returning Oliver to his healthy, youthful complexion. My eyes widened, and my heart soared.

Oliver released my sister's wrist and panted.

Lily hugged her damaged wrist and backed away.

Oliver began sitting up, and I reached out to stabilize him, but he pulled me into his strong embrace. I wrapped my arms around his neck, and beneath the stench of rot, blood, and sickness sweat, Oliver's familiar scent filled my nose in comfort. I sobbed with relief.

"Daisy, you're okay. I was so worried."

I smiled, tasting my tears. "About me? You were the one dying on the floor."

He pulled back and gave me a quick kiss on the lips. "I'm always worried about you."

Lily cleared her throat, and Oliver met her gaze with appreciation. "Lily, right? We met briefly at Megan's funeral. Pardon my need for a shower."

My sister nodded stiffly. She was reluctant to be near him. She was afraid of him, but why?

"Thank you for saving my ass." Oliver rose and easily lifted me to my feet. He displayed his palms in a gesture of friendliness. "I'm not going to hurt you."

"It's not you I'm worried about," Lily said, meeting my eyes.

"What's going on?" I asked her.

"Have a seat," Oliver said, gesturing to the stools at his bar. The perpetual host in him kicked in, as if he wasn't just seconds from death. "Ignore the mess. I was out of it for a while." Oliver swooped around the bar and cleaned up the surface. He set out a line of glasses and poured tequila from a brand new bottle.

"I'm happy to help you, but I can't stay," Lily said, backing further away.

"I haven't seen two minutes of you in months," I said. "Please stay a little while. Let me thank you."

"It's not safe for me. You may have noticed I'm the cure," Lily said slowly. "I'm the only remaining cure. Vampires will want to keep me locked up as an insurance policy. And everyone who wants vampires dead is going to kill me if they find out. Including Pierce."

That explained her terrified reaction to Pierce at the funeral.

"I'm not going to take you prisoner, Lily," Oliver said, lifting a drink to his lips. "A human owns this place, so you're safe in here."

"You don't understand." Lily approached me and fastened her hands to my arms urgently. "I'm the cure. You're the weapon."

Oliver choked on his tequila. "Excuse me?"

# 20

# The Choice

**Daisy**

After being reassured Oliver wouldn't lock her away, my sister accepted a drink from the bar and downed it in a single swallow. She dropped onto a stool and knitted her fingers together in nervous anticipation. If I weren't in shock over her revelation, I would've joined her. Instead, I closed my mouth to avoid catching flies and waited for her to continue.

When we were little girls, we were the best of friends. One sunny afternoon, we both fell off our bicycles, and Dad praised Lily for trying, but he criticized me for failing. Lily would stand up for me only to be told it was great she wanted to help others, but Daisy needed to learn for herself.

I spent my youth vying for Dad's approval, not understanding the damage he was causing. That directly fed into my seeking strangers' approval when I saved their lives, and I wasn't ashamed that Dad's lack of affection influenced me so much. But Lily never felt that rejection and pain, and when I grew up, I was grateful she had been spared. There was a lightness, a wanderlust she always carried with her, making her magnetic to all those around her. Especially me.

Perhaps that magnetism wasn't her gentle personality. Perhaps I wanted to finally learn why I was treated differently, what was wrong with me. Breaking free from the recesses deep in my mind, a sharp jealousy grew, but it was inappropriate to unleash my frustrations on my sister. It wasn't her fault Dad thought she was perfect. It wasn't her fault I was considered less than. Her having information about Dad's secret work didn't surprise me, but that jealousy could never return to its cage.

My sister turned to Oliver and wiped her lips with the back of her hand, face grim with the truth she'd exposed. "Dad's been experimenting on vampire captives for a while. Only when Newt told him the truth of his work did Dad refuse. So, Newt sent Soren to kill Mom, and Dad suddenly got on board with mass murder. He used our blood, Daisy, *our* blood, in his twisted recipes."

"And he disclosed all this to you without a word to me," I said flatly, the jealousy having popped out.

"He thought that by using us, he was protecting us." Lily set the glass on the bar.

That didn't help. "I'm older than you. Why would he hide this from me? Does he really think I'm incapable of handling this? I'm dating a vampire!"

Oliver took my hand in his, and the sweet affection calmed me down for the time being.

"You have roots here—friends, a home, a job you love, and a man you love." Lily glanced at Oliver, acknowledging his prominent role in my life. "So, now you see why we can't stay together. It's too dangerous. I'll disappear again and start fresh."

I wasn't going to lose my sister again. "You can't leave. We can help each other. When Oliver's not on death's door, he's strong as hell. He can protect us."

"I do my best." Oliver lifted a second drink to his lips to hide the thick layer of sadness drawing his features, but he didn't need to worry. I wasn't leaving him. I would never choose to leave him. Oliver was my love, my partner—the one I could always count on, but he wasn't infallible. That made me love him more.

"And you were pretty close to dead, no offense," Lily said to him dismissively. "Daisy, the only way you can protect us is by accepting your witch DNA. Witch power can keep us safe."

That was ridiculous. All I'd accomplished was *maybe* knocking over a tiny green army guy, which wasn't proof of anything, and a glowing hand so dim it was likely a hallucination driven by intense desire. "How is that supposed to help?"

Lily stood up. "Think of it like a tenderloin steak."

"Interesting choice of metaphor," Oliver said.

Lily ignored him. "Not everyone has one, and those who do sometimes don't realize what they have. As a Barrett, your steak's been sitting on your grill, doing no harm, not interfering with your day-to-day life, just waiting for the perfect time. When that time arrives and you turn on the flames, that steak changes. It's seared into a different flavor, a different texture. Its molecules are changed forever."

I couldn't figure where she was going with this. I shared a quick glance with Oliver, whose complexion suddenly turned pale, and I frowned at my sister. "You're saying I have a steak, and I don't know it?"

"By turning on the flames of your witch DNA, not only do you wield actual power to protect us, but more importantly, your base blood is changed, preventing you from being used to make more of Dad's poison. Don't you see? The ability to make the weapon would cease to exist."

I wasn't the only Barrett in the room. "If witchcraft is in my DNA, then it's in yours, too."

"I can't become a witch because my blood would change, too. Don't you see? As long as the weapon exists in its current state, I have to keep the cure viable. If I activate my witch DNA, the cure is gone forever."

Oliver paused in his swallowing.

I stared at my sister.

"I'm sorry," Lily said. "To prevent myself from accidentally destroying the cure flowing through my veins, I have to stay away from all this—the danger, the drama, Dad's experiments. I have to stay away, so I can't be around elves and vampires. Now you know why." Lily pulled away.

"Wait!" I called after her, but with sadness on her face, she turned and left in a hurry, closing the door behind her on the way out. "Did that just happen?" I stared after her, dumbfounded by the information she'd kept from me.

"Daisy," Oliver said, regaining his senses. He swept my hair over my shoulder and tipped my chin to face him. "Your sister is trapped between warring factions she didn't ask for, but she's right to go. If the elves catch her, they will kill her so the weapon can continue without resistance. Because of your father's own hand, she must stay far from the elves."

I shook my head, unwilling to believe Dad had deliberately cursed her like this, forever keeping my own sister away from me. My father couldn't be that depraved.

"Listen to me," Oliver continued. "If vampires discover the weapon flowing through your veins, they will want you dead. There's something you need to know. That night we met at the bar and I—" Oliver cleared his throat suggestively "—stayed over, I saw the drawing on your wall."

His charcoal drawing of the three witch friends, including my ancestor, and Allison and Jamie's ancestor. "It's yours, isn't it?"

"Lily spoke the truth. The witch gene flows through your DNA."

I frowned. "You knew I had witchcraft in my veins, and you never said anything?"

"Between your possession of my ring in a spell-infused box, the grimoire, the friendliness of your roommates, who are witches, I had a feeling—a dreadful pit-of-despair sinking feeling—but I wasn't certain. At first, I thought you were a witch with your memories tampered with, but now I believe Lily's right. You're a dormant witch, and if you activate that gene, you will be unstoppable, capable of protecting yourself from both elves and vampires, including me. I'm not indestructible." Oliver tented his shredded shirt covered in dried blood to make his point. "There's something Lily didn't tell you or doesn't know. Unlike Pierce, I want you to make the choice for yourself, but I don't want you walking blindly into your decision. Witchcraft isn't without its side effects."

Of course, nothing was ever easy. "Like heart palpitations, increased thirst, dizziness, and a warning to avoid operating heavy machinery?"

Oliver smiled. "There's that sense of humor I've missed." His smile faded away. "It's an innate desire to hunt and kill vampires. Love in your heart won't win that war in your mind, and it takes time to learn control. We could leave this all behind and travel the world. I'm sure there's somewhere you've always wanted to see."

"You're telling me my choice is to live my life on the run, getting hunted by vampires who want me dead and elves who want me locked up for my blood, or become a witch and kill you against my will?" I shouldn't have been dabbling in the craft with my roommates, bringing me that much closer to becoming Oliver's enemy. They must've known about this, and they deliberately withheld it from me. Encouraged me, even.

"It is a choice, just not a good one."

"If I were to take a global vacation, it would be for happy reasons. This is my home. I'm not leaving." I gripped Oliver's hands. "And there's no way I'm following the witchcraft path, not if it takes me from you. I can't live without you."

"I'll protect you from everything always, down to my last breath. I imagine it won't be easy." Oliver's pale eyes softened, and his lips found mine. His arms wrapped around me, and I relished having him alive and in my embrace. He was everything to me.

"Good thing I like it hard," I teased to lighten the mood.

Oliver's eyes flashed, and something grew, pressing against me. "You have no idea what I want to do with you right now. But don't worry about your sister's warning. We'll figure out something."

For now, I was safe. Vampires couldn't get inside, and the only elf I was aware of was Pierce—who still had my necklace. We'd figure out something. Our mouths connected again, slowly exploring, and my hands slipped up his firm chest. At the ragged threads, I pulled away. "Your shirt is absolutely destroyed."

"I should've bought the dry cleaners on Carney Avenue."

I smiled, remembering his delirious statement in the suburban torture dungeon. "And I should've bought stock in stain remover."

"Seriously, I should ring my tailor."

"I don't think anyone can fix this shirt." One button at a time, I exposed his taut chest, smooth and unmarred, with a soft dusting of dark hair. But behind the tattered dark fabric, he was covered in dried blood from his numerous stab wounds and whatever else Evangeline had done to him.

Oliver groaned in anticipation, watching my nimble fingers work to uncover his sexy body in desperate need of a shower. "Daisy?"

"Hmmm?"

"Where's my shoe?"

# 21

# Call Me a God

**Daisy**

Upstairs in his bedroom, I slipped the ruined shirt off his firm shoulders, and my fingertips brushed along his sticky biceps. Only a bumpy scar remained from Dad's gunshot, as if it had happened months ago. All the stab wounds were healed into thin lines. Magic had healed the physical wounds, but I couldn't compel away the pain and torture. The best I could do was make him temporarily forget.

I unlatched his belt buckle, and Oliver dropped his pants, exposing endless miles of perfect man shape, including a bulge in his boxer briefs. My hands glided along his perfect curves, and I squeezed the luscious, firm ass. A throb accumulated between my legs, anticipating his touch and his mouth lighting my body like a spark plug roaring an engine to life. My lips lifted, amusing myself with a metaphor Oliver would appreciate.

"What's the smile for?" Oliver's broad palms slipped my shirt free, and he reached around for my bra hooks.

"Just thinking of the vibration of your car."

"My car? I'm stripping you naked, and you're thinking of my Shelby?" Oliver tilted his head to the side, amused. "That's the second sexiest thing you've ever said."

"What's the first?" I asked with a coy grin.

He freed the button of my jeans and unzipped the fly. I shimmied my hips as he dragged the tight fabric down. "If you have to ask, then I'll jumpstart your memory."

Oliver settled me inside the massive shower and turned on the waterfall. He slipped his hands over his body, rapidly washing off the blood, sweat, and iron residue, and after a vampire second, he turned, caging me against the wall of the shower with powerful arms, water dripping down his face from his hair, looking perfectly ravenous.

I meticulously brushed away the dripping strands, paying the closest attention to every inch of his face. My heart skipped a beat. He smiled, and I knew he was listening to my physical reaction to him.

"Now, where were we?" His lips found mine, and I rose up on my tippy toes as water pattered around us. His erection pressed against my naked hip.

"Something about a jumpstart," I mumbled between kisses.

His lips trailed down my throat, and my breathing became deep pulls. Soft lips and warm breath left a cool trail along my skin, and he discovered the tightening of my nipples.

"Sounds about right." His mouth sucked my nipple, and I arched into him with a gasp.

He chuckled against my skin. "That's the spot."

I laughed and raked my fingers through his wet hair. "There are more uses for that mouth of yours."

"You never complained about my commentary before. What's changed?" he asked playfully and took that moment to graze over my body with his slick hands. Oliver kneeled, resuming a trail of kisses down my stomach to the crest of my hips.

I liked his pillow talk, but I answered him seriously. "For the first time, I was afraid I would lose you today."

Oliver paused, his mouth inches from my clit. He tilted his face up to meet my steely gaze. "Daisy, our world is dangerous for humans. I'm not going to lie, but you're strong and capable. You saved my ass, and I'm never going to leave you. We'll always figure out something."

His words brought tears to my eyes, but they were invisible in the shower. Oliver's compassion took over. He climbed to his feet and wrapped his arms around my naked body. "I love you. I'm not going anywhere."

I sniffled, and his length pressed against my hip again, not asking or begging for entrance. It was just there, ready for me when I wanted it. Well, I wanted him now. I needed him inside me. "Take me now, please."

Oliver kissed my lips quickly. "You don't have to beg. I'm yours anytime, day or night." He bent at the knees to reach the right angle, and his length found my opening. I opened my legs further to grant him entrance, and he gently thrust against me.

I arched against him again, and a moan escaped my lips. His thick arm lifted one of my legs, and he leaned me against the tile wall. He slowly pulled free, and I met his thrusts as he worked his way deeper and deeper. Steam billowed around us. Slick hair pasted to my face and neck. He sheathed himself fully, and a loud groan of pleasure vibrated in Oliver's throat. "Engine jumpstarted. Stand by for acceleration."

I laughed. "Just fuck me already."

"Your wish is my command."

Oliver thrust slowly at first and then faster, building an impressive regular momentum, endless with his inhuman stamina. His fingers reached down to my throbbing cleft, and he ground his thumb against the swollen, sensitive tissue. Heat and a toe-curling, muscle-clenching build from his fingers left my body clenching. Loud, punctuated noises of pleasure escaped my lips, and I exploded in release. "Oh, God. Oh, God. Oh, God! Oliver!" I cried out. The man was talented and so very generous.

His fingers continued moving slowly as I rode the waves, and he stopped the moment before the sensitivity became too much. I opened my eyes to gaze upon the beautiful man before me, and I realized Oliver hadn't come yet. "I'm sorry. Shit."

He hushed me. "Don't ever apologize for your own pleasure. Anytime, anyplace, I'm yours. But if you're done, I'm already satisfied. The number one sexiest words passed your lips."

In the throes of passion, I didn't remember what I said. "What were they?"

"You called me a god. Uh, three times. What better compliment is there?" Oliver wrapped his arms around me, erection remaining fully inside me. He brushed slick hair off my face.

Heat bloomed within. "You're beautiful, generous yet protective, and your stamina is to die for, so to me, you are a god. There's no one or nothing else that compares."

Oliver's lips spread wide in a grin. "And you're human, yet you have the lips of an angel, the body of Venus, and the patience of a saint."

I laughed. "Now who's exaggerating?"

Oliver's smile slid away. "My godliness was an exaggeration? Come now, be honest."

I smiled wistfully. Only minutes ago, this seemed like only a dream. "I wish this could last forever."

Oliver shut off the water. Drips splashed onto the tile floor. "You are my forever."

"Easy for you to say." I met his thoughtful eyes and backpedaled. I didn't mean to offend him. Becoming a vampire wasn't his choice. "I didn't mean to dismiss..."

"I can make you a promise." His hands curled around mine, and he brought them to his lips. "I promise when you've had enough of humanity's bullshit, when you'd rather shake a stick at children than hug them, when you'd rather toss the newest seventeen-G cell phone into the bay, I'll be there with you, and together we'll cross that rainbow bridge."

"You hate children?" I extrapolated, avoiding the heavier conversation.

"You know what I mean," he said softly.

Understanding his promise had me furrowing my brows. "I can't let you kill yourself when I'm old. Life is a gift, and so few people get a second chance. Don't waste yours on my account."

"I've lived a long time, far more than natural. You are my life, and without you, I don't want to be here any longer."

Who was cutting onions around here? I blinked back tears. His devotion was beautiful, but I couldn't think about that promise. "I wish we had more time."

Oliver leaned closer and kissed my forehead. "There is one way."

"What is it?"

He shook his head, and he slipped free from between my legs. "I shouldn't have said anything. Forget it."

I didn't like his retraction. "What is it?"

The sexy vampire brushed the water off my shoulders, focusing on it harder than needed. "I made a promise to myself that I'd never turn anyone. I broke it once in desperation."

I made the leap. "Evangeline?"

"And you can see how that ended. A baby vampire needs an adjustment period. Over a hundred years ago, it was easier to stay hidden while learning to fight the new urges, and random animal attacks were easier to accept. Nowadays, with higher populations and viral information, staying hidden is very difficult. Not to mention the intense desire to murder every human in sight without regard."

That, and drinking blood, giving up food, and avoiding the sun added to the list of reasons never to choose to become a vampire, no matter the alternative.

"All it takes is one slip, and there's a new witch hunt, rounding up vampires to burn. The only difference between Peshtigo 1871 and today is that I'm more afraid we'd end up in labs like your father's and later destroyed like rats. Being a vampire is inherently too dangerous, and I couldn't live with myself, knowing the woman I cared about most left me to rampage all over Europe, killing hundreds—thousands—of innocent people for fun."

My stomach curdled. "That's what she did?"

"Those deaths are on my hands. When she'd returned from Europe, I thought I had killed her, ending her homicidal streak, and that pain had stayed with me. Only after she escaped the lab did I learn she'd been captive all these years. I couldn't place that burden on you, and I couldn't kill you even if it meant saving thousands."

I would never turn into someone like Evangeline. I was an EMT, a saver of lives, a lover of people. There was no way a blood-drinking murderer would spring free from the depths of my psyche just because a strange virus infected my system. I'd been deprived of a loving, close-knit family, and I craved that. I wanted children someday, but I didn't know how to reconcile that with Oliver. If I were turned into a vampire, it would never be an option. "Well, you're in luck. I already decided a while back I never wanted to be a vampire, and you've just convinced me it's the worst thing imaginable."

Oliver smiled. "With that settled, are you up for round two?" His fearless erection waited, hard and veiny, jutting from marvelous hips.

"Clear your calendar." I sent him a sly smile, and his lips crashed down on mine.

# 22

# Revenge Best Served Cold

**Oliver**

Sex with Daisy was always amazing. Sex with Daisy knowing I'd never have to turn her into a beast like me and worry about her slaughtering innocent people, exposing the vampire race to another witch hunt? Priceless. I was far more energetic than I'd been in ages, but I still held back. She was a delicate human, after all. My only regret was never getting to experience the full strength of her in my arms, as a vampire, and completing a blood bond ritual with her.

But sometimes sacrifices had to be made to keep the ones I loved safe.

I admired Daisy's sleeping face as she cuddled up alongside my naked body. My arm had long since fallen asleep, but I didn't care. I treasured every moment we had together, because in the end, there was never enough time. I was honest when I'd said I would follow her to the Other Side. Without her, I was nothing, and I would fight for her until my dying breath.

I'd just planned that to be much, much later on, and my run-in with her dad brought that worry too close to home.

By taking her necklace and rummaging in her mind, making her a prisoner while being aware of it, Pierce Evansson had broken our truce, which was a shame...for him. I lifted off the bed, carefully sliding Daisy off my dead arm, and I shook life back into it. I stepped into my walk-in closet and selected an appropriate suit for my festive mood.

Daisy stirred and groggily sat up.

"I didn't mean to wake you," I said, setting my garments over my wingback chair and quickly slipping into them.

"Where are you going?" She rubbed her eyes.

"I have an errand to run."

"I'll go with you." Daisy threw the sheets aside and curled over, picking up her pants off the floor. She wriggled back into her pants, and I very much enjoyed watching.

I adjusted my suit collar and tugged at my shirt sleeves. Giddy at my errand, I tried to hide the smile on my face, but I couldn't. "I'm not picking up the dry cleaning, Daisy. It's better if you stay here. He already stole too much time from me, and I'm going to end this. Then we have our whole lives before us."

"He?" Daisy put her bra back on, unfortunately, and pulled her shirt over her head. "Are you talking about Pierce?"

Her slight hesitation meant she was worried about her father. "I won't hurt your dad unless you want me to, and don't worry, there will be no guilt or hesitation on my end."

"He's an asshole, but no. Please don't. I'm grateful you asked instead of going half-cocked at him. He'll get his someday. I used to believe in second chances, but I think I'm hoping more for karma."

"I only do things full-cocked." I waggled my brows at her playfully.

Daisy laughed, but it quickly faded as I prepared to go to war with an elf for Daisy. "Then you should know Soren rescued me. Pierce caught him before he could escape with me, but he gave me your sun ring to return to you. I hated the whole situation, but I couldn't help. He told me to go to you—he made me go. It's dark out now. Soren never came home, did he?"

I glanced at my hand, noticing I wore the mystic gem. The thoughtful bastard. I would've felt my brother's vampire presence if he'd returned, and I always woke easily with unusual sounds within these walls. I was certain he'd never come home, but I reached out with my senses now to double-check, and I felt nothing but a very human Nicole, confirming Daisy's assumption.

Anger surged through my veins like a pulsing heat of energy waiting to be spent on someone's face. Pierce had already broken our truce, but if Soren died by his hands, he would wish he'd never met me. "I'll get Soren back."

"I'm still going with you." Daisy stood by my side.

"Daisy." I reached out and cradled her smooth face. "This will likely get messier than I'd expected. I can't bear anything happening to you."

"Ditto," she said, pulling my hands away and tangling my fingers with hers. "We're partners, remember? To me, that means both inside and outside of the ambulance."

I didn't want her anywhere near the elf, who clearly had no boundaries, but I respected her choice. That didn't mean I couldn't take advantage. "One condition."

"Name it."

"We need to move fast, so I'll carry you to Greg's house to get my Shelby."

She opened her mouth to object, but I pressed a finger against her lips. "And no kissing my ears and throat while the vampire is in motion. All hands stay above the belt for your safety and mine."

She smiled. "Is this a ride in your arms or a test drive in a dangerous car?"

"I do have one impressive engine."

Daisy beamed, her cheeks flushing. "Deal. Let's go."

I led her out the front door and scooped her up into my arms as if I were about to take flight. She tried smoothing her hair after our long day of sex and several hour sleep. Night had fallen, so I didn't worry about prying eyes seeing us. The speed a vampire moved would be nothing but a blur to a human. After a blink, there was no trace. At those speeds, Daisy's efforts were in vain.

"Don't bother. This ride is going to be windy. Besides, I like your bedhead."

She reached up and kissed my lips.

I pulled back sooner than I wanted to. "That's one of the rules."

"You didn't say lips."

I thought back to my conditions. She was right. "Well, I need to see where we're going."

"For being in a hurry, you sure are taking your time."

That was true too. I didn't want to literally carry her into danger, but the longer I delayed, the worse Soren could be. I had to save my stubborn little brother and punish the elf. "Hold tight."

Daisy wrapped her arms around my neck, and I zipped off down the sidewalk. I lived only two miles from her dad's house on the bay, so we arrived within seconds. I set Daisy down at the passenger-side door of my car, and I opened it for her. She climbed in on wobbly legs, and I dropped into the driver's seat and fired up the Shelby, thankful the elf had left my keys above the vanity.

"I'll never get used to that speed, but it sure comes in handy." Daisy checked her hair in the mirror and buckled in.

"Like someone I know, I prefer hard, fast, and rough. All three at once is the olive in the martini."

Daisy blushed. I shifted into gear and tore off to the elf's house. With my horsepower and single-track focus, I arrived in mere minutes. Plus, small town. I pulled to the curb behind my brother's Prius and assisted Daisy out of my car. If she weren't here, I'd be so much faster, but I didn't regret having her by my side.

And the elf's house didn't have a barrier. Declining my usual standards of propriety, I kicked the door open, breaking its lock. I reached out for a barrier anyway, since Daisy had called this home for however briefly, but there was no invisible block for me. From the darkness of the interior, I listened for sounds of panic, murmurs of torture, whimpers of pain.

Nothing.

I didn't know whether that was a good sign or not.

"Daisy, find your necklace. If you see Pierce before I get to Soren, scream."

"No problem." She slipped into the darkened kitchen.

I sniffed the air, and I couldn't pick up the scent of an elf, but Pierce always wore the same floral scent, easy to pinpoint, but harder to distinguish between him and the bottle in his bathroom. Then I reached with my heightened senses to find a vampire's presence, but I couldn't pick up anything. That left me canvassing the house the old-fashioned way, room by room, in case my brother had been magically concealed.

The elf better pray Soren's heart still beat.

## Daisy

PIERCE WAS MANY THINGS, but sneaky wasn't one of them. In his bedroom, on top of his chest of drawers, was a jewelry box with a ribbon on top, the kind someone received with a jewelry store purchase. I slipped off the cover and smiled at my locket. Predictable. That was Pierce. I removed it from the box and lifted it over my head, and immediately I felt relieved. Now I just needed Oliver to make the chain indestructible.

My hand was clamped by an ironclad fist.

"Not so fast." Pierce's voice sent a shiver down my back. "Where's Soren?"

"He's not your concern." Pierce still didn't let go.

Oliver hadn't found Soren yet. We needed more time. All I could do was reason with him. "Why can't you accept that I don't want you? Let me go and find someone else to coerce into being your wife, because it's not going to be me."

"You and I were meant to be together. It's our fate."

If fate said I had to mate with an elf and give him offspring only to be abandoned, well, fate could kiss my ass. "I believe in choices."

Pierce dragged me to his bed and pushed me down. I motioned to get up, but his hand stopped me. "You don't understand."

The longer my ex jabbered on, the more time Oliver had to find Soren unimpeded, so I humored him with gritted teeth, but if he attempted to touch my clothing, I'd scream until the dead rose. "Then enlighten me."

Pierce sat next to me, rocking the mattress and forcing me to lean toward him. I scooted farther over. "Our families go back almost two centuries. Your ancestor, Henrietta Barrett, was best friends with Edith Johnson, my grandmother. Our families have been linked for generations. Stop trying to fight *us*."

His argument was flawed. "Oliver's mother, Rose Watson, was the third best friend, so your argument doesn't mean anything."

Pierce's jaw flickered with frustration. "Your father agrees with our match."

"My father can take a flying leap or pound sand, whichever you prefer."

"Your roommates support us, too."

First, why was everyone else's opinion more important than mine? And second, Allison and Jamie had told me elves were worse than vampires, so why *did* they support me and Pierce, if superficially? When Allison had seen Oliver's drawing on my bedroom wall, she'd told me that Edith Johnson was *her* relative—she was related to Edith Johnson. "Wait. How can you and my roommates be related to the same woman?"

Pierce sighed. "Edith Johnson and Logon Larsen bore my father, Evan Logonson, and she was freed from service afterward, so the witch line continued with a human progenitor. They weren't lying to you. What more must I do to prove to you we're soulmates?"

*Treat me like a person instead of an object?*

Finding out my roommates were his relatives was a surprise, and I believed Pierce told me the truth, but I'd long since given up trusting him. "Nothing. There's nothing you can do. I love Oliver. Why can't anyone accept that?"

My ex's fists clenched. "Because he's an abomination! He feeds on people—"

"He taints your breeding stock, you mean?" I interrupted. After my roommates explained what elves really did, just being this close to him disgusted me. I wished he hadn't healed me twice. He still didn't know about Oliver's torture-chamber bite. I slyly shifted my injured wrist out of his casual view.

"Who told you that—Oliver? I'm going to kill that vampire."

I jumped away from his side. "You're not, and he didn't. Seriously, you can't control me. I want the life that I want, and that doesn't include you."

Pierce stood up, rocking the bed, and I tilted. "That's where you're wrong. *Elves* choose their breeders, and I'm going to kill that scourge and make you mine. This will be easier for you if you behave."

I wanted to vomit. "You and my dad aren't getting away with this."

"Daisy," Pierce breathed my name in a patronizing tone. "You still aren't getting it. I'm a hundred and thirty years old, not much younger than your bloodsucker and his murderous brother. My grandmother was taken by an elf and bred, and I'm glad, otherwise I wouldn't be here now."

The curdling in my stomach wasn't getting better. "You're glad she became a cow for you to be born. I wonder what she thought of it. Oh, that's right. Her memory had been erased. Isn't that right? So where is she now?"

Pierce shrugged. "She died a century ago. I grieved, and her passing doesn't faze me any longer."

I couldn't temper the anger and disgust flowing through me. "So that's your plan for me—breed me until you get your spawn and abandon me like your grandmother had been? Then dismiss me entirely and not give a shit about everything I suffer?"

"It's not like that."

"Then explain it, because I'm really struggling to understand."

"Daisy." Pierce reached for my hands, but I pulled back. "Remember Abby's wedding when I left you to get you a drink?"

I remembered that, but nothing afterward. Oliver had told me we met there, and Pierce erased my memory twice. That compulsion still hadn't broken. So I fibbed, "I remember dancing with Oliver, and you erased my memory of it." I wished that evening had gone differently. If only Oliver would've rescued me from the elf then, I could've avoided so much stress and heartache.

Pierce pinched the bridge of his nose. "I was asking your parents for permission to marry you. Don't forget, Oliver was there to kill my dad. He only danced with you to piss me off."

Oliver had told me the story of how he exacted justice for his sister's slaying. Although I didn't agree with his method, he had admitted to his actions, and he had shown remorse, which was leagues above Pierce. Besides, I trusted Oliver. I trusted him to tell me the truth. As for Pierce, I scoffed. He thought so little of me that no other man could possibly be interested in me. I wished I had a stake and could wield it effectively.

"Daisy, I've always wanted to marry you and make a bunch of babies with you. I promise I would never take them from you or erase your memory of it. Yeah, I'm an elf, but I'm not a Neanderthal like generations past. I'm always here for you, and I always will be. Come with me. We can talk this out over a real meal. You know, because I can eat. I can make one hell of a breakfast spread, including *homemade* waffles." Pierce paused, watching me process.

Every time I needed Pierce, he'd shown up. He did things to protect me from the dangers I wasn't aware of. He wanted to marry me and give me a normal life. Sometimes he crossed the line, but I could excuse that as *cultural* differences. "Jamie is a great cook, too." Not that I wanted to defend him right now.

Pierce added, "We can be a happy family, a real one, not the nightmare everyone spreads—you and me and a bunch of kids. The whole elf clan would love to meet you, and they'd welcome you, too."

"I thought humans were forbidden."

"They make an exception when I ask."

I squinted at him. "Are you something special to them?"

"You could say that, and there's many more of us. Then you can see the real elves, not the stories." Pierce smiled, reminding me of when we had been happier together. I missed that about him—the sweetness—even if he missed the mark frequently. For example, I hated daisies.

It was a lot to process. A big, normal, happy family—something I never had and craved desperately. And he'd told me all of that with my necklace on.

A dull thump rattled the walls. Pierce snapped to attention. "I'll be needing this." He stole my locket and bolted like a lumbering giant out the door.

That wasn't good news.

# 23

# A Twisted Alliance

**Oliver**

I COMBED EVERY INCH of this house except for the primary bedroom. Since Daisy was arguing semantics with Pierce, playing a lovely distraction for me, I rested easily, knowing she was safe for the time being. As much as I hated the elf, he wouldn't physically harm her, and I was close enough to intervene the second I grew suspicious.

More concerning though, Soren wasn't here. I exited the front door and scanned the residential area. Still dark. No flicker of movement caught my eye. I sucked in a deep breath and picked up his scent. How had I missed it before? The vampire's signature came from Soren's own car. He'd escaped the elf's clutches and hid for the daytime in his Prius. A bigger relief than I'd expected. My brother was fine for now.

A strong and swift breeze rustled my suit, but it was too quick for me to act. A bone-crunching wallop to the spine tossed me through the air, and I smacked against the exterior of the house. I dropped onto the porch and rubbed my head.

Evangeline stood over me, legs spread, arms folded over her chest, and a smirk worthy of *Villains Today* magazine.

With a grunt, I climbed to my feet and pressed a hand against my aching-but-healing back. Now that I was cured and well-nourished, she was less of a threat to me. "Evangeline, a 'hello' would've sufficed. What are you doing here?"

"I see you escaped my captivity. Curious—where did you find the cure?"

Feet thundered down the stairs inside the house. And that meant the moose was on the loose. I hoped Daisy was okay and had the reservation to stay safely away. I braced myself for whatever came next.

Pierce filled the doorway. "Angel, catch." He tossed a sizzling necklace to Evangeline. My ex caught it, and her flesh sounded like bacon on a stove. With a grimace, she popped open the locket and dumped out the contents—vervain and black nightshade. Evangeline placed the sizzle-free necklace over her head and positioned the locket front and center of her chest. I didn't like Daisy not having her protection.

"Angel? Since when are you two on nickname terms?" Images of the elf with my ex were an impossibility. I shook the nightmarish thoughts from my head.

"That's none of your business," Pierce said.

Fine. I'd rather not hear the details anyway. Since the players on the board changed, Pierce's punishment would wait. I needed to get Daisy and Soren out of here. "That's it?" I asked Evangeline. "All you wanted was that necklace?"

"Angel, go inside—" Pierce stopped. He'd caught Daisy's scent at the same time I did. My love stood in the doorway behind his bulk. Pierce shifted aside to allow her to pass. "Daisy, there's someone here who wants to meet you."

This was bad news if I ever heard any. "Daisy, stay inside. Pierce and I have some issues to work out." With my fist, and if he compelled her again, with my fangs.

Daisy ducked under Pierce's bulk and popped out onto the porch. Clearly, the elf hadn't compelled her to stay during their chat. That was almost forgivable.

"I'd rather not stay in there. Who wants to meet me?" She turned and found Evangeline cleaned up and smirking. Daisy's eyes widened, and she made a move toward me.

Evangeline stepped between us, and Daisy, ashen with fear, said, "You clean up nice."

Evangeline smiled warmly. "Now that I've had the feral washed off, thanks to your dad, it's a pleasure to make your formal acquaintance." The vampire addressed Pierce. "The little human still has her memory intact. I'm surprised." Evangeline gripped Daisy by the wrist and flung her off the porch and into the front yard.

Before I could dash after her, a meaty fist locked on my arm, freezing me in place. I growled at the elf. "Let me go, Pierce."

"I will." Pierce reeled back and decided to rearrange the angle of my nose. I buckled over at the flash of white pain in my face, and Pierce's self-satisfied grin pissed me off. I glanced at Daisy, and she was chatting politely with Evangeline. The weirdness just kept getting weirder.

I leaped at the elf and shoved him back against his own house. The walls shook with the force, and Pierce crumpled to the porch in a massive heap.

"Our truce is over. If this is what you want, then come get it," I taunted the elf.

"Good." Pierce rose to his full height. "I've been wanting this for too long."

Pierce dove at me, and for the first time in decades, I unleashed my full strength on him.

## Daisy

My wrist sparked with pain, and I was going to feel my hip tomorrow. I'd never felt more like a useless toy than when a vampire showed her true strength. I didn't even know if she had to try all that hard. Humans really were inferior, objectively speaking.

"You don't know anything," Evangeline said, hands on her hips. My necklace taunted me from her exposed skin on the low-dipping blouse over hip-hugging jeans. I hardly recognized her without the disheveled hair, messy clothes, and feral snarl. I had to admit, she was stunning. Tall, leggy, with cascading curls out of a storybook.

I climbed to my feet, understanding his attraction all those years ago. But years of isolation and torture in a lab left the woman needing help, like a padded room and medication.

No one should have to survive what she'd endured and try to reintegrate into society alone. That didn't excuse her attacking me before, and she wasn't exactly offering me milk and cookies now.

She was trying to stake a claim on Oliver, and that pissed me off. "I know that Oliver and I don't want anything to do with you."

Evangeline's eyes flashed in anger, but she maintained her composure. "He and I have a long history with many bumps in the road. You, I'm afraid, are nothing more than a filler. Now that I'm back, you are no longer needed to keep Oliver occupied in my absence."

I looked at the porch, and Oliver and Pierce were talking things through. Maturely. This wasn't going how I'd expected at all, but on the whole, I was proud of Oliver and confident in his love for me. "I'm certain he's long since moved on from you, and your continued attachment despite his rejection is...unhealthy. Do you think he'd really take you back after you killed so many people in Europe and then locked him up and tortured him?" And I thought my family was dysfunctional.

Evangeline stiffened. "Getting poked, prodded, and experimented on for decades is unhealthy, but who's keeping score?"

Remembering when she'd pounced on New's throat, guilt pressed on me. The longer I could keep her talking, the less chance she had to use her fangs, and I wanted to keep my throat in one piece. I was the weak link in this group, so I waited for someone else to break the status quo. "My dad did this to you, and I'm sorry. If I had any idea, I'd—"

"What?" She interrupted. "Save me? You were there in the lab with lots of opportunities. I freed myself. Not you."

I had been occupied, but I never did check the other doors for other captives. "I'm sorry. Really, I am."

Evangeline moved closer and stared hard into my eyes with glowing red irises. Hunger or compulsion? I focused on her nose. Her voice deepened, threatening. "Do you really think two words can undo all the decades of torture?"

Guilt, shame, the usual. I trembled with her so close, but keeping her talking was the extent of my defense. "It doesn't, but I don't know what else I can do."

"Stay right here," she ordered.

In confusion and reflex at the benign answer, I met her gaze, and the glowing irises captured me. "You stay right here," she repeated.

To test the dread curdling in my stomach, I tried to take a step, and I couldn't. When I got out of this mess, I was going to need my own supply of vervain, so I couldn't be kneecapped at any second. I hated being helpless, watching her stroll up the porch, unimpeded.

Pierce patted her shoulder as if tagging a partner to leap into the ring, like they'd planned this out. The elf marched down the stairs toward me while Evangeline had Oliver's attention. Pierce's bulk blocked my view of the vampires.

"Do you mind moving? I can't see through you."

Pierce smirked, but he didn't move. "What did she say to you?"

"Why do you care, and since when are you and her friendly?"

"She and I have similar wants."

I cringed. A vampire and an elf? "And what is that?"

Pierce grinned. "Revenge."

Her obsession with Oliver wasn't about winning him back. She'd already tortured him. Was one day in that suburban hellhole not enough? I supposed that to her, it wouldn't be. I remembered his blackened body, stabbed all over, blood puddled and coagulated on the floor while his head lolled to the side, unconscious. That was what she wanted. More pain. More suffering. Anger burned through my body, trembling my limbs, and I needed a release. I needed to punch something, pull some hair, but I couldn't leave this spot. If I punched Pierce, he'd laugh, and I couldn't take more of their superiority.

"Get that psycho away from Oliver." I demanded.

"No," Pierce said with amusement on his lips.

I gritted my teeth in agonizing frustration. "Why can't the two of you just get along?"

"Isn't it obvious?" Pierce touched my chin and tilted my face up to meet his.

I squeezed my eyes closed, unwilling to be rendered more of a puppet. "Obviously, it's not."

"He toys with women. It's a game to him. Can't you see what he did to Evangeline? The girl's off her rocker. I want you, Daisy, and I'll take care of you. I have since the moment I first saw you. You remember, don't you?"

I dragged the locked memories from their dusty chest. "Last year's Halloween party at Fully Loaded. You sat next to an empty barstool, dressed as an elf." I just realized the pointy ears he'd displayed weren't a costume. I'd been so blind, unwilling to absorb the truth before my eyes.

"Easiest costume there is." Pierce smiled.

But I definitely remember he'd excluded the grand finale. "And the wings?"

"They're dramatically more show-stopping than elongated ears, so I kept them under wraps. Do you remember what I said to you?"

"You gave me the worst pickup line in history." I couldn't help but chuckle. But apparently that was news to Pierce.

His face fell. "You didn't like it?"

I recited his words. "You're such a delicate flower. How do you lift that heavy hand of yours all day? I can hold it for you."

"That was beautiful." Pierce frowned.

"I distinctly remember laughing."

"I thought you swallowed wrong."

He really didn't get it. He was so obtuse when it came to anything emotional, as if his communication detector needed re-calibrating.

After failing med school, I'd worked at the bar, scraping together the funds to finish an emergency medical services diploma while dodging my dad's judgmental criticisms. With my free time absorbed with studying, I wasn't *gung ho* about holidays. And unlike Allison, when I was off the clock, I didn't hang around work. So on my night off, why did I go to the bar's Halloween party in the first place?

I dug around in my memories, seeking a logical explanation. And there it was: Dad had told me to go. He'd said that I might meet someone, and I couldn't let that opportunity go to waste. Because meeting an elf had been more important than my replacement studies. "Did you and my dad set me up?"

"What? Why would you think that?"

"Dad wasn't a social butterfly. In fact, I think he hated the bar scene entirely, and he thought parties were a breeding zone of disease, so why would he suggest I go, unless he had a reason?"

Pierce squirmed.

That was all the confirmation I needed. "This whole thing between us was a setup from the start. Is anything about you honest?"

Pierce grabbed my hands. "Everything I said in my bedroom was true. There's so much more you don't know. So much more that might change your mind about me."

I pulled until I freed myself. "If tonight was the first time you were honest with me. I don't know how much clearer I need to be when I tell you there is nothing between us and there never will be."

"Don't overthink everything so much, Daisy. Everything will work out in the end."

A thump came from the porch, and Pierce shifted to see what had happened. Now I could finally see. Evangeline and Oliver were still arguing, but she'd been thrown onto the porch.

I'd never been more afraid in my life.

## Oliver

I KEPT MY EYE on Pierce lurking over Daisy. As long as he stood in the yard, she was safe. I didn't appreciate his hulking form blocking her from my view, but I had other issues to contend with. Evangeline closed the distance between us. I couldn't tell if she wanted to kiss me or bite me, but I noticed she'd reclaimed Daisy's necklace.

My ex-girlfriend chose to swing at me, and I dodged it easily. If I could get Evangeline to calm down and talk this out, I could collect Soren and take Daisy home. "As much as I love our recurring rendezvous, I do have demands on my time."

"I survived in that lab only because I believed you were going to rescue me." Evangeline swung at me weakly, just enough to keep my attention focused on her.

I dodged it again. "When I found you by chance, I never thought for a second of leaving you in there. Evangeline, please. What do you want from me?"

She leaned forward aggressively. "After decades of travels and adventure and fun all over Europe—learning control by myself—I returned to this small town for *you*. Instead of a loving embrace, you staked me and left me to die alone. Except that wretched, cold-blooded killer of a brother of yours, with no remorse for what he did to me in 1880, took me."

I gritted my teeth. "You were dealt a shit hand, and I'm truly sorry for it."

"For forty years, I'd been in a continuous state of torture, hoping beyond hope that every day you would come rescue me—so I could kill you. I even escaped twice to speed up the timeline, but Soren had gotten in my way. I'm not sure which of you brothers I hate more. Truly, I couldn't decide. And now the moment where all my dreams will come true has arrived, but I'm feeling a little—scared. Will ending you satisfy the ache that I've built up for so many years? I doubt it. Then what will I do afterward?" Evangeline smirked and glanced toward Pierce.

I wouldn't stand in her way if she really wanted the elf. Good riddance. "Evangeline—"

"Since you didn't let me die as a pure, innocent human in love with a monster, a balancing of the universe is in order. Now your replacement girlfriend will instead."

Fury roared from my head to my heart and funneled strength into my fingers and toes. Over my dead body would my ex-girlfriend touch Daisy. I might've done many terrible things and turned my head when I should've acted, but Daisy was innocent. "You didn't deserve any of that, but she doesn't either."

Evangeline lunged at me, but I gripped her throat and held her far enough away. She couldn't do anything but scratch me with her fingernails. I was older and therefore stronger. I'd recently replenished my strength with fresh human blood. She couldn't beat me. I lifted her up off her feet and slammed her back first onto the porch. The wind flew out of her lungs, and her breathing hitched. All that did was shut her up.

"Just stop. We don't have to do this," I said. She was suffering. I didn't want to hurt her. If I let her get a few good knocks in, perhaps she'd calm down enough to process this logically and just go, leave with the elf, and never come back.

Wide-eyed, she stared, and after a few beats, she gasped and sprung to her feet. "That's where you're wrong. So very wrong."

She lunged at me again, fingernails curled into claws, and I side-stepped. My ex whirled on me.

"Evangeline," I said in a warning tone, "I'm offering you a truce."

She reeled back a fist, and I caught it in the air and spun her into my arms, embracing her with her fist behind the small of her back. She panted, her heaving chest pressing against me.

"Maybe you're right," she said breathlessly.

Finally.

"I only needed to blow off some steam, and now I can see what's right in front of me." Her face nuzzled my throat. I frequently had that effect on women. So, instead of flat-out recoiling at her touch, I softened my grip on her, ready to talk sense.

Evangeline ducked low and spun away. In a flash, she snapped a wooden baluster and staked me in the abdomen. With a shocked gasp and two hands on the fatal wood, my body stiffened with shock and blinding pain. But that wasn't enough for her. Evangeline angled the stake up toward my heart and shoved with her full might before releasing me.

I folded over, collapsing to my knees. The pain paralyzed me, and now I counted on the traitorous elf to keep Daisy safe from my homicidal ex.

Screams like razor blades tore through the night.

# 24
# Unwanted Desiny

**Daisy**

Oliver's ex-girlfriend, in cute casual clothes, with a smirk on her face, strolled off the porch. Oliver dropped to his knees and fell to his side. A hunk of wood jutted out from beneath his ribs. I stared and blinked in disbelief. That...that didn't just happen. Oliver wasn't moving. After everything we'd been through—after almost losing him to the vampire weapon, after fighting off Pierce's manipulation—we were happy. A few short hours of sweet bliss, and now... It couldn't be over. She didn't...

Oliver still didn't move.

My breath rushed in and out of my lungs in shallow gasps. No, that—that didn't just happen. I didn't just lose him forever. An immortal in perfect health, who survived almost two centuries, couldn't be gone just like that. He couldn't be gone...My head swam, and my chest squeezed with pure, blinding anguish. The crushing agony tore my heart out.

I dropped to my knees in the grass, and I screamed so loud I couldn't hear anything but the pounding of my shredded heart.

A vice-like squeeze on my skull kicked the ground out from under me. I collapsed onto my side, curled into the fetal position, begging the pain to recede. This wasn't anguish. This was elf compulsion breaking—an old memory unleashed.

At my cousin's wedding, Pierce had erased Oliver from my head twice, but I knew that because Oliver had told me. I also knew Oliver had gone to avenge his sister's murder and that the act was regrettably humiliating. It was deplorable and unforgivable. Revolting—that was the word. I knew all that. So why was it disgusting me so much now?

Evangeline gripped my hair and lifted me to my knees. My scalp felt like it was pulling away from my flesh, a searing hot pain. I cried out, and fury raged within me. I could think of nothing but wanting to kill her. The evil vampire, who'd slaughtered innocent people all over the world, needed to die. I needed to protect humans from her.

But how?

Pierce wormed his way between us and made her release me. I held myself up on all fours, painting as my scalp's fury eased.

"Daisy wasn't part of the deal. Once you've dealt with the vampire, you leave."

"Things change, big guy." Evangeline slammed her palm against Pierce's chest. The elf tipped backward, but recovered.

"Then our deal is over." Pierce slipped a hand into his cargo shorts, and he revealed a sharp stake. The one he'd always carried as a 'hunter'.

Evangeline's eyes widened with surprise. "Traitor!"

The rapid speed of betrayal and destroyed trust baffled me. How had these people survived so long? From one second to the next, a longtime friend became an enemy, a respected lover became a betrayer, a good friend bartered the lives of others.

I had enough.

I was going to stop this right now before more people got hurt. I climbed to my feet and jutted out my arms, funneling all the fury to my hands like I'd practiced, hoping for something stronger than the little army guy and more intimidating than the nightlight fist.

"Enough!" I roared.

The elf and vampire flew backward and landed in the grass, the wind knocked clean out of their lungs. Panting with surprise, I didn't have time to think about what I'd just done. I rushed toward the porch, and halfway up the stairs, something firm knocked me sideways. I hit the wooden railing and flipped over, landing in the sharp shrubbery.

My ears rang—a high screaming that came from nowhere and everywhere at once, and my vision sparkled with black dots and returned to a fuzzy blur. My thundering heartbeat drowned out the ringing, and all I could remember was severe blood loss, the growing panic that I was bleeding to death, and that I couldn't move a muscle.

I looked up at the covered porch and admired the sleek paint job—no peeling paint. But I wished I would've turned the light on so I could see better. So I could see my attacker. My hand went to my throat. Huh. I wasn't paralyzed. I pulled my fingers back, and I wasn't bleeding. The pain of the bite wasn't registering yet. I touched again on the other side. Still no blood. I frowned and looked up at the porch light fixture. This...this wasn't my porch. The paint was too new, and Soren wasn't dragging me by the hair.

I gasped and panted, air finally dragging back into my burning lungs. My head rang, but I sat up and pressed a palm against my temple. What just happened?

## Oliver

THAT DAMNED VAMPIRE. I couldn't trust one further than I could throw one—which, in all honesty, was pretty damned far on a good day. After the initial shock of my staking wore off, I securely gripped the wooden baluster with both hands and ripped it out of my abdomen. Blood spurted for a few seconds.

Apparently, Evangeline had skipped anatomy and physiology on her jaunts through Europe. She'd missed my heart, but not my much. The pain cased, and I panted as my body hyper-healed within seconds.

I climbed to my feet, carrying the soiled weapon. Evangeline reached for Daisy, who rested uncomfortably in the bushes. She was dazed.

I sped to my ex and threw her flat onto her back on the lawn. She landed hard, and I kneeled on her chest, threatening her throat with the bloodied stake.

Evangeline chuckled. "Do it. Do it, you son of a bitch, and do it right this time."

She hated herself as much as I'd hated myself, but Daisy had saved me from those dark thoughts, taught me I wasn't a monster for what I was, and that I could control what I did. And that people deserved second chances. Evangeline never had that love and support.

"I'm sorry for everything, Evangeline. We were supposed to be together. You were the light of my life, but I never meant to take your choice away from you. And because of you, I've never turned anyone else, and I never will."

"Is that supposed to make us even?" My ex snarled at me.

"Not even close. I'm sorry. I really am, and I've thought of you nearly every day since that night in June."

The strain and fight eased from her body, and the anger twisting her features into something monstrous faded. She said softly, "The fourth."

I smiled and damned tears sprung to my eyes. "That's right. After my farming duties were complete in the morning, I worked at the lumber mill in the evenings until I could buy you an engagement ring, and when I finally had it in my pocket, I was going to propose that night. Soren didn't agree. He couldn't see how a vampire and a Puritan human could make it work. Ultimately, he was right. Don't blame him for this."

The parallels between her and Daisy weren't lost on me. At least we'd settled the major difference: Soren accepted her, and regardless of what might happen, Daisy would remain human. "I'm sorry for all the pain I caused you. If I could take the burden from you, I'd carry it until my last breath."

Evangeline held back a sob. "You can."

"Are you sure?" I wouldn't normally hesitate, but I did have feelings for the woman once, so very long ago. After all I did to her, she deserved the choice, and to be sure of something she couldn't take back later.

Her arm freed the locket around her neck. Since it didn't burn her skin, it had to be empty. She held it out to me. "Do it," she said softly.

I took the necklace and tucked it into my pocket. With a shaky breath and tears in my eyes, I gently pushed the stake through her heart. She gasped, and her mouth popped open. The gray pallor of death swept over her like a blanket. I sucked back a sob and swiped my eyes clear. "I'm so fucking sorry, Evangeline. I'm so sorry."

A car trunk slammed shut. I craned my neck and climbed to my feet, dashing tears from my eyes.

Pierce gripped Soren like a hostage. He was weak, bruised, and bloodied. Tortured.

The fresh pain curling in my chest morphed into unadultcrated hatred. My voice wasn't my own. "Release him."

The elf approached, dragging a weakened Soren like a stubborn dog on a leash. "For many years, we picked off each other's family members. I know you want me dead after my latest attempt to subdue Daisy, and I don't blame you. You are what you are, but it has to end. I'll make you a trade, one last truce. You give me Daisy, and I'll give you Soren. Then we leave each other's loved ones alone."

For colluding with my ex to kill me, I should kill Pierce now. But Soren was in his grasp, and even as an elf, Pierce was fast, and the bastard had wings.

"What's going on?" Daisy said, scrambling through the bushes. She'd taken a nasty knock, and as she found her wobbly footing, she pressed a hand to her temple.

"Daisy, stay back," I said, terrified to lose her too.

Several feet away, she stopped. My aching chest swelled with relief and gratitude, but she wobbled again, as if about to fall over. I rushed the last few steps to steady her, and I held her tight. I only ever needed her. She was my one and only. My forever.

Daisy frowned and pushed against my hold. "You were dead. I saw it. What's going on?"

I pulled her closer, but she pushed me again. "No, don't. Don't...touch me right now. Something's not right. I...in fact, I need you to back up."

I covered my mouth in shock, horrified and terrified. My heart crumbled, and tears rimmed my eyes. Her anguish had activated her dormant witchcraft. "It's true."

"What?" she asked. "What's happening?"

"You're a witch," Pierce said, answering for me. He wasn't broken up about it.

"What?" Daisy spun to face Pierce and looked at her hands. With a lilt of disbelief, she asked, "Are you sure? I mean,

I might've been able to almost do something, but I wasn't sure, because I could argue that I'd imagined what I thought I wanted, but they said I did it, but I didn't…" Daisy trailed off. "Oh my God, you have wings! How? How can I see them? Are you finally showing me?"

She'd suspected, just as I had. Now she was changing. Swallowing back the emotion clogging my throat, I opened my arms for one final embrace. "Daisy, give me a hug and you'll feel it."

She slowly stepped into my arms, face curling with confusion. I pressed her against me, sighing, fully allowing myself to grasp the last few seconds of pure happiness.

For the last time, I felt her warm body fit against mine. I wrapped my arms around her like a fortress, unwilling to give up its queen. As her arms pressed me against her, the warmth of budding magic trickled through the contact like a steady but growing electric shock.

The tears returned, and I kissed the top of her head. My lips tingled at the touch. I loved her, and now I couldn't go near her. The urge to kill would grow rapidly, and she wouldn't be able to help it. For now, this was the end, but I would wait, and I would hope. "It's not your fault what you are. It only matters what choices you make," I whispered, reciting her line to me a while ago.

Daisy pulled away, frowning. "What are you talking about?"

"That urge to punch or kick me?"

Daisy looked at the grass as if introspectively assessing herself. "Yeah. Yeah, I'm pissed that you killed Pierce's dad in a humiliating way at my cousin's wedding, and that you teased me with a beautiful dance twice just to mock him. Pierce erasing my memory was a blessing."

Pierce stiffened.

I exhaled. The magic was taking over. She had to mean my erased homicide had been a blessing, not my seducing her, surely. "That urge will only grow. Your witchcraft needs to kill vampires. It can't be helped."

Disbelief flitted across her features. "What about Allison and Jamie? They didn't try to kill you."

"They trained to control their power for many years, likely since they were kids. Only the witches you see in public after dark have learned it."

"I'm not going to be a recluse in a cottage in the woods. Even if it takes years, I'll learn to control it too." Tears shimmered on her eyelids.

"Daisy..." I started with defeat in my tone.

"We've survived so much, but now you're giving up. You're saying goodbye, aren't you? Just like that?" Daisy stepped further back, the hurt twisting her features and wetting them with tears.

"Come back to me when you're ready. I'll wait for you, however long it takes, because you are my forever, and I'll always love you." I swiped away my tears.

The odds weren't in our favor, but I needed us to part with hope for her sake. Maybe someday she'd be strong enough to welcome me back into her arms, but I knew it was false hope. And after everything I'd done to Soren, my family, Evangeline, and now Daisy, and however many others,

I deserved the coming centuries of torment and anguish. Daisy didn't, but once her magic took full control, she'd think nothing of me.

For now, Daisy stared at me with her broken heart on her sleeve.

"There is no other option." I turned to Pierce and said the crippling words of defeat that I would regret every day. "Give me Soren. We have a deal."

Pierce bodily shoved my unconscious brother, and he landed at my feet in a heap of limp limbs and ill-fitting clothes.

"What?" Daisy asked, looking between us both. "What deal?"

"Daisy," I said and held out the necklace. It was empty. No sizzle, no burning, no pain. Lifeless. "As a witch, you can't be compelled by anyone anymore, but this will stop vampires from biting you until your magic is strong enough to protect you. For your sake and mine, take it and refill it. I'm sure the elf has plenty of vervain to share."

Pierce nodded proudly.

She leaned forward and snatched it from me as if I were poison. I might as well be. My chest squeezed as if my Shelby slowly rolled over me, pausing at the apex of my sternum, but my heart wasn't willing to give up the fight.

"You won't regret this, Daisy. Let's go." Pierce gestured for her to follow him back inside his meager house.

I stayed standing right where I was, not objecting to his orders.

"What's going on? I don't understand." Daisy's pleading eyes broke me all over again. I dashed away tears.

"Pierce can keep you safe now. I love you." I wanted to tell her to take care of herself and fight against Pierce, but he couldn't compel her into submitting. Admittedly, he was formidable, unrelenting, and he'd protect her against the likes of Newt and Evangeline, and I had enough other enemies out there.

"No, no. I'm not doing this. Turn me," Daisy said in desperation. "Turn me and we can be together, right?"

I shook my head. She didn't mean it, and even if she did, that wasn't an answer. Evangeline's ancient gray corpse was slowing turning to ash a few feet away. "You know I can't do that."

Pierce urged her to go with him. With a teary frown, she wrenched her arm away from his touch and led the way into the house. The door closed gently behind them.

## Oliver

I LIFTED SOREN IN my arms and carried him to my car. In silence, burdened by a hollow ache where my heart used to be, I drove us home and dropped my brother on my leather chaise lounge. He was battered and bruised, swollen in places vampires shouldn't be. He'd been bled out to sustain this level of damage, preventing his healing. But he was alive.

"What happened?" Nicole asked, rushing to Soren's side.

"The elf. I'm getting refreshments." I bolted down to the basement and filled a box with blood bags. My stash had been replenished, thanks to Nicole.

I brought the box to Soren's side and tore open the first bag. I pushed it between his lips and squeezed. Instincts had him swallowing. I'd expected and dreaded this day since the first night Daisy and I'd slept together, when I'd found my drawing on her wall, the grimoire in her dresser next to a spelled box, and my ring on her finger. When my repeated attempts to steal my ring had her stealing my heart, I hoped we could've avoided it, but it was inevitable. I didn't expect it to hurt so damned much.

"Is there anything I can do?" Nicole asked.

"The blood is enough. He'll be fine." At least, I hoped so. There were no traces of the serum on his skin. If the elf had some, he would've used it.

At least vampires wouldn't be hunting her to prevent its manufacture, but I didn't know how much more was out there already. I sighed.

Nicole's hand rested on my forearm. "I meant you. What happened?"

"Evangeline staked me, and Daisy turned into a witch and moved in with Pierce." I stopped at that, not because I didn't want to tell her, but because my voice wasn't strong.

"I'm so sorry, Oliver. Have you discussed her turning into a vampire?" Nicole's gentle hand rested on my forearm. "It would be an easy solution."

I focused on my brother's swallows. This wasn't a conversation I wanted to have. "No."

"You're so damned stubborn, you know that? I would've been by your side, out there helping you and Soren, in my prime with enhanced...everything, but you'd turned me down all those years ago. Now look what that got you—an old woman, wise beyond her years, but useless when she's needed most. Now you turned down Daisy, and where did she end up? In your enemy's arms. One of these days you need to set aside your fear and trust that people can be everything you hope for, that not everyone is Evangeline."

I snapped. "Don't you think it's not on my mind all day, every day? Evangeline didn't want it, but it was forced on her. You know how she ended? She begged me to kill her tonight, so I shoved a stake into her chest and watched her die."

Nicole listened grimly.

"Daisy doesn't want it. We'd already discussed it at length. No matter how much she begged tonight, she'd never forgive me. I respect her choice, but it doesn't matter now. It's over. She went with Pierce. So, if you don't mind, I'm going to heal my brother, so the elf's torture doesn't kill him."

I stuffed another bag of blood into my dying brother's mouth. That elf broke my number one rule for the last time.

# 25

# Surprising Hosts

**Daisy**

While Pierce snoozed peacefully on his bed, I'd tossed and turned on his lumpy couch. In the same breath, I'd thought Oliver was killed by his ex, and I became his mortal enemy. Now my magic—this stupid magic I'd wanted and encouraged—needed to kill him and any vampires I encountered. This was worse than if Oliver had died. Truly. Rather than having a place I could visit to talk to him, knowing he was at peace, now I could see him, hear him, feel his presence, sense his pain, but I had to stay away. With mastering my new abilities, the urge would fade from uncontrollable homicidal tendencies to justifiable hatred, but I might never be free from the urge to kill. Since I failed more than I succeeded, that meant forever.

For the first time, I thought my dad would be proud. Instead of crafting a fatal weapon, I became the fatal weapon. The only thing we had in common.

As a witch, no one could compel me ever again, so I felt safe knowing my choices were mine to make. Oliver had told me to go with Pierce. If I were in any danger, he never would've agreed. And since the elf didn't know about Oliver's bite on my wrist, I was now immune to elf breeding too. Needing to get away and clear my head, I halfheartedly accepted Pierce's offer to show me something about himself he'd never shared with anyone. I thought he was going to pull out a family photo album and show me the embarrassing highlights. I didn't expect he'd drive us through town, across the powerful Menominee River, into Michigan, and down a county road out of town.

"Does that hurt?" I asked, now able to see his wings precariously folded behind him and brushing against the roof of the SUV.

"It's mildly uncomfortable."

I remembered the gold-tipped feather I'd found the night Soren had attacked me. "Do you save your shed feathers to make pillows?"

Pierce cast me a bewildered side-glance. "No."

In a sleepy wooded area, far from other homes and farms, he steered the SUV onto a gravel driveway, camouflaged with weeds. In a neglected clearing, a squat building had rotting wood siding and peeling yellow paint. This place looked like a long-since abandoned motel. I'd streamed many movies and creepy television shows over the years, and my Spidey-sense blared like a foghorn. "Uh, this doesn't look right."

Pierce smiled reassuringly. "Things aren't always what they seem."

The tires crunched over the gravel, and Pierce slowed the vehicle to a stop at what appeared to be the main entrance.

We unbuckled and climbed out. As Pierce led me to the front door, there were no lights on or any human activity nearby, but after a beat, something bothered me. I could feel something. What was it?

Pierce watched me with a close eye as he held the door open. "It's okay. Come inside."

Reluctantly, I crossed the threshold ahead of him. My eyes adjusted, and I blinked. No kidding, things weren't what they seemed. This building wasn't an interior room at all—more like the entrance to a garden. There was no carpet, which I expected to be musty, torn, and worn. Instead, the flooring was pale stone. The ceiling above was open to the sky. Just ahead, a fountain rumbled and hissed, luring little songbirds. Green potted plants decorated the area, and ivy climbed the surrounding white walls trimmed with shiny gold. On the far side, an arched and gated door led away from the impressive garden. Clean, majestic almost. I never would've guessed, and based on the exterior, I couldn't fit the opposing pieces together. I turned to Pierce, a calm wonder settling over me.

I gasped at the unexpected sight. "Pierce?" My lips parted in awe. He was...beautiful. His elongated ear tips and gold-flecked white wings were suddenly saturated with color, flickering against what seemed like his own source of light—majestic and magical. Angelic. His folded wings extended a few inches above his head, and sweeping white feathers tickled at the backs of his knees. "What am I seeing?"

"As a witch, you can see through our glamour." Pierce sent me a gentle smile of approval, as if he'd been wanting to show me for a while.

"Why were they so...muted or...muddy earlier?" The contrast was hard to explain. Frankly, I was completely baffled by the whole thing.

"Your magic complements ours, and you're growing stronger by the minute."

I wasn't giving up on Oliver. In fact, the more I understood, the faster I could master it, but this new world fascinated me. "What is this place?"

"Those of my people who refuse to integrate into human society live here. We are but one clan of many. Let me introduce you to my family."

That was it. The eerie, foreign feeling was the presence of elves everywhere, but I couldn't see anyone.

Pierce called out, a language indecipherable to my ears, and a dozen or so curious boys with pointy ears and folded white wings appeared, all wearing different types of plain T-shirts, knee-length shorts, and bare feet. A couple of adult men appeared out of thin air and quickly scolded the children to glamour themselves. If they did, I could still see their elf differences. They were cute—so innocent and curious.

A broad-shouldered, intimidating elf with a square jaw and a headful of sleek gray hair stepped in front of the others. Despite the clear advanced age on his face, his wings retained the angelic shade of white. The strands of gold glinted in the light, just like Pierce's. He approached, towering over me and Pierce, with a frown on his lined face. Clearly, this was the elf in charge. "Evansson, why have you brought a human among us?"

With complete confidence that he hadn't just pissed off these people, Pierce said, "This is Daisy Barrett, the woman I wanted to introduce you to." His eyes connected with mine. "In hopes of changing her mind."

I should've guessed. Pierce was nothing if not patient and persistent. And I noticed he didn't tell them I was a witch or in transition to becoming one.

"Daisy," Pierce added, "this is our leader, Logon Larsen."

I struck out a hand to shake, and the elder elf hesitated. Pierce nodded, and Logon finally acquiesced moments before it became awkward. His grip was soft, as if he were ill or had never shaken hands before.

Pierce added, "My grandfather."

"Oh." I blushed. This was the elf who bore a child with Edith Johnson, who must've known Oliver's mother, and my ancestor, Henrietta Barrett. I was flustered as if I'd just met a celebrity. "It's nice to meet you. I'm sorry about what happened to your son, Mr. Logonson." No one deserved to die like he had.

"Thank you, dear. My grandson tells me you're a healer for your people."

Pierce had told them about me already. My face burned bright red. "I'm an EMT. I drive the ambulance, you know, the meat wagon." As Dad condescendingly referred to it. "Stay safe, or you'll see me again."

Logon Larsen tilted his head in confusion. Right, elves healed themselves and others—Mr. Record-Breaking Paramedic over here.

I sheepishly added, "Or not."

The elder elf laughed. "I like you. Come, dine with us." He wrapped a thick arm around my shoulders. His wings rustled like a bird's, and I glanced over at Pierce. My ex-boyfriend had a look on his face I'd never seen before. Softness, warmth, and caring all radiated from him. He nodded for me to go, and he kept pace next to us. The curious elves followed in step behind us.

We walked by the small fountain, songbirds fluttering overhead, and headed into an arched tunnel. This was a slice of paradise tucked away in my small hometown. "I've lived here my whole life, and I never knew your amazing world was right under our noses. How long have you guys lived on this side of the river?" Menominee wasn't that big of an area. Certainly someone would've noticed them at grocery stores or the bars.

"Chased from their homes in Scandinavia five hundred years ago, many of our ancestors settled in these lands of the Upper Peninsula. With wars among the Natives, France, and Britain on all sides, we formed smaller clans in hiding and opted out of human squabbles. We privately maintain our culture, even the aspects that modern human society deems unfit."

He must've been referring to the breeding and abandoning thing. At least he recognized we thought it was disgusting.

"Magical boundaries protect us from accidental discovery, and as you've noticed, we can conceal our true nature." Logon Larsen smiled and glanced at Pierce.

Pierce resembled his grandfather—strong bone structure, deep brown eyes, and broad shoulders. There was a gentle giant-ness about them. Pierce was an attractive man, always was, but the spark of passion was never there, and that he'd dismissed my graduation ceremony still angered me. We had our issues, like all couples. I'd always felt like there was something missing between us, and I wasn't willing to settle.

I remembered Pierce had told me he wasn't a Neanderthal with the breeding and abandoning thing. Couple that with seeing all this and meeting other elves, I didn't think Jamie knew much about them—like he'd regurgitated old witch lore passed through the generations. Elves didn't sound as horrible as he'd led me to believe. Now I had answers, but they only led to more questions.

Logon's choice of words caught my attention. Now that I wasn't exactly human, and I had more questions than ever, I didn't know where I stood in this new world. Knowing I wouldn't be killed on sight if they discovered what I was would be a relief. "Magical boundaries? You work with witches?"

"We have a few abilities of our own, nowhere near what witches can do, but they don't understand us, so we stay out of the way."

So, not exactly friendly, but at least Pierce hadn't placed me in a dangerous situation. "Are you in hiding from them too?"

The end of the dark tunnel was draped in ivy, glowing in sunlight. Logon Larsen swept the soft greens aside and guided me through. I gasped at the courtyard of exotic flowers I'd never seen before and more songbirds flitting around an even bigger multi-layer fountain. A four-story building of rooms with walkways and railings, like a hotel, surrounded the lavish fairy tale in the center. The stone floor, white walls, and gold accents continued. Everything looked new and clean. Magical.

"Do you call this hiding?" Logon asked with a sly grin.

More elves appeared at the balcony railing on all levels, old and young, just as curious about me as I was about them. None were female, but I never felt safer. I didn't need to ask why they preferred living here to the tri-city area of Menominee, Marinette, and Peshtigo. This place looked like someone had carved it from an imaginary utopia. I knew too-good-to-be-true when I saw it. I frowned. "Is this real or a glamour?"

The elder elf laughed, a deep bellow rumbling in his chest. "It's real, with one embellishment. Those fluted flowers streaked with cherry and lime green that look like poisonous stars?" He pointed, but the flowers he referred to were obvious and stunning, and beginning to haze over and change color. "Those are Mystica Amaryllis, a tender perennial with a lifespan longer than most humans. I love the look of them, but they don't grow up here."

"Then you have a great imagination." Why didn't Pierce glamour himself a nicer place to live? Not that it was any of my business, but his house was so...normal...humble, even. Was he trying to make himself fit in by not turning heads on a paramedic's income?

Pierce reached out to a blossom and picked one. The glamour finished fading rapidly—from an exotic flower to an ordinary spike of tiny purple flowers. "Give me your locket."

I slipped the empty and useless locket off my head. Pierce crushed up the flower and stuffed it inside. "Now you're protected from their bites once more."

Vervain. The elves had a sea of vervain at their disposal. I shivered.

"Right through here." Logon guided me across the stunning garden and through an arched doorway at the far end. I glanced over my shoulders to watch them pass. The elf wings fit the curve of the doors, shaped just for them. I smiled, and then I stumbled on a stone underfoot. Pierce caught me by the wrist. My face burned bright red, and I freed myself from his grip rapidly and hid that wrist. This place was a stunning wonderland, but I had to be more careful.

The doorway opened into an expansive dark-wood dining room filled with long lacquered tables. Overhead, wagon wheel chandeliers, which were wired for bulbs rather than candles, hung from an exposed log ceiling. It all reminded me of a Viking dining hall. I looked thoughtfully at Pierce. Logon had said they were Scandinavian, and the style was very old. Jamie had told me elves were immortal.

"How old are you?" I asked the leader, so amazed by everything. His flinch told me I'd blundered. "I'm sorry. I didn't mean to offend."

Logon smiled. "Since you're Pierce's friend, I'm six hundred years old. Pierce is, what? About a hundred and thirty these days?"

Pierce said, "Close enough."

"Dinner will be out in a moment. Pierce, allow the lady to accompany you. Beg my pardon, but I must assist in the kitchen." The leader of the elves parted on friendly terms, leaving through yet another door deeper into the building. Metal clanged and clattered—the kitchen. I was surprised the man in charge assisted personally. He was so unlike what I expected a leader to be. He was, ironically, normal, and despite the stunning wings, completely down-to-earth.

Immortality without the blood drinking, but with magical glamour and healing. Unlike vampirism, this sounded like a good deal.

Pierce pulled out a thick wooden chair for me to sit, and he pushed me in before settling in the seat next to me. Other elves filtered in through various doors and filled the seats in the great hall.

"I can't believe this," I said, watching the men and their sons chattering, so polite and friendly with each other.

"Daisy, I thought I could win your heart by pretending to be something I'm not. But what I pretended to be wasn't what you wanted. After you learned about our hidden world and recent events changed our dynamic, I brought you here for a second chance. I hope that by showing you the real story behind the elves—the real me—you can then decide for yourself what you truly want."

I blinked back tears of appreciation and waited until I was sure the clog of emotion in my throat was clear. The sweetness was so uncharacteristic but opposed to what I knew. I needed to change the subject. "Your grandfather really likes flowers. That interest didn't pass down the family line, I see."

Pierce looked hurt. "To me, a flower is only petals and colors that need sun and water. That's as far as my botany experience goes. I thought I was being cheeky giving you daisies. You don't like them?"

I supposed I never told him the joke was tired. "They're great, really. Just...overdone."

"I can see that. You must have buckets of men lined up to hand you daisies, each hoping to be more clever than the last." Pierce nudged me playfully.

I didn't miss the sly compliment. Pierce was trying hard to win me over, much harder than I'd ever seen from him. I had to ask what had burned in the back of my mind for a long time. "Why didn't you come to my college graduation?"

"I suppose you should know the truth—that's part of this whole experience." Pierce exhaled. "Your father asked me to stay at his house because he had a credible threat against your mother."

Newt had ordered her death, and Soren was sent to do the deed. He'd drained her and snapped her neck. I checked my rising anger. "You were her bodyguard?"

"Your mother's life was a bargaining chip to buy your father's compliance. When he didn't comply—"

"If you were supposed to stay at my mom's side, then how did Soren get to her?" I swallowed back bile, threatening to make an appearance with trumpets and confetti.

"She convinced me to let her go run an errand, and I'm sorry. I should've forced her to stay a prisoner in her home where I could watch over her, but I didn't. I trusted her to do what she needed to do and to come right back."

"If you had gone with me to my graduation, you could've kept me safe during my accident. But you skipped it for bodyguard duty, which you also failed to do." The wind flew out of my lungs as if I had been punched. I bent over, facing the shiny lacquered table, and I focused on my breathing.

"I'm so sorry, Daisy." Pierce touched my arm in sympathy.

I held out my palm to stop him from talking. I couldn't handle hearing another word, or I was going to break down in hideous sobs.

A series of elves brought dinner out on rolling carts and rested plates in front of the community. I tried to focus, to regain my composure, so I wouldn't draw attention. The chatter in the hall quieted down.

"We take turns," Pierce said, pointing to the kitchen staff. "Every day, a different group prepares the meals. It's a great system."

I was grateful for the change of subject. A bowl was set before me. Beef stew, one of my favorites, and one I rarely ever made since meat was so expensive. At this point, I wondered if Pierce had tipped off the chef. The chunks of meat, potatoes, and carrots smelled inviting, but my stomach churned.

"Sometimes things don't go how we plan, but we all play a part around here," Pierce continued. "Are you surprised by the menu?"

"By many things." The little brown bits bobbed, trying to calm down after the jarring of the bowl, and the beef stock sloshed, just like my stomach. Guilt for rejecting their meal tore through me, but I couldn't eat. "I need to go home."

"Now?" Pierce looked hurt, but I couldn't stay.

"Yeah, now. I'm sorry. I just can't." I rose and pressed a hand to my stomach.

"Sure, okay. It's no big deal." Pierce set his napkin next to his plate and gazed longingly at the untouched food.

After my dad rejected the meals I'd prepared for him each day, I couldn't let good food go to waste, and I didn't want the chef upset. "You know what? You stay here and eat. I'll wait in the car."

Pierce smiled. "You're the best. I won't keep you waiting."

And he didn't. I guess an elf could pack it away faster than a starving linebacker.

# 26
# Dark History

**Daisy**

After a night's sleep that I couldn't describe as good or not, I finally felt...refreshed. Clearheaded. I could think objectively about what I'd learned at the magical elf clan. If there was anything on this earth I was sick of, it would be lies, so I'd appreciated Pierce finally telling me the truth. My mom died because he trusted her to be safe. I had to respect that, even if doing his job would've kept her alive instead. I've made plenty of mistakes that almost cost me my life. She hadn't been as lucky as I have been, but luck wasn't going to get me back into Oliver's arms.

As Allison instructed, I reached forward, palms up. I visualized my emotions from my broken heart building onto my palms. I missed Oliver so much it physically hurt, so I easily pooled the pain. My palms hummed with energy, and the ache in my chest eased. The magic was a physical force, even if I couldn't see it. Now I understood why people liked to shoot things to work through their pain. I wanted to shoot magic and break everything if it meant feeling less.

"Excellent. Now, drain the energy back inside you *without* releasing it," Allison said.

I finally felt lighter, free, and my hands trembled, awaiting the release. "I can't take that pain back."

"You must learn control. Remember the little army guy you knocked over? Well, now your abilities are a hundredfold stronger, maybe a thousand. You have to do this, or you can kill someone with a sneeze."

I blinked, surely having misheard. "You're kidding, right?"

"Not at all."

I waited for the punchline that didn't come. Since I didn't want to murder someone—by accident or not—I closed my eyes and focused on the power gathered in my palms. I willed the humming orbs of power to slide from my hands and—

A loud clatter of kitchen pots startled me. I lost focus, and from my hands the orbs of energy coalesced into a terrifying strike. The beam of energy hit a framed photograph on my TV stand. Glass tinkled as it fell and clicked with the temperature change settling. Good thing I didn't have a pet hamster or something.

"Oops."

"Sorry, Daisy," Jamie called from the kitchen.

I rushed over to the debris and picked up my collateral damage—the picture of me and Pierce smiling. I brushed away broken glass, and it looked as if I'd shot it with a high-caliber rifle. In no time, I'd gone from a puff of air to a sniper. I had to be more careful.

For a while, I'd wished to dispose of this photo. At the elf clan in Menominee, Pierce had asked for a second chance.

Now clearheaded, that urge to forgive and please was strong. But he was incapable of loving me, and I didn't love him. If I wanted children badly enough, could I settle for that—a mutual, passionless, partnership agreement? While he only wanted me to give him sons, he'd promised he wouldn't take them or erase my memory of them. But he'd lied to me about what he was, what his kind did to women, and he'd colluded with my dad to win me over. Could I trust his word? I shook out the last glass shard and placed the frame back on the TV stand.

Oliver and I loved each other, like nothing I'd ever experienced before. It was mutual, full of passion and respect. The only time he'd lied to me was when he'd been ashamed of himself, not trying to manipulate me. The blood drinking was an issue, but we managed it. Sure, he couldn't have children with me, but that wasn't a factor right now. Maybe it would be later. So, the only hurdle remaining right now was this damned magic keeping us apart. The only way I could ever feel his arms again, the touch of his lips, the caress of his fingers...was to master this damned ability.

Jamie brought over a broom and dustpan. We both crouched together, cleaning up the mess. "Is there a way to give this stupid witchcraft back?"

Jamie snorted. "If you ever wanted to quit a musical instrument, or abandon a drawing, or quit a foreign language, the only consequence is wasted time. If you quit studying and practicing your magic, people's lives are in danger. Besides, only those who persevere reap the rewards of their efforts."

"So, that's a 'no'," I grumbled to myself. There had to be an easier solution because, like Oliver had said, I might never gain enough control to be around him, and I wouldn't accept that. "Has anyone found a spell to reduce the urge to kill vampires?"

Jamie darted me a skeptical look. "As far as I'm aware, no one's ever wanted one before."

Allison turned pages in a witch's grimoire, preparing for my next lesson. I repeated my question to her.

She pushed thick-framed glasses up her nose. She had a shift at the bar tonight, and it was librarian night. "I know this is hard for you, Daisy, but it's best for everyone if you accept yourself as you are."

That was dismissive, and I didn't appreciate it. "I do accept what I've become, and I like the possibilities," like fixing the plumbing, "but if vampires and elves have been trying to coexist all this while, can't we make a sacrifice—undo the spell forcing us to hunt the vampires—avoid tipping the balance? I mean, how am I supposed to go grocery shopping, knowing at any moment I might be forced to throw a ball of magic down the snack aisle? I can throw a decent cornhole, but what if I miss? Innocent bystanders could lose a foot. This is a public health issue."

The corners of Allison's lips lifted, and she closed the book. "This is about Oliver, isn't it?"

*Yes.* "How would I explain invisible magic destroyed shelves and removed limbs? Would you post bail for me? Because the money train's been broken down in the desert for years." I shuddered at my student loan and mortgage balances in comparison to my paycheck. Nope, couldn't afford jail. Jamie carried the dustpan of glass to the kitchen trash.

"Come sit with me." Allison lifted off the floor and sat on the couch. She patted the cushion next to her. "It's time you understand the war."

While I sat next to Allison, Jamie brought us all rum and Cokes before sitting on the plush chair across from us.

I'd been inside this secret world for a while now, but I still felt like I knew nothing. "Is this a long history? I have a shift starting in a few hours." I sipped the alcoholic beverage, careful of my intake.

Jamie smiled. "It's very long, but it doesn't take long to tell. The relevant event takes place in the late 1600s. Vampires appeared in the area of what's now called Salem, Massachusetts. They fed on the innocent and turned a few unlucky fellows. Town elders were furious and blamed the witches' magic for drawing in the fanged monsters. Our magic doesn't draw anything, but the humans wouldn't listen to the wise old women. So, the elders rounded up every witch known or accused, including plenty of innocents. Some witches were given a joke of a trial and were hanged. Others died of disease, waiting in jail. All of it was for public show, a secret warning to the fanged monsters to stay away, and a blatant warning to witches to hang up the caldrons, candles, and herbs."

"I had no idea that was the truth behind the Salem witch trials. How did they end?" I stared at my roommate completely fascinated.

"Those in particular? The witches who'd escaped scrutiny hunted down the vampires at large until the rest fled. The clergymen's evidence of supernatural occurrences began to be doubted, and their accusations fell apart. The Salem witch trials had officially ended, but similar have been recurring for centuries before and since. Every time a new batch of vampires feed and kill, the witches are destroyed for the crime."

"I haven't heard of any recent witch trials. No one believes witches have real power."

"We proactively fight the vampires before things with humans escalate. That's why our hidden world needs to stay hidden—to protect our very-much real magic from discovery and destruction."

"Then why does their population grow?"

"Because society said we have to pay bills, and public service isn't exactly lucrative," Allison said.

All of this made perfect sense, and hope tickled the strings in my heart. There was one big, glaring piece of the puzzle left. "You said vampires had moved into the area and their affliction spread. Are they the result of a contagious disease, something completely curable by science?"

"I'm afraid not, or we would've eradicated them decades—if not centuries—ago."

Hope? *Poof*.

"The witches of their village created vampirism as a capital punishment. The expectation was that the cursed perpetrator would destroy his or her family and step into the sun from overbearing guilt."

Picturing Oliver attacking his family, my lips parted. "That's horrible."

A sinister smile flickered across Jamie's features. "It's a forbidden spell, lost to time, and as you can see by the population growth over the centuries, it wasn't exactly successful. Vampirism is difficult to contain. We hunt as best we can to slow their spread and prevent a repeat of the witch trials. I'm sure today's trials would be very different."

"I don't think they would drown us," Allison said dryly. "So there's a minor consolation."

History was ugly. All I wanted was Oliver's comforting arms. I knew his affliction was never his fault, but since the origin was magic, then the solution had to be too. And I happened to have some at my disposal. "Can the spell be undone?"

"You're talking about curing vampirism." Allison swigged her drink.

"Seems more effective than hunting them down one at a time."

"Effective? Maybe. But not even remotely easy. There's rumored to be only one copy of the spell, and no one knows where it is, or if it even survives to this day." Allison stood up. "Refill?"

"I'm good, thanks," I said.

Jamie waved away the offer.

"Where does the hate for elves fit in with this?" I asked.

"If elves kept their procreation among themselves, we wouldn't have a problem with them at all, but they don't. Women and witches are fair game, but witches can't be compelled, so if they choose it, they can. Humans don't have that choice, so if we see it, we can't stand to let it happen." Jamie leaned back and finished his drink in a large gulp.

Except my roommates hadn't stopped Pierce when I'd first met him. Jamie and Allison couldn't claim they didn't know. They could see at least a haziness of the truth and, according to Pierce, they were distantly related.

Was the potential discovery of the hidden world enough of an excuse?

I needed them to teach me how to function in public. I needed to grow my strength to protect myself. And I needed most of all to control my urge to kill vampires. But there was this blanket of frost between my once-trusted roommates and me. I rubbed at Oliver's bite mark on my wrist.

# 27

# Impossible Choice

**Oliver**

WHEN I HAD PRESSING matters focusing my attention on business, I kept myself pleasantly occupied. But when I didn't, like now, I would've been upstairs focusing on my work in progress, almost as satisfying. Ever since I'd made the trade with the elf, I hadn't found a moment's peace. Too frustrated to sit still, I paced the long hallway of my house back and forth and back again while Nicole and Soren sat on my couch, watching me, making my frustration grow.

My niece hugged a bowl of popcorn, and her obnoxious crunching grated on my ears. I paused to snip at her. "It's rude to eat popcorn while I'm thinking."

Nicole crunched harder and slower to spite me.

Soren nursed AB-negative in a rocks glass. At least he couldn't eat, and so far, he wasn't slurping. "My brother, you've been pacing for days. I think you've made a rut in the hardwood."

"Thank you for your wise observation," I said dryly. Their pointless interjections only broke my concentration.

"Have you decided what you're going to do?" Nicole asked. "Because I don't think you want contractors mucking around in here."

Stuck between the proverbial rock and a hard place, I spun on her. "Is my plight entertaining to you?"

"Not at all." Nicole crunched another bite with a small grin on her face. "But I am waiting for an answer. Are you staying, or am I reopening the books for reservations?"

Daisy wasn't mine any longer. She probably wouldn't be for the rest of her life, but while she worked on mastering her magic for me, an elf meddled in her life. I was stuck here waiting, tearing through paper and pencils in frustration, wallowing in regret at having given up Daisy for anything. I glared at my ungrateful brother. Or I moved on, and that meant...away. She was human—*a witch*—but it didn't matter. I was a vampire. As Soren had taught me, I should just pack up and go. Find yet another purpose in life.

But I was immortal. Why should I make that choice now? "This bed-and-breakfast is not reopening."

"With that settled, now what?" Nicole lifted a brow. ·

"If I go to her, the love of my life will kill me."

"Yep." Soren slurped.

I gritted my teeth. There had to be something I could do.

"What's the alternative?" Nicole asked.

"Never seeing her again." I had prepared myself for the inevitability of her latent witch genes activating. Now that it had happened, the torture of being so close, yet so far, was unbearable. Worse than death. My time was plentiful, but hers wasn't.

After Pierce had done a number on Soren, I expected his healing to take longer, but he'd been chugging down my replenished blood stash for the last few days, and although hungrier than usual, he was back to his old self.

Soren rolled his eyes. "Then the choice is obvious, and you're being dramatic. She's a new witch. Give her time to settle and learn her craft. Once she has a modicum of control, she won't kill you on sight."

"Oh, for Pete's sake," Nicole said. "She can use her words. If it's not safe, she'll tell you. Then you leave, but at least you would've tried. Fretting about it gets you nowhere. Just go talk to her."

I wanted to believe my niece, but Soren had a point. "Even if she doesn't want to kill me, her instincts will force her. She may not have the choice of warning me." What I feared speaking out loud was—what if Daisy was no longer my Daisy at all?

"She's a young woman who doesn't know the power at her fingertips. That's your warning. You have vampire speed and strength. Your love can reason with her, or, you know, take a few shots and run like your ass is on fire," Nicole said and chewed another painfully slow, obnoxiously loud bite.

"I hardly survived the last two scrapes—her dad's serum-laced gunshot and Evangeline's stake—so I'm done underestimating those who wish to do me harm. Deliberately inserting myself into this one is...suicide."

"Don't be so dramatic. If she's at work, focusing on saving lives, she'll be distracted enough for you to talk this over," Nicole said. I wanted to believe her.

"Your funeral." Soren swallowed down the rest of his blood. So far, he was more convincing. "For future reference, did you want your ashes spread on the Menominee River or buried in the family plot? Or even, for the lazy among us, spread in the backyard? We could make this a tourist destination. Open up this place for newlyweds and show them what happens when communication goes to shit. You know, like a couple's therapy session."

When I thought I had opposing views to consider, they'd been on the same side all along. I checked my watch. "If I'm not back by morning—"

"Yeah, yeah, she killed you, and I'll sprinkle your ashes in the backyard." Soren rose and stretched. "Well, that was the worst entertainment I've seen in ages. Time for a refill and real scripted TV." My brother headed to my bar.

As my unwanted audience dispersed, I rushed upstairs and dressed in the itchy blue uniform of the EMS department for Borealis Medical Center. I smoothed my collar and combed my gelled hair in front of my bathroom mirror. If she killed me tonight, I was going to be buried in this hideous outfit. I brushed away those depressing thoughts because Nicole had to be right—Daisy had to give me sufficient warning.

I charged downstairs and received a friendly wave goodbye over Soren's shoulders. He was eyeballs-deep in trash TV and nursing a vodka blood with his caveman feet on my coffee table. At least this time he wore his own jeans and T-shirt. As much as he seemed to enjoy his bachelor lifestyle, after I'd experienced the other side, I believed my brother to be hiding loneliness, but that wasn't something for me to fix.

I had to fix my own first.

I parked the Shelby on the hospital's surface lot and checked my watch again. Our shift started soon, and now a silly lump formed in the pit of my stomach. What if she already had a new partner? What if she recoiled in horror from me? Least of all, if she killed me on sight.

*Only one way to find out.*

I climbed out of my Shelby and fondly touched the candy-apple red fender. "This isn't goodbye, old friend. I'll see you soon." After a deep exhale and squaring my shoulders, I pushed through the employee door and wove my way to the emergency services breakroom on silent and swift vampire feet.

Daisy stood with her back to me, stirring a cup of coffee. As always, she stole my breath. The woman I wanted to spend the rest of my life with was right here, so close, yet so far. She turned sharply as if sensing my presence.

Her face crumpled with fear. "What are you doing here?"

"I'm your partner." I approached cautiously and held out my hands to her.

She stepped back and shook her head. "That was before. You can't be here. I...I..." Daisy set down the coffee and covered her mouth with a hand. It trembled.

"I know you can do this. You're stronger than anyone I know. Fight the urge. You know me." I gave her my sweetest, flirtiest smile, straight from the Rockwell Handbook of Charm.

Daisy fastened her hands together and stared at them, terrified. Tears flooded her eyelids, and her hands reached out to me in a slow, offensive gesture. "I can't."

I closed the distance between us and reached for her hands, but she stepped away from me again. "You can. I know you can. You can beat this."

The door to the breakroom swung open, and footsteps rushed away. I didn't bother to see who it was because they were of zero importance to me. Instead, I held out my palms in surrender and inched closer to Daisy. "Concentrate on that urge. Suppress it. Tell it to go away, that it doesn't own you."

Her lower lip quivered, and her voice broke. "I can't."

"Yes, you can." One final step and I gripped her hands in mine. Power pulsed through her like a generator powering a whole house. My skin heated with the magical current. I didn't care. I healed quickly.

"I love you," she said. The sadness in her tone broke my heart all over again.

"I don't accept 'goodbye'. You can fight this. We can beat this together. Fight it." I released one burned and blistered hand to touch her cheek. She didn't nestle into my palm like she usually did. Instead, she shook her head, slipping away from my touch.

"You have to go." A sob broke through. She tried to free her hand, but I wouldn't let her.

"Go now, please," she desperately repeated her demand.

"I'm not leaving you. I love you, Daisy, and I trust you." New witches were powerfully dangerous to vampires, but Daisy didn't know spells yet, and she couldn't bend her energy to her will until she trained for it. A few off-the-wall blasts of power might buckle the drywall in places, but hey, this breakroom was in serious need of remodeling, anyway. And if she hit me? I'd take every lick if it meant staying by her side.

"Kiss me," Daisy begged in a whisper. "Then stop me from hurting you forever."

My chest squeezed at her defeat. "Don't give up on me."

"I can't fight it anymore. Please!" Daisy's body trembled hard with the effort. She wasn't going to win.

The tingles of electricity climbed up my flesh from hand to chest, rapidly growing in strength and speed. My muscles burned with her power, and I tensed. Steam lifted off my skin, and tears reached my eyes. I knew what I had to do. With her power increasing rapidly, I had only seconds before she'd put me flat on my back, burned to a husk. She really would kill me, and now I was just as defeated.

Our time was up. One last goodbye kiss. I pressed my lips to hers, and the sizzle of electricity burned my mouth, my face. Far too soon, I pulled back, brushed the hair off her neck, and extended my fangs. I had no other choice but to stop her—as she requested.

Daisy's terrified eyes watered, pleading with me. "Do it," she whispered.

I bit down into her throat long enough to inject the venom that froze the vocal cords down to the toes. The electric surge burning my body lessened and vanished. I released her and licked the trail of blood leaking from the pair of wounds.

I cupped her face with both hands and brushed tears from her cheeks. Her beautiful face carried sorrow and regret, and as her balance shifted, I caught her in my arms and carried her to the breakroom couch. It wasn't good enough for her, but there was nothing softer to wait out my venom's effects.

I kneeled on the floor at her side and brushed the hair out of her eyes. "Is there anything you need scratched?" I tried gentle humor, knowing she couldn't respond.

The corners of her eyes wrinkled with laugh lines, while tears slipped down the sides of her face. I would give anything to hear her laughter again.

"I'm sorry. I'm so sorry. I gave you the least amount of venom I could. You've got about five minutes before it wears off." I sent her an apologetic smile and checked my watch. "In four minutes and fifty...two seconds and counting, I'll leave."

Daisy's breath blew from her chest in what I could only hope was a sigh of relief. If she thought I'd reconsidered turning her into a vampire, she was sorely mistaken.

The breakroom door opened again, and I still paid it no mind. Daisy was my priority, forever and always.

"Get away from her, you animal," a familiar voice ordered.

Well, now the intruder had my attention. I sprang to my feet, ready to shield Daisy with my body, especially now that she was helpless. What I found both confused me but sent me into a rage—Dr. Greg Barrett flanked by Pierce Evansson. Now that was an unwelcome surprise.

"What are you two doing here?" I asked, annoyed.

The doctor pointed at me in accusation. "You're supposed to be dead. The better question is how did you survive my weapon?"

As if I would give my enemy more fuel to use against my kind, the arrogant prick. "There is a zero percent chance I'll tell you that, and since you aren't authorized personnel, you need to leave."

Pierce stepped forward, proverbial chest feathers puffed, with support on his side and plenty of innocent bystanders beyond these weak walls. "You compelled the boss to give you this job, didn't you? Is there no limit to your entitled arrogance? You never even attended medical classes, not that you're here for the scraps of a paycheck."

I couldn't help laughing. "You're only here for the immediate access to vampire bite victims. Don't kid yourself, Evansson. I grew up on a farm; I'm familiar with the odorous fertilizer coming from that high horse you rode in on."

Pierce shifted his weight, as if deciding to risk making the first move. "Either way, you don't belong here."

I gestured at my uniform. "This is my shift with Daisy, so you can go now."

"I'm not leaving until I have Daisy secured far away from you," her dad said.

"She's safe with me, and since I'm the only one in this room who's trustworthy, Daisy stays with me." Even if she wanted to kill me—but one problem at a time.

"She's not safe until all vampires are dead. Pierce?" Greg ordered his muscle to attack. At least he was self-aware enough not to take me on himself.

I poised myself for the defense and parried a right hook to my flank. "You don't have to do this."

"You can't beat us." Pierce struck again, and I parried once more.

"Both of us lived our own lives and left each other alone for months. We had peace around here," I said, attempting to take the high road, but my efforts weren't successful, and the longer this dragged out, the less likely it was to work. But in three minutes, Daisy would regain her movement and could defend herself. Pierce kicked my knee, and I grimaced, buckling down in pain, but I recovered with vampire speed and leaped across the room.

"As long as you stand between me and Daisy, there will be no truce," Pierce said, approaching me with menace.

"Can you ever keep your own word? No wonder Daisy doesn't want you." As if that weren't obvious by now.

"You don't seem to get that doesn't matter," Pierce said, and I hoped Daisy absorbed every honest and dirty word.

I chuckled. Elves—such disgusting cretins. "You've erased her memory more times than I can count, because that's what you do instead of discussing things with her. But she keeps pulling through your compulsion, because she's stronger than you think. Who Daisy wants does matter. She didn't choose you."

She chose me. She loved me just as I was, and that was worth dying for.

Just not by these two swine.

Daisy murmured behind me, and I glanced over my shoulder to check on her. Greg lifted her up over his shoulder, grunting and straining under her weight. As the venom wore down, Daisy's head turned from side to side, trying to fight him. Her dad was a vile insect, worse than a mosquito who deserved nothing but my windshield, but he wouldn't get far.

After this encounter, Pierce would make sure Daisy had never heard my name before, so I needed to subdue the elf before they both ran away with her as a prisoner.

The elf slipped a stake out of his cargo pants, and with a quickness I admired, he lunged as I shifted to dodge. The wooden stake, hand-carved, protruded from my chest. Excruciating, paralyzing pain burned in my chest and stole my breath—worse than any magic. I touched the wet wound on my navy-blue polo and pulled back...blood. My only consolation was my quick dodge prevented it from being a fatal blow.

Pierce wore a smirk on his ugly face. Answering my unspoken question, he said, "Vervain dipped wood, the perfect weapon. Well, second only to the doctor's invention."

Daisy screamed.

An explosion rocked the foundation of the hospital, and the ceiling collapsed over us in a hailstorm of drywall, insulation, and, unfortunately—the plumbing. I covered my head against the debris, but a metal beam crushed me to the floor. Could this day get any worse?

# 28

# Saving Myself

**Daisy**

THERE WAS A METAPHORICAL line in the sand, an invisible limit, that when crossed was the point of no return. Everyone had one, but not everyone had to test the integrity of that line and question its placement. Dad belittled my career choice, insulted my educational failures, tricked me into dating an elf, and tried to kill my boyfriend just because witches cursed him with fangs and the need to drink blood. Through practice, I'd solidified my line.

I'd made excuses for my dad inching close to the line several times, most notably, he'd been protecting me, his own daughter. Protection was his love language—one that I was intimately familiar with as Oliver's was the same. The difference in their approaches was stark. Oliver's protection was warm, selfless, and he'd sacrifice himself if it meant I'd be happy for even a short while. My dad's felt cold, neglectful, and self-serving, as if I were a pawn in a bargaining agreement, and protection was equivalent to a get-out-of-jail-free card.

Oliver came here to help me—and fulfill his duties as my partner. My dad.... Well, Pierce had popped in and run off to alert my dad like a brown-nosing tattletale. My dad had shown up and ordered Pierce to kill Oliver as a distraction. While my love was preoccupied staying alive, my dad carried me off—all in the name of 'protection'. He'd planned to give me to the elf after the dust settled, knowing full well what Pierce's intentions were, after both he and Pierce ignored my relentless and clear rejections. And still, I flopped, partially paralyzed, over his shoulder and painfully bounced with his steps, unable to stop him.

Pierce was only doing what benefited Pierce. Perhaps he still thought his actions were in my best interest. He'd shown me the elf clan and told me the truth of my mother's murder, but it wasn't enough to balance out all the terrible things he'd done. Tonight, Pierce was just being...an elf. Whatever.

But I expected more from my dad. No father could harm their child to the extent mine had and still claim to care. When I added up all the choices he'd made, I decided he'd crossed that line in the sand. More like he'd taken a giant leap over it.

No longer would I be vulnerable to manipulation. No longer would my dad stab me in the back. No longer did he deserve the respect of an explanation about my love for Oliver. Stick a fork in me, I was done. Dr. Greg Barrett wasn't the man I thought he was. He wasn't the man I'd hoped he could be, but I accepted he didn't love me. My dad was my biggest threat, and he carried me off as if I never had any say in my life.

Still partially paralyzed from Oliver's welcomed bite, I'd screamed in frustration and defense—the only thing I could do—and accidentally unleashed an explosive force of magic. My dad had dropped me as he crumbled to the ground and the building fell from above.

Staring at what remained of the ceiling, I blinked and gasped, sucking wind back into my lungs. The ringing in my ears cleared. Water pattered on the floor from the broken pipes. Insulation fluff fell to the floor like snowflakes. A cloud of drywall haze settled in what was once the breakroom.

I sat up, pressing a hand to my head. I'd decimated several rooms and hallways as if a wrecking crew had gotten drunk and come in here to have unrestricted fun. Luckily, there were no patient rooms nearby. Still, several staff rushed around, assisting patients and other staff nearby. I hated to wonder what could've happened if I had been at full strength.

The heaviest of the explosive damage had missed me, by sheer luck or my magical field, I didn't know. Besides some cough-worthy dust, I was physically fine. I pushed the fallen drywall off my body, groggily climbed to my feet, and half-heartedly brushed myself off.

My dad pitched a board that had fallen on him and climbed to his feet with a groan. He removed his glasses and wiped the lenses clear. Popping the frames back on his nose, he sighed with relief when he saw me. "Daisy, I'm so glad you're okay. Let's get out of here. I need you at the lab."

Fury swirled around me like an invisible tornado, lifting locks of my hair, ready to unleash a fresh warpath of destruction. Giving me to the elf was bad enough, but the lab? I wasn't a daughter to my dad. I was a thing to be tested, modified, and milked at his convenience. This cow was closing shop, and my full strength had arrived. "I'm not going to any lab."

He flicked his wrists at me as if I were a lost puppy. "Don't be insolent, kitten. I don't have all evening."

The derogatory nickname infuriated me. How could I have been so blind all this time? What he'd always thought of me was right there on his tongue. "I'm not a pet. Don't ever call me that again."

Dad stumbled his way through the debris toward me, but his footing wasn't stable, and he smartly gave up before twisting an ankle. "This isn't you. At PDI's lab, I work to save lives, just like you. In the end, that's all I care about."

I already knew that.

"But I need your blood to continue my work."

"I thought the weapon was perfect as it is." I repeated the words he'd said to me and Oliver when he'd pointed and fired a loaded pistol right next to me.

Dad ignored my statement. "The brothers took it all, and you're different now. You're the star of the emergency services department here—"

He understood I was a witch and wanted to make a new serum with my new blood. I was so angry I struggled to see straight. "I drive the 'meat wagon', remember?" I spat out his insulting phrase for my career choice.

"I know you care about saving lives as much as I do. I refused to see things clearly until Newt opened my eyes, and I have since come to understand my place. Come with me, and together we can rid the world of the demons among us, and partner up with the elves, whose healing could save even more lives." He flicked his wrist again. "You'll understand your place soon."

I glared at him, and pure red hatred seeped from my skin. The wind of my magic, a high-pressure system aching to fly into action, whipped my hair into a frenzy once more. I focused on Greg's chest, where a heart should've been, but instead, there was nothing more than a gaping hole. I needed to fill that hole for him. So I filled it by expanding that sad sack called a heart.

That hollow smile of his morphed into confusion, and as the pressure on his heart increased, true horror. Greg clutched at his throat and pressed a fist to his chest. "Daisy," he gasped. "What are you doing? This isn't you."

Memories of happier times between me and Greg flitted through my head. They were short and fewer than I expected to recall—he brought me a candy bar after work one night as an apology for missing my birthday party; in mom's stead, he'd brought me and Lily shopping for homecoming dresses, but he spent the whole time on his phone, nodding blindly at the preferred styles we'd tried on. Lily and I had fun, anyway. Greg and his selfishness made me this way, and I had no regrets. His abuse made me powerful.

Greg's tiny gasps were drowned out by the pattering of water from the broken pipe in the corner. Eyes red from burst capillaries, he fell to his knees, still clutching himself. "Daisy..."

I should've felt awful. I should've regretted harming him, but I couldn't conjure any connection between us that was worth saving. He was truly dead to me. Greg's face turned an unpleasant shade of purple. The magic within continued my purpose—poor old Greg was having a *heart attack*. Unfortunately, a lot of life-saving equipment had been damaged.

Shucks.

Pierce rose up from the debris and clambered to my side with fear on his face. "Daisy, stop. What are you doing? He's your dad."

"Tell him that," I said, still holding my magic where I wanted it.

"Daisy," Pierce said, gripping my arm painfully. "Stop now. This isn't you."

I grunted at the crunching of his grip, and Greg collapsed onto a debris pile. "Go away. You're ruining my concentration."

Pierce forcefully threw me over his shoulder. A new surge of fury rose. With my magic, I pushed him over—little green army guy several thousandfold in strength—but I landed on my feet while Pierce landed on his face. My ex sprang up like the damned daisies he always bought me, and he glared. I was amused rather than terrified by his lame attempt to kidnap me, because I could finally save myself.

"I've been bitten twice without you healing me, so I'm no longer a contender for Pierce's incubator." Now maybe, he'd leave me the hell alone.

"Is that all you think I see you as?"

Guess not.

"We have nothing in common, and there's no passion between us—never has been. You admitted you can't love, and I deserve better than that. So I have no reason to waste my time with you."

Pierce's face crumpled. "Waste your time? What time? You want the silver wedding bells and the babies? Newsflash, he can't give you that." Pierce pointed to where he and Oliver had fought. Oliver was buried in the debris—not moving, and I didn't sense his vampire essence. A flutter vibrated through my chest.

"I can give you that. I could've been enough for you," Pierce insisted.

I shook my head. "I don't want good enough. I want great. I want passion. I want—" *Oliver*.

"That's it then?" he asked, lips pressing into a thin line.

"That's it," I repeated, relief flooding me. He'd finally accepted my answer.

"We do have something in common, whether you like it or not." Pierce held out his palm for me to take, an invitation to go with him willingly. "We have an enemy we need to take down."

"What enemy is that?"

Pierce frowned. "Vampires. As a witch, you're bound to destroy them—it's in your magic, and as an elf, it's my obligation to protect my kind, and I'm not going to lie, it's fun to hunt them. To fight. Together, we can end the plague on humans. We need only a new supply of your blood." His hand still hung in the air, unanswered.

I looked at my palms. "When I see a vampire, my instinct is to kill, but I don't want to. I don't want to, so I'm not going to. That's the difference between us." I glanced at Greg's lifeless form on the rubble. "Are you going to heal him and continue this unnecessary tirade against Oliver's kind?"

Pierce sighed. "I can erase injuries, I can delay natural causes to get a patient into surgery, and fully heal vampire bites and accidents. Not witchcraft." There was some long-awaited good news. Pierce's hand still waited, pleading. "Come with me. We can do this together—a team at work and a team at home. I can give you everything you want, and I'll deny you nothing."

Except my freedom.

I glanced at my love's still form and still sensed no vampire essence. But I brushed away thoughts of his death. I'd experienced his almost dying so many times in the last few weeks, I couldn't handle another. Not right now. And this building couldn't afford another of my breakdowns.

Pierce's hand bounced, urging me to accept. The brothers, Oliver and Soren, I presumed, had taken and likely destroyed the remains of the weapon. With my blood changed, Lily could come home now. She was safe, no longer at risk of being hunted and killed by elves for the cure in her veins. My dad was dead, along with the rest of my family. As I took in my demolished surroundings, Pierce couldn't blackmail me into helping. "My blood doesn't work now that I'm a witch, and I'll never join you in the lab."

"Then I only need you to be the mother of my sons, filling our house with happy smiles and laughter. If you change your mind about hunting, I'd love to share a mutual hobby. Not many couples can also claim to be best friends. Regardless, I'll always be there for you, Daisy. Always."

Not all vampires were evil. Soren had confessed something pretty close, but he'd been helping me break Pierce's latest compulsion, and he'd been under a witch's control when the damage had been done. I didn't want him dead for that, and I wasn't going to be responsible for starting a war. Nothing good ever came from war. "Never."

"Then you leave me no choice." Pierce's meaty hands reached for me like fishhooks, as if to force-heal my bites or kidnap me. Probably both.

Using my magic, I thrust an invisible, focused beam at his chest, and he flew backward and slammed against an exposed concrete wall with a bone-splitting crunch. He crumpled to the floor. Compromised concrete rained down on his body. Maybe this time, he might've gotten the hint.

Fire truck sirens filled the air. People's footsteps scurried around, helping those who were scared, startled, or otherwise in need of medical attention.

I reached my senses out into the room, feeling if any vampires were around to trigger my homicidal urges, but I still felt none. Which meant...

I scanned the debris field in the breakroom. A light fixture dangled and sparked. A mangled I-beam had fallen from the ceiling, and I followed its path to the floor, buried in debris. At the base of the iron, still fingers reached above the drywall and boards. A twist of pain in my stomach had me rushing, and I scraped up my legs in my hasty hunt to reach Oliver. I threw aside boards and thick pieces of drywall. I brushed away insulation and gasped.

The I-beam crushed his chest, and right next to it, Pierce's wood stake protruded. No, not again, not like this. Crouching down, I tried lifting with my legs, but I couldn't budge it. The beam was still connected to the ceiling. But I could take out the stake, for what that was worth. I gripped the handle and pulled it from his flesh and threw the bloody thing aside. I fell to my knees. My fingers brushed the dust off his beautiful face. This was all my fault. Oliver was dead. The one man I'd ever loved was dead, by my own hands.

I stared at my open palms and urged every spiky knot of searing pain to accumulate. The crushing pain in my heart eased as the emotion funneled into my fists. I focused on the mangled, monstrous I-beam and visualized it lifting and moving away. I used my hands to direct the energy just right, and the I-beam trembled with my force, but it didn't lift. My hands shook with the tremendous effort, trying beyond all reasonable measure to move a heavy piece of connected foundation off my love's chest, but it was no use. I used up all my stores.

I leaned over and kissed his cool lips. "It's gone now. It's safe to wake up. I'm sorry. I'm so sorry for all this. I love you. You are my forever. Please wake up."

He didn't move. With a piece of debris, I scratched my wrist and pressed it to his mouth. I forced drips between his lips, but still he didn't move. I was too late.

I roared in anguish and sobbed, climbing sloppily to my feet. Pain refilled my chest like a mug under a waterfall.

Pierce was a broken heap of unconsciousness in the corner. He would get up eventually, but I never wanted to see him again.

"Daisy!" a nurse called to me. She was young, dusty, and had cuts on her face from the explosion. I did that to her, and a sock to my gut had me bending at the waist. I hurt her. "Come, let's get you checked out."

"Did anyone die?"

"I don't know yet, but come with me. You're bleeding. You need to be checked out." She urged me forward.

I shook my head and retreated, stumbling backward. Silently, I screamed for Oliver to move. My strong, inhuman, nearly two-centuries-old love couldn't be the only fatality from my mess. I couldn't be the one to kill him. I had to get away from here before I hurt anyone else.

"I'm fine. Really, I'm...fine." No bigger lie had been spoken.

I rushed out of the building and sobbed until my tear ducts were dry as the Sahara.

# 29

# Hope Returns

**Oliver**

Vampirism offered many perks: increased speed, heightened senses and emotions—including anger and love, and depending on the day, immortality could be considered a positive.

Like today.

The only things truly lethal were a wooden stake to the heart or beheading. But there were downsides. The blood drinking was, unfortunately, the worst—a necessary inconvenience. I couldn't go to the grocery refrigerators and fill a cart with my preferred flavor of the week. I, like all vampires, managed the hunger as best I could, some of us deliberately better than others. Vervain was the second worst. Not only did it interfere with our mind control, but ingested, it left the human inedible until the substance passed through the human's system. Plus, it was poisonous to us, and at high enough volumes, it could kill.

Like today.

Pierce had staked me with wood, but he'd missed my heart when I'd moved, which an elf paramedic with an understanding of anatomy should've accounted for. But now I knew why he was sloppy about the staking. The amount of vervain was enough to kill a roomful of vampires.

Me included.

I'd long ago lost count of how many times I'd died over the last century and a half, but vervain ranked among the least pleasant. To humans, it was as benign as a dash of parsley over their meal, but for a vampire, it caused necrosis of muscle and organ tissue that, unfortunately for me, regenerated just slightly slower than it disintegrated, leaving me in lengthy fits of anguish as my body fought the raging death from lack of oxygen. The irony would be enough to chuckle about if I weren't suffering through it again. I couldn't recall how many times I'd wallowed in the slow vervain death, but remembering the pain made the anticipation worse each time. All I had to do was wait out the inevitable.

I resurrected with a gasp of pain radiating from every inch of flesh on my body, and I coughed. The scent of blood on my lips wasn't my own. I licked it clean and smiled. Daisy had tried to feed me. I loved that woman so much.

I took mental inventory and counted approximately seven shattered bones, mostly thanks to the I-beam on my chest, knitting themselves back together. I shifted my tired arms and shoved the thing off me. With a grunt, I climbed to my feet and checked my ruined polo. The stake was gone. A half inch to the right and I'd be dead permanently. That had been too close. Speaking of the elf, I'd turned to find Pierce in a limp heap against a concrete wall. The corners of my lips lifted in satisfaction. She kicked his ass.

And I couldn't have been prouder.

In my precarious condition, I couldn't wait for the elf to wake up to gloat on her behalf, but I was in no shape to fight, despite my owing Pierce for breaking my number one rule too many damned times. Right now, I needed to feed before the instinctual demands forced me to hurt someone for my own sake. I shook the dust from my hair and used my impaired vampire speed to reach the hospital's refrigerators. With the lovely selection, I chose a few of my favorites, A-positive, and ducked into a broom closet. I popped their ports and slammed them down like pain pills.

I'd heard every word Daisy said, but I couldn't respond at the time, and she hadn't waited long enough for me to return to her, but that was for the best. As soon as I resurrected, she would've had to kill me again. That would've been much harder to explain to witnesses prowling around helping survivors. I'd had enough humans to compel into forgetting as it was.

I checked the phone she bought me, but the screen was shattered. Not very durable things, as she'd warned. I stuffed the broken unit back into my pocket. After taking my fill and healing, I moved from one witness to the next and cleared their memories.

I should've made Pierce do it, but I couldn't take the chance he'd wake up too late.

Power surging through me, I found the hospital executive's office, and after admiring the man's well-cut suit, I gave him a believable excuse for the foundation collapse and convinced him there was no need for a structural engineer to assess the damage and discover the source of the explosion. That would only lead to questions no one would be answering. I told him to hire a construction company to begin repairs at once, and I would personally fund the entire cost.

He was thrilled, of course.

I almost paused to ask him the source of his suit, but decided my tailor was the best in the state, and I had no need for inferior clothing. I found Daisy's boss and told him I quit. He apologized as if it were his fault, and he asked if there was anything he could do. The man was good people, so I told him to take care of Daisy. The boss smiled and wished me well. I'd be sending him a fruit basket this Christmas.

No more itchy polyester polos for me. I went home and showered and changed into a clean suit. Daisy didn't need me by her side any longer. She was powerful enough, and I trusted her to keep herself safe, but a hollowness seeped into my bones. Where would I fit in her life now? Until I could be in her company without her killing me, I didn't fit at all, and I feared there was nothing I could do but wait.

I strolled downstairs and adjusted my watch around the sleeve bunching over it. I was technically back to full strength, but I didn't feel all that energetic, so I stepped behind my bar to mix a stiff drink.

"Oliver?" Nicole asked, rounding the corner with her telltale limp. "Ah, there you are. I see the young woman left you intact."

"Of course." Hardly, but she didn't need that detail to fret over. I pulled her into a bear hug.

"I heard there was an explosion at the hospital. Gas line or something, and the foundation got damaged. Witches did it, didn't they?"

There was no fooling my niece. So then how many others figured it out? "Just one angry, uncontrolled witch versus her traitorous dad and the elf."

"Oh, dear. I'm sorry I convinced you to go. Don't tell Soren he was right. You know how he gets."

"I can always find the voice of reason, even when I don't want to hear it. If I hadn't been impaled for the best part, it would've been marvelous to watch Daisy, but I know she did me proud. She took them both down by herself." A new witch's strength was nothing to be underestimated.

"They're dead?" Nicole's hand covered her gaping mouth.

I poured myself a glass of tequila. "The doctor is. I didn't wait to find out the elf's condition, but either way, this deserves a celebratory imbibing. Care to join me?"

Nicole craned her neck, as if expecting to see Daisy stroll around the corner. "Where's Daisy now?"

"Home, I suspect. I'm not sure what to do about us until she can get her powers under control. In the meantime, I'm going to bolster mine." I downed my drink and refilled it. Daisy didn't need me anymore, and I was going to need many, many drinks over it. "Do you want tequila?"

"No," Nicole said.

"I do," a familiar voice interrupted at the same time I sensed a vampire's presence. But it wasn't Soren.

My hands froze in place. My beating heart took a momentary vacation, and I turned my head at the same time my niece did. Neither of us said anything. I stared, shocked into a state of uncomprehending stillness. Nicole didn't move either.

I couldn't find my legs as a lean woman sauntered up to my bar wearing a skirt suit ready for a business meeting, with waves of familiar brown hair tumbling over her shoulders, and a secretive smile lighting the room. There were definitely secrets here. Zipping through recent memory, trying to find the last ones I had of her left me cloudy and confused, but I did find my tongue. "Stacey?"

"Hi, Oliver. I've missed you." My business acquaintance—specifically my real estate agent—smiled casually, as if we were best of friends. "I'll take tequila on the rocks."

Keywords of familiarity snapped me out of my shock. I poured Stacey a drink and handed it to her with a cocktail napkin under it. "You died when Dr. Barrett angered the wrong witch." My eyes tracked to her hand, and she wore a sun ring just like mine, among several other types.

"I was supposed to, but thanks to your brother, I remain on this side of the dirt." Stacey tasted and set her half-empty drink down.

Vampire Staccy Barrctt. I nccdcd another drink. I wanted to picture the shocking delight on Daisy's face, but all that came to mind was the horror of her magic wanting to kill the mother she'd just gotten back. "Does Daisy know about...this?"

"Why do you think I'm here?"

"To offer me another lucrative property?" I quipped and sipped. "We've had a good run. I'd hate for this current situation to change that."

"Don't you worry about your business ventures. I have no intention of leaving my work. How else can a vampire earn money than by walking into mystic-barrier-free properties and selling them for a nice cut?" She lifted her drink and finished it. "I guess I'm lucky I only lost my life and not my livelihood."

She *was* lucky. Most humans-turned-vampire had to learn survival from scratch, like my siblings and I had. Becoming a vampire in modern times was likely both easier for the options and harder from a lack of invisibility. "If you're looking for Daisy, why did you come to me?"

"She's not ready to see me like this. You've done a great job introducing her to the life, but I need you to give my daughter something to help her warm to the idea of me on my feet." Stacey Barrett slipped one of the rings off her finger and set it on the bar in front of me. "This will suppress her powers for two weeks. Use it wisely."

My brows lifted. Frankly, I was both flabbergasted and completely suspicious. "What's the catch?"

Stacey smirked. "No catch. Just take good care of my daughter. Oh, and thank Soren for releasing me." Daisy's mom turned on her high heels and sashayed out the door.

I was simply stunned. After dealing with Soren and his anti-humans-with-vampires viewpoint and my personal struggle with it, I never expected anyone to encourage our relationship, let alone Daisy's own mother.

Nicole blinked. "Did that just happen?"

"The question is, how did that just happen?"

"Do new vampires have new tricks?"

"I hope not." I picked up the ring off the bar—a round onyx gemstone with gold spiraling outward and knotting on itself before curving around the base of the setting. Perfect spiritual symbols of self-control.

Suspicious or not, I wasn't going to let a good thing go to waste, assuming Mrs. Barrett, the lovely wife of the unfortunate Dr. Barrett, didn't have something else in mind. The only one from that family I trusted was Daisy.

"You think she's honest about that ring?" Nicole asked.

"That's the priceless question."

If I placed this on Daisy's finger and it destroyed her, vengeance would cower in my shadow. If instead Daisy destroyed me, then Stacey made herself the worst enemy imaginable.

But if the ring did as described, then we had two weeks—a mere blink of an eye in my lifespan—but it was an offer of hope I didn't have before.

Only one way to find out.

# 30
# Crippling Pain

**Daisy**

I DROPPED MY CELL phone on the coffee table and collapsed onto my couch. Calls went straight to voicemail. Texts were left unread. I refused to believe I'd killed Oliver. While waiting for the time when my boss arrived at the office, I composed myself, trying to sound functional. Then, when I thought I could handle the news, I called him. Immediately, I began pacing across my living room.

"Daisy, how are you feeling?" my boss said grimly.

"I'm fine." *Not.* "What happened? Is anyone hurt?"

My boss cleared his throat. "Many people had bumps and bruises. We had a few casualties. I can't believe a gas leak caused all this. You'd think the inspectors would've noticed a defect capable of such catastrophic damage."

"Who?" I said, voice shaking. "Who died?"

"The police aren't releasing any names until next of kin have been notified, but I will say, prepare yourself, Daisy. I'm so sorry."

Names, plural. Prepare myself? I stopped pacing and held back a sob.

"Take the next few days off. The department is going to need a lot of reconstruction and rearranging to be functional again. The volunteer squad is going to help, and we're pulling in nearby units to pick up the slack in the meantime. You need the rest."

"Thanks," I said in a quiet voice and hung up.

I stared at the black screen, which showed my dirty reflection, and I stood there, frozen, mind-numb. The silence was deafening. I'd made more mistakes in one day than most people made in a lifetime. *Names, plural.* I was a monster. I couldn't wield magic safely or appropriately. I couldn't be subtle because I couldn't control it, so I didn't want it. Moreso I didn't deserve it.

I threw the phone onto the couch and stared at the hands that destroyed my life—the place I was proud to call my job. Greg—even if we had our disagreements, did I mean to *kill* my dad? What was wrong with me? And Pierce—he could heal accidents and injuries in humans. Could he heal injuries to himself? He'd said, 'Not witchcraft.' So, my throwing him across the room with magic meant he couldn't heal. How many others died at my hands?

The only person I needed to know about was Oliver, and my boss's use of the plural only crushed me. Last I saw my love, his lifeless hand protruded from the rubble, and my magic sensed no vampire essence in the area. My blood couldn't revive him. Oliver had already been gone. Now he was gone forever.

Without this cursed magic, Greg would still be alive, thinking up new ways to convince me to be his lab rat, but Oliver would be alive, helping me plan and plot against his attempts—and we could be together right now. In his loving arms, caressing and soothing me or taking a drive in his Shelby. He never got the chance to teach me to drive a stick. Or in my bed, free of clothing, with hot kisses trailing along our bodies and sensual touches, leaving soft gasps in their wake.

There was only one solution.

"Take it away," I whispered to Allison, who watched me closely. "Take it all away."

"I understand how hard this is for you." Allison approached, apparently believing I wasn't a hazard to her health.

"Do you?" I snipped, but my anger and revulsion weren't aimed at her. That didn't mean she wouldn't become yet more collateral damage in my wake.

My roommate sighed and gestured for me to sit on the couch. I picked up my phone, tucked it into a pocket, and dropped down. Allison sat next to me. "I had to learn to harness my magic, too. It wasn't without mistakes."

I looked her in the eyes and waited for the side of her I didn't know, and for some sliver of reassurance that I wasn't the only one to destroy everything that mattered.

Allison collected my hands in hers. "When I was young, something startled me awake. I snuck out of bed and tiptoed down the hallway and watched Dad pace the living room and kitchen. He was clearly troubled, but something about Dad's seething anger told me to stay clear, so I stayed quiet. A few beats later, my mom walked in through the front door. She told Dad was pregnant, and she was leaving him."

My eyes widened.

"That baby was Jamie and not my father's. Dad hit her. Knocked her right off her feet, and when she didn't get back up, I screamed for her. My magic exploded through the house. On the kitchen counter rested a wooden block of knives. They were swept up in my power."

I squeezed her hands in horror. I'd always thought Allison tucked the block of knives into a cabinet for aesthetic reasons, and now I couldn't imagine what a young child had to see.

"My dad had no chance of surviving that. But Mom lived, and she raised me with Jamie and his dad."

"How horrible. I'm so sorry." I squeezed her hands in support.

"My mom introduced me to our family lineage then. I was too young to understand most of what she explained, but I followed along with the basic lessons for control. Jamie had joined me, mostly to be included, since we didn't expect him to ever awaken his own magic. For a while, it was too hard for me, and I begged my mom to take it away, too. I didn't want to hurt people only because I was upset. I didn't want to kill anyone, ever. But, like me, I can't take your magic away. It's part of you, but it gets better with practice and time."

Children accepted change much more easily than adults. Maybe if I'd activated this latent power when I was a child, I'd have had a chance to work through the bugs. Instead, I was a grown-ass adult with way too much power to control. But my only choice was either to learn control or to kill more people. I'd already lost the love of my life.

How was I supposed to keep my mind on the intricacies of the incantation, not to mention the whole meditation aspect, when the soul-crushing guilt in my chest left breathing a near impossibility? As long as my brain was a slurry of scrambled eggs—whipped, cooked, and sticky—and my heart was broken into tiny irreparable pieces, I didn't see how I could focus. And this chaotic magic wasn't going to wait for me to heal.

The only solution I could see was to uncook my scrambled eggs and glue my heart back together. Then I could help my boss clean up, help others in need, and prevent another disaster with a clear head. I could be what Allison needed me to be—a functional witch. I squeezed my eyes shut and made my final plea with a shaky voice. "Erase my memories."

"What?" Allison said in disbelief.

"It's the only way. For everyone's sake, take Pierce away. Take my dad's death away. And...take...take...Oliver Rockwell, too." I swallowed back a sob, knowing I was sacrificing my happiness, even if it was nothing more than a memory now.

"Elf and vampire compulsion won't work on you." Allison touched my shoulder gently. "And I can't spell another witch to forget."

My heart had already been crushed into the dust of the explosion I'd caused. Why not squeeze all those little particles further, adding thousands upon thousands of times more pain? How was I supposed to survive this? How?

"But," Allison added cheerily. "We might find some kind of spell to help. We don't know until we look."

Hope blossomed in my chest for an answer that made sense. Witchcraft got me into this mess, so it had to get me out. "Finally, some good news."

I rose, taking Allison's hand with me, and pulled her to her feet. My heart thundered in my chest with excitement. I'd almost forgotten what it felt like.

"Now?" she asked.

"Right now."

Allison smiled. "Okay. Let me get my supplies." She fished out her witchcraft storage container and brought it upstairs to my bedroom.

I followed behind and dragged out my box of Aunt Lisa's things. I opened the sun ring box inscribed with witchcraft symbols. Oliver's ring had been in here. I stroked the velvety interior. I missed him so much, and now I fought back another wave of uncontrollable sobs. Soon...soon the pain would be over.

What did these symbols on the box mean? That was a puzzle for another day, just like humans rebuilding the hospital, the elves dealing with Pierce—dead or alive—and the medical examiner situation with Greg, a problem I'd have to resolve with lawyers. But Aunt Lisa's grimoire had to have the answer for today. I knew exactly what I was looking for.

Allison sat across from me and rummaged in her big box of supplies for a grimoire. She opened the pages. "I can't take away your magic, and I can't erase your memories, so what's the plan?"

I opened the cover of Aunt Lisa's grimoire and skimmed the text. "I'm bringing Oliver back to life."

Allison frowned, disapproving instantly. "Whoa, hold on. Are you sure Oliver is dead?"

I inhaled deeply to get the depressing sentence out in a single go. "I couldn't sense his vampire essence in his lifeless body, under the rubble, with an iron I-beam crushing him, after Pierce staked him in the chest. His skin was gray, too. So, yeah, I'm pretty sure." The image would haunt me until the day that I died. "And his phone is going straight to voicemail."

Heat burned my hands, and I released the book before it caught fire.

Allison set aside her book, frowning at the glow on my hands. "Daisy, you have to control these emotions before you have another explosive episode. I can resist your force, but the rest of your house wouldn't be as lucky. I'm pretty sure homeowner's insurance doesn't cover accidental magic explosions."

Okay, she got my attention.

"Concentrate on the chaos within—atoms *zinging* all over, smacking into each other as if heated by a microwave. Streaks of color trailing in their wake, casting a blur of colors, muted by their disorganization. Picture your emotions lining up, single file, and turning the jumble of colors into a smooth, harmonic rainbow of brilliant tones. Move that rainbow into a harmless area, like your elbows."

"My elbows?" I asked, temporarily amused and...distracted.

Allison nodded.

I closed my eyes and concentrated. Taking her advice, I pooled those painful thoughts, organizing them into a beautiful rainbow, and pictured them gliding along the neural highways of my body to collect at the harmless area. My elbows heated and tingled as if I'd banged my ulnar nerve—the funny bone. That was something I could tolerate, and infinitely better than the pain in my heart or blowing my house to smithereens. I rubbed my elbows against my thighs to alleviate some of the discomfort.

"How's it going?" she asked.

"Itchy and tingly." I rubbed, and a spark caught on my jeans. I reeled back and patted out the tiny flame. Wide-eyed, I stared at my roommate.

"It's still power. You must be careful." Allison smiled, and with a twirl of her fingers, she fixed the singed hole in my pants, just like she'd fixed my torn dress from Evangeline attacking me. "Treat it like chickenpox—no scratching."

"Good advice in many situations."

Allison laughed. "I suppose you're right." She scooted over to the container and set up candles in a circle.

I didn't know what she had in mind. "We haven't found a resurrection spell yet."

She poured a ring of salt onto my carpet. "Magic doesn't grow on trees. It's a part of you and finite. Each spell draws you down, and it requires time to replenish the well. Think of it this way: when your bank account is running low, you're careful about which bills get paid when, and you don't buy that shimmery new top at the store."

I totally understood that.

"And just like magic," she continued, "you have to be mindful of your usage, spend accordingly, and don't waste it. As you perform more spells and refill the well, your well expands. You become more powerful—capable of more magic in shorter timeframes. Right now you're still very green and lacking in the control department. Doing a resurrection spell of this caliber is incredibly dangerous. So, we're going to throttle your power, make you less dangerous."

I frowned. This wasn't what I had in mind.

"It isn't going to do Oliver any good if you tear his head off after you revive him."

"Good point. Thank you, Alli, for helping me and looking out for me. I really appreciate it, and so does Oliver."

Allison set the last of the candles in the circle. "Every new witch needs an Obi-Wan Kenobi to learn from."

I didn't think Allison was a Star Wars fan. "Do I get a lightsaber?"

Allison snorted. "Never in your life. Now, focus right here. I want you to channel that elbow power to your fingers and ignite these candles. Only these candles. Remember, homeowner's insurance doesn't cover arson."

"It's not arson if it's an accident," I grumbled.

Allison shifted aside, leaving me plenty of room to work without accidentally setting her on fire. I focused on the pain, anger, and guilt tingling at my elbows. It was much easier now that hope had grabbed hold of my heart and allowed it to soar. I was getting Oliver back after this, and I wasn't going to hurt him. As I guided the colorful emotion down to my palms, I could've sung in elation, but I focused. Holding the pain in my fists like invisible fireballs, I imagined releasing them from my hands—delicately. The first candle blew over and rolled away toward Allison's feet.

Allison retrieved my first failure and repositioned it. "Close. Less power next time."

I exhaled and repeated the process, but instead of gliding an invisible fireball's worth, I trickled less rainbow, enough to make a small flame, a lighter's worth. I released. The candle didn't tip over, and the wick still didn't light.

"Try a little more power. You're getting close. You can do this."

I wasn't so sure. Somewhere between fireball and lighter was…little green army guy. I conjured up the amount of power it took to move the little toy two inches. With that amount of flame, I aimed it toward the next candle in the row and focused on heat, not force. It lit without falling over.

I jumped up, fists pumping the air, and I yelled and laughed and spun around. "Yes! Did you see that? I did it! Oh, my God, I can't believe it! I did it. Ahhhh!"

"Of course you did." Allison beamed at me proudly. "Be careful of too much excitement. It's almost as powerful as pain."

Adrenaline surged through my veins, and I panted with excitement, my breath tearing through my lungs. For the first time, I thought I could do this. But I was going to be excited, or afraid, or angry in the future—I was human. I had to be able to control my magic while still under the grips of emotion—regardless of which kind.

"When you center yourself again, light the rest of the candles." Allison directed.

Okay, okay. The lesson wasn't over yet. I focused the same little green army guy amount of energy and thrust it toward the next candle. It lit. Then the next, and the next, until the whole row flickered with tiny flames. I stared wide-eyed in wonder.

"You're on the right track, and you did great—a natural even."

A natural. Who would've known?

I beamed, and Allison pulled me into a bear hug, but I could hardly stand still. I wanted to show off. I couldn't wait to demonstrate my new chaos-to-rainbow control to Oliver. He would be proud.

Allison released me. "Now, I need you to stand in the circle and repeat a chant."

And the lesson continued. I almost needed a break to jog around the block and ease some of this explosive excitement, but I followed my teacher's orders. "What's this for?"

"A twofold spell. You're planning on resurrecting the dead. Necromancy is a difficult path. Many who start down that road never recover, so I'm going to throttle down your power until you have full control, and infuse luck into your spells. Trust me, you're going to need it." Allison gestured for me to climb inside my flaming circle.

Obedient to my Obi-Wan Kenobi, I did, and when she began chanting, I listened. When I picked up the pattern of sounds, I joined in. Together we cast a spell of good fortune on me—Lord knew I needed all the luck I could find, and

I was eager to learn control faster and easier. When Allison stopped, I did too.

Energized and ready to roll out my plan, I leaped out of the circle. Power hummed within me. I was too damned excited. "I feel...electrified. Ready to take on the world." I sat on my carpet and blew out my successful candle ring. Now, for business. I placed Aunt Lisa's grimoire back into my lap. If necromancy, or whatever, was so dangerous I needed a spell for extra help, would it be sitting here so easy to access?

"Is there a resurrection spell in one of these books?" I asked Allison, suddenly doubting the ease of my plan.

"If we can't find exactly what we need, there's always something similar. We just have to take the time to find it. I'll have Jamie bring us coffee and come help." Allison stepped over to the doorway and hollered down the stairs. Jamie called back. My roommate took a seat across from me and took up her book too. I'd never appreciated a friendship as much as I did right now.

We both turned pages in our respective delicate books. I didn't know any keywords to search for or the names of any relevant spells. "What exactly should I be looking for?"

"Ingredients that include personal effects and dirt from a grave."

Strange. "Whose grave?"

"Oliver's."

The idea that he'd already been presumed dead and buried centuries ago made my stomach flip, but what if they pulled him from the rubble and buried him again? "His original grave or his new one?" I never thought I'd ask a question like that before.

"Older is better."

I realized I didn't know where his grave was located. There were no obvious markers on the bed-and-breakfast property. I remembered Oliver's story about his family trapped in a cave during the 1871 Peshtigo Fire. Skipping the part where the newly turned vampires had fled in the night, likely, the townspeople would've presumed them dead from the blaze. *They* would've buried the Rockwells...

Not far from Oliver's current home in Marinette, and just outside of Peshtigo, was the rustic hunter's cabin—near the location of my car accident, and our emergency shelter from the coming sun on our escape from the lab. He'd known it was there, and he could enter without permission. As a guess, he could've buried his sister Sadie there, after she'd been hunted by Evan Logonson. It makes sense he was familiar with the area if it had meaning to him. It was a place to start.

"I think I know where to look." That stretch of highway still gave me nightmares, but since I had no reason to go to Green Bay anytime soon, it was a jitter I could ignore.

"Great, then we just need the spell."

Jamie appeared in the doorway to my bedroom, holding a pair of steaming mugs. "Digging for a spell? My favorite way to spend a Saturday."

"Grab a book and start reading," Allison said.

Jamie crossed the room and handed us both the mugs before curling up on the floor with a grimoire himself. We turned the rustling, delicate pages mostly in silence, occasionally reading aloud some ingredients or a spell's name if it had one and sounded tantalizing.

"How about this one?" I asked. Both my roommates paused their search to listen. "Titled 'Healed with Vigor'. Ingredients include a photo of the deceased, dirt from a grave, four raw chicken eggs—"

"At least it's not lizard eggs or something much harder to find," Jamie interrupted.

"True," Allison said. "Have you ever tried chasing a black iguana? Very humbling experience."

"I did," Jamie said. "Spring break in Florida a few years ago. I told you, or I thought I did. I was smashed that week. But at least those little bastards don't eat meat."

"How would you explain that in an obituary?" Allison asked as she and her brother derailed my finding. She mimicked an announcer's voice. "James Franklin Harris died unexpectedly after being run down by a black iguana at twenty miles per hour and eaten alive limb by limb."

"Like mini raptors," Jamie said and curled his fingers into tiny claws. "Never go backpacking in the wilderness without a satchel of food you can toss and run the other way."

"Excellent tip," Allison said.

"Are you guys done?" I asked. My roommates stared at me as if they had been caught talking in class. "This spell also requires something called Dew of the Sea. It sounds rare and mystical. Either of you know what that is?"

Jamie blinked. "Rosemary."

"Who?" I asked, not wanting to waste more time on some wild goose—or lizard—chase.

Jamie laughed. "I think boxed waffles are the greatest shit ever made, but even I know rosemary is a seasoning. You'll find some in your pantry. Clearly, I'm the only one who uses it."

"Oh." My cheeks heated. I had cooked dinner for Greg every day, but that one wasn't used in my rotation. "All right then. I'm going grave hunting. You get the eggs and rosemary. Deal?" I closed my book and settled it back into Aunt Lisa's box.

Jamie slapped his book shut. "Deal. Alli, want a drink?"

Allison closed her book and stacked it back into her storage container. She rose and took the supplies with her. "The coffee's still buzzing. Besides, it's too early for that."

Jamie shrugged. "It's five o'clock somewhere."

"When do you *not* use that line?" Allison waited for Jamie to follow her downstairs.

"When I'm not judged for day drinking." Jamie and Allison left my room together.

Preparing to get dirty, I tucked away the box and changed into jeans and a T-shirt. I went to the kitchen and rummaged for a suitable container. Satisfied with a four-cup liquid measuring cup, I jumped into my car.

I could do this.

It was just dirt.

# 31

# Grave Intentions

**Daisy**

I crunched gravel as I rolled my car to a stop at the hunter's cabin in the woods. With a deep exhale, I climbed out of my car with the four-cup measuring cup and headed straight into the woods. Leaves and twigs snapped underfoot. Fresh pine filled my nose. Sunlight penetrated the canopy overhead and sent beams of light onto the forest floor. It was almost magical—if I weren't hunting for a graveyard that might not exist.

The pitter-patter of critter feet stopped me on the regular. I wasn't paranoid or afraid, just trying to remain vigilant. Cautious steps brought me to a clearing, and I brushed aside the climbing weeds and slipped through.

I'd found a very small, long-forgotten cemetery with weeds overgrowing many of the time-worn markers. Approaching the first, I stilled. In a few days, I had to pick out a headstone for Greg. Picturing his name, date of birth, and date of death formed a lump in my stomach. I did that to him. Me. I would handle that when it came, and I could handle it much better with Oliver at my side. Focus.

I brushed at the face to read the name engraved on the stone. I didn't recognize it. Careful of where I trod on the land, I weaved my way through the secret cemetery until I realized the next grave marker had already been cleared. Flowers had been placed here recently. I approached and read a familiar name.

"Rose Watson, dedicated spiritual leader, and forever in our memories, 1821 to 1871." The year of the Peshtigo fire. How many Rose Watsons had been around at that time? This had to be Oliver's mom. Some still cared enough to bring her flowers all these decades later.

I sighed. My own mother had been distant, aloof, and never home. I'd spent years pining for family vacations, meals out together, hell, even watching a movie together, curled up on the couch. Mom had always been absent, but she was still Mom, and I missed her. Nothing could ever bring Stacey Barrett back.

But I didn't want my real mom. I wanted a fantasy I never had, a second chance at a caring mom. I rested my hand on the raised stone, imagining Rose Watson to be kind, just, and a very hard worker, always there for her children. Working her magic to keep them all safe and to keep food on the table. We could've spent quality time together. I would've loved to meet the woman who crafted such a remarkable man.

Shame she'd perished in the fire, racing back to her sacred space. No one deserved the agony of dying from smoke inhalation in a fire. I shuddered, remembering the flames licking up the sides of the car while I had been too weak to escape. I'd almost died that early pre-dawn morning. If it weren't for Rose Watson's amazing son, I would've.

I had to save Oliver.

I patted her grave one last time and kept moving. The next grave was Sadie Rockwell. Oliver's sister. So I was in the right place, but her dates were confusing—1853 to 1871. She was a vampire murdered by an elf forty years ago. Whoever had this marker made didn't know the truth.

I moved along. The next stone in the row was overgrown. I pulled aside the climbing weeds and ripped off tough vines. My hands were filthy, sore, and cut, but I couldn't quit now. I was very close. Panting from the effort, I read the next name and gasped. I found what I'd been looking for, but seeing his name on a headstone still squeezed my heart.

"Oliver Herman Rockwell. *Herman*?" A sloppy snort passed my lips. That middle name didn't suit him at all. "Beloved by all, we will meet again one day, 1841-1871." So very true. My eyes watered. Who wrote such sweet words to him? Someone who didn't know he'd survived the fire, either. The world assumed he was dead. The world was right.

For now.

I spun on my heel and marched across the clearing to a patch of wildflowers. Tiny white and yellow blooms were perfect. Ripping up a fistful, I returned to his grave and set the bunch before the stone. My head dipped low, and I rested a hand on the grave to hold myself up.

"There's no excuse for losing control, and I'll be sorry forever, but it's going to be okay. Allison throttled my power, so when I bring you back, we can be together. I know I can do this. Please forgive me for desecrating your sacred space."

I waited for a response that wouldn't come. His body wasn't here. For all I knew, he was in a cooler at the morgue, waiting for Soren to identify him and claim the body. Or he was ash, swept up with the construction debris and dropped into a commercial dumpster for hauling to the city dump. I really hoped his ring was on his finger, because that visual made me want to vomit.

I kneeled in the thick patch of weeds. Using my bare hands, I brushed and tore at the stubborn grass, fighting to reach the sod. It wasn't going well. I used the mouth of the measuring cup to scoop, but the plastic was too weak. I needed a spade or a trowel or something if I had any hope of tearing up sod to reach the dirt beneath.

In the winter, it was common to get stuck on unplowed roads and in parking lots. I always kept a bag of sand and a small metal snow shovel in my trunk, just in case. Never thought it would be used for digging graves, but here I was. With a sigh of frustration, I marched back through the woods to my car and stopped short at the cabin.

I dropped the measuring cup.

My lips parted.

I'd recognize that Shelby anywhere, as I was sure nearly everyone would. The problem was someone—Soren or Pierce?—stole his car for a joyride, or I was hallucinating. Under the glistening sunlight, the candy-apple red paint glowed like a beacon of hope, and I didn't know who to be angry with.

I reached out with my senses to find a vampire's essence. Soren had to be lurking around, maybe feeling nostalgic about his brother's untimely death and wanting to visit the family graves. I wasn't picking up anything. Unless it wasn't Soren. I reached out again, seeking elf essence, and gritting my teeth at the audacity, but I still picked up nothing. Did Allison throttle my power too much? Honestly, I wouldn't complain about that.

I gazed upon the beautiful Shelby, but I needed to hurry, so someone else could have privacy at the cemetery, because why else would they be here? I popped my trunk and collected the metal shovel.

An overpowering awareness pressed on my body like an invisible boulder. A vampire was nearby, and I sucked in a breath at the intense alarm. He was way too close. My fingers gripped my trunk lid painfully, blanching my knuckles. I shouted a warning, "Please back away. I'm almost done here, and then it's all yours."

I wasn't angry, but it was as if my body had built a fury or an offensive weapon all on its own, taking control of my magic. The urge to lash out and destroy whatever was near pounded in my skull like a tormenting spirit, relentless and unwavering, maddening. My hands trembled as untold magic poured into my hands—not like a mug catching a refill under a waterfall. Not like trying to swim upstream at Niagara Falls. I was the waterfall. The power was suffocating, and I needed air.

I felt...*unnaturally strong*. And this was throttled?

I slammed my trunk closed and held the shovel, but I wasn't sure what I'd do with it—stop the visitor or stop me? I spun, expecting my fanged friend to be awkwardly close. But I still saw no one, yet the pressure stayed strong. I scanned the area. The critters of the forest were silent. My instinct told me a vampire had to be here, but there was nowhere to hide.

Except the cabin. Since Soren didn't have a sun ring, of course, he'd wait there. Not a wise place to shelter from...me.

I pushed my palms toward the door and unleashed the overloaded magic trembling through my body. The door flew off torn hinges and landed on the forest floor. I stepped inside and gave my eyes a beat to adjust. Blankets were still nailed over the windows. A disheveled mattress lay on the floor. I crossed to the refrigerator and found a single bag of blood in it, but no other signs of life.

"I know you're here. Come out."

No answer. No sounds. Then where was he?

I stepped outside. "I know you're here."

Leaning against the Shelby stood a glorious Oliver in a fine suit. Sunlight reflecting off the car's paint lit him up like an angel. I blinked several times. My magic rebuilt, demanding to be satisfied. But it didn't understand hallucinations.

"Oliver?" I asked, disbelief clear in my voice. Had I lost my mind with grief, or could hope be this powerful?

The vampire rose to full height and slowly approached. A wistful but wary smile crossed his lips. "You're not going to attack?"

"I killed you," I said tentatively.

"Pierce staked me, but you know I'm immortal."

I knew all that, so my hallucination would too. "I saw you buried. You were dead at the hospital. How is this possible?"

Oliver strolled closer, cautious in his steps. "Death doesn't stop me. Only a stake to the heart—"

"Or decapitation," I finished for him.

I remembered the shovel in my hands. I tossed it away. My heart thundered with relief. Warmth filled my chest, and I rushed to close the distance, needing his touch, the feel of his arms around me, holding me securely. I needed his lips on mine. I needed him.

"You're really here!"

My surging emotions rapidly refilled my magical well. That instinctual fury within gripped my muscles and drained all the emotion from toes to scalp, directing it to be used as a weapon. I tried to pull it back, but I couldn't stop it. It flooded through me like a broken dam. This wasn't right. I was supposed to have less power, so I'd have more control. Instead, I was much, much stronger.

I stopped in my tracks, trembling. Swallowing back the pain of the demanding magic.

"What is it?" Oliver asked, worry creasing his brow.

"I can't hold it. You have to leave. Get out of here before it's too late!" My hands pulsed with burning heat, ordering me to release. At this point, I was terrified I'd melt my car, so I couldn't go. He had to. "Hurry!"

"I'm not leaving you." Oliver stepped closer. Rays of light glistened off his gelled hair. Sadness pulled at his pale gray eyes.

"I can't stop it. I can't. Please go." I held back tears. I'd just gotten him back. I couldn't lose him again.

"I believe you can. I believe *in* you."

Tears welled in my eyes, obstructing my view of his beautiful face. Life wasn't fair, and my pain only fueled the witchcraft further. "I can't hold it back. You have to go," I said weakly. My arms reached out toward him. Not for a hug, but to aim and fire. A sob broke free. "Please."

Oliver shook his head.

A stream of power unleashed from my hands. This was not the meek lighter flame, nor the massive fireball. It wasn't even the door tearing off the hinges. It was worse—the precision and concentration of the little army guy, dialed up a thousandfold, but I couldn't turn down the volume.

Oliver dodged behind his car. "I know you can do this. You can fight this."

I shook my head as another wave of energy refilled my hands, and I fired at his cover without warning. Oliver dodged in a blink, but my blast blew out the Shelby's windows. Glass shards twinkled in the sunlight and rained down on the gravel. Oliver's mouth dropped open. "What did my Shelby ever do to you?"

He was joking, but I couldn't join in the fun. "I didn't mean to. I told you I can't stop this. Please go, Oliver." Another refill of energy pulsed through me. "Please get out of here."

He stupidly approached instead. "I'm not running away. I know you can do this. I trust you."

I shook my head, and my face pinched in sadness. "I can't. I can't."

Oliver stepped closer.

My magic blasted in his direction again, but Oliver sidestepped. Targeting wasn't my forte yet, but I was afraid he was training it. He was only a few feet away from me, but the closer he got, the less time he had to dodge. The less accurate I needed to be. "I thought I'd killed you once. I can't survive losing you again."

"The only way you can kill me is with a paralyzing spell and access to a stake. That shovel over there is metal. Hurts like a bitch, but not lethal." Oliver reached out and gripped my hands. "And now you can't pick up any of the random sticks lying around."

He tried for levity, but fear tore through me, and touching my skin was a mistake.

The power surged directly from me and into him like a conduit. Oliver gritted his teeth against the electrifying current. He ground out, "You can do this."

I shook my head, unable to free my hands from his. My magic no longer fought to release because it had a direct connection to him. My heat made his skin glow, and micro-flames danced along his skin. He was paling, burning up. In horror, I asked, "What's happening?"

Oliver stiffened his spine and clenched his jaw through the pain. "You're magic is destroying what it had created—my sun ring."

Ash flaked off his hands. His suit blackened and steamed.

A sob broke free. "Get inside the cabin and heal up. I'll run into the woods and wait until you can get safely away. If my magic pulls me toward you, I'll run away until I wear holes through my shoes. Go now!"

As I expected, he didn't move. He said gently, "You're not a failure, Daisy. This is all normal. I know you'll control it someday, and as I promised, I'll wait for you. But in the meantime, this will help." Oliver's stubborn fingers shifted in my hand, and a ring slipped up my finger.

The urge to destroy him eased rapidly and vanished. As if my magic had been snuffed out, I easily released him. I gazed at the miracle I'd been hoping for—a magic spell to reduce the need to kill vampires. Unlike Allison's, this one seemed to be working. Oliver had it in the shape of a black onyx twisted into a gold setting. It was simple, but beautiful. "It's all gone. I'm me again!" I laughed.

Oliver visibly relaxed. His half-grin made me snort with happiness. His skin and the magic within his sun ring healed at once. He was my Oliver again—perfect in every way. I brushed my fingers over his firm chest and snagged the tattered remains of his suit. The damage looked like it had been incredibly painful. "I'm sorry I ruined your clothes again. Send me the bill for the replacement and the inconvenience."

"My tailor has been getting overtime pay. He's happy. And now that we know the ring works, I need you...closer."

He didn't have to ask twice. With a broad grin, I jumped into his arms, and he squeezed me against his chest as if I would float away. I wrapped my legs around his hips and crushed his lips against mine. Oliver wanted me to overpower my magic on my own, but he knew, deep down, that I couldn't yet. He had a backup plan, which I was grateful for. "Thank you. I'm never taking this ring off."

Oliver's eyes met mine. "Let's make the best of this, okay?"

I bit my lower lip. We had been apart for far too long. I needed every inch of his body on mine, in mine. "There's a mattress in the cabin."

Oliver grimaced. "For so many reasons, which include my brother sleeping there, I would rather pass. Let's go home to pack. You've had a rough time lately, and I'm taking you someplace deserving of my queen."

*My queen*. I liked the sound of that, but I wasn't in the mood to entertain patience. "I'm not picky."

"I think you'll find it's worth the wait. I'll meet you at your place in an hour." Oliver kissed me deeply, and a throb started down low.

The teasing was unbearable. And after everything we'd survived the last few weeks, I never looked forward to a mini vacation more than now. "You'd better deliver," I said gruffly in his ear.

"I've never disappointed you yet, have I?"

Confident bastard with magic fingers and a glorious snake in his pants. I loved every inch of him. "Not even remotely," I said with a sad smile. "But I'm really sorry I ruined your favorite car and another suit. I keep destroying your things—I'm a mess, while you have the looks and patience of an angel. I don't deserve you." Reluctantly, I slipped down off his hips.

"Don't say that. The magic is new, and that's just glass. I can replace things, but I could never replace you. Daisy, you mean everything to me, so stop apologizing for things out of your control." He brought my knuckles up to his lips and kissed them.

My eyelids fluttered closed at his delicate touch. I didn't want to let go of his hand, but I had to. "I love you, Oliver."

"You are my forever." My vampire slipped free. "You have one hour, then you're mine." He opened his driver's door and brushed out glass shards from the bucket seat. He climbed inside and started the engine, but he waited for me to go first.

I collected the shovel and tossed it into the passenger seat of my car. I steered out of the gravel space and drove out onto the highway. Oliver stayed on my tail, and we sent flirty glances in our mirrors and leap-frogged down the road. Clearly, he was nerfing the Shelby, since my car would never stand a chance, and with his reflexes, he could outrace me blindfolded with his hands tied behind his back. I loved his playfulness, but how he managed driving at freeway speeds and no windshield was beyond me. My eyeballs hurt in sympathy.

When we reached town, we split up to our respectful houses with a friendly wave, but I detoured for a special gift before heading home. And when I got home, I packed a backpack and, as I rushed down the stairs as promised, Oliver was at my door wearing a fresh suit and a charming smile. He truly didn't want to waste one second of our mini-vacation.

# 32

# The Fairy Tale

**Daisy**

In the time I'd bought Oliver a gift and packed a bag for the surprise vacation, Oliver'd had the windows replaced in the Shelby. That service had to carry a steep premium, but Oliver insisted it wasn't a burden. Guilt weighed heavily anyway.

He'd taken me southbound on Highway 41, and I focused on Oliver's warm hand, forcing myself to picture puppies playing in a yard instead of the fiery accident scene as we passed the site. Someday, that location wouldn't bother me, but until then, I avoided leaving the tri-city area as much as possible. Oliver's big surprise required a trip south, and I didn't want to spoil his excitement.

Exiting the highway in a suburb of Green Bay, the Shelby rounded a circular drive at the ritzy Courtyard Inn. I'd heard of it, but never had a reason to stay here—nor could I afford it. Above the French door entrance was a cloth awning inscribed with the name. Green ivy grew along the brick exterior, and the sharply sloping roof gave the place an antique, classy feel. The five-story resort had immaculate landscaping—a water fountain, shaped hedges, and flowers in several colors dotting along the perimeter. The whole thing just screamed Oliver's style. No wonder he'd chosen this place.

Oliver stopped the car, and a concierge rushed around and opened the passenger door for me. I climbed out awkwardly, and he closed the door behind me.

A valet in a stiff uniform and straight spine held out his hand for Oliver's keys. "I'll take great care of it as always, sir."

Oliver smiled. "I know you will." He handed the man the Shelby's keys and a folded tip. The valet blushed and bit back a grin, nodding appreciatively. He quickly ducked into the antique sports car.

Oliver approached me with his arm hooked, and I fastened myself to his side. The sexy vampire led me through the French doors, split open simultaneously by a pair of doormen.

If the rare occasion required it, I stayed at budget motels where a pool was considered a luxury amenity. This was something from another world to me. I took in the luxury interior as we stood in the foyer—walnut-accented cream walls, brown leather furniture in the lounge, anchored by a massive woven rug, which looked new, not wrinkled or well-worn. And the massive fireplace at the center of the room contained a crackling fire.

A porter rolled a cart over with a friendly smile. I hesitated, unaccustomed to this lofty service, but at Oliver's gentle prodding, I let the stranger take my bag. Oliver tipped him as well, and the porter rushed off with our stuff. How did he know where to take it? Mind readers everywhere.

"It's like we're royalty here," I whispered to him, out of earshot from the staff.

"I suspect we are," Oliver said, patting my hand and bringing us to the lacquered check-in desk.

"Why is that?"

Oliver didn't answer. His attention was on the beaming receptionist, a mid-thirties blond with a pressed white blouse and an identification tag clipped to a breast pocket. She gave Oliver her full, undivided attention. "Good afternoon, Mr. Rockwell. The usual room tonight?" Her voice lilted like a merry songbird, and she offered a room card as if knowing Oliver's preference and had prepared ahead for his arrival. The service around here was fantastic...and creepy.

Not only had Oliver washed up, changed his suit, fixed the Shelby's glass, but he also had time to make reservations at a luxury hotel. I was impressed, to say the least.

"Thank you, Lauren." Oliver accepted the card and tucked it into his breast pocket.

"Have a fantastic night. Call down if there's anything you need, sir." Lauren waved us goodbye.

Oliver acknowledged with a nod and brought me to the elevators.

The elevator brought us to a suite on the top floor. The theme of creams and beiges and dark wood continued up here. Colorful floral arrangements of ruby peonies, golden amaryllis, and sprigs of mauve heather filled the living room and kitchen, similar to what he'd brought me when I had been at work, and I'd used a bedpan as a vase. They were even more beautiful now, in proper glass vases, and the quantity was stunning. I stuck my nose into the nearest bouquet and inhaled the sweet aroma. I turned in place with a massive grin hurting my cheeks while Oliver watched me.

I headed to the picture window. Our room overlooked the back of the hotel, a field of wildflowers, a river, and a garden below with a pergola and swing. It was serene and jaw-droppingly beautiful. "This place is a storybook fairy tale, and everyone treats you like a regular."

Oliver stopped at my shoulder to admire along with me. "I am a regular."

"These flowers are so beautiful, and with such short notice... Thank you. How did you manage all this so fast?"

"Many things happen quickly when you offer people money."

I supposed that was true. "What brings you here often enough to be a regular?" I'd never seen Oliver with a day job, and now I was curious.

"Whenever I need to relax, I'll swing by here for a few days."

With student-loan brain, I snorted.

"What's funny?" he asked, genuinely perplexed.

"Oh," I said, caught off-guard. Oliver didn't live in the real world like us peons. "Affording a vacation is so far down my list of priorities, I couldn't imagine spontaneously getting away for a weekend. When things were really tough, I had to ration my anxiety meds. Let's just say I'm very grateful my roommates are dependable and we get along." Mostly.

Oliver turned to face me. "American humans are told to become independent by an arbitrary eighteenth birthday—tossed out on their own to earn enough money to quit their jobs by an assumed 'retirement' age. According to those metrics, I've lived three lifetimes. If I hadn't figured out how to make myself independently wealthy, what am I still doing here?"

I had to laugh at his silly tone. His bed-and-breakfast, his Shelby, his fine, custom-tailored suits that he had no issue constantly replacing, this massive pile of out-of-season flowers. Sure, I figured he had money, but I never thought much more about it. "Okay. No more comparing. What have your three lifetimes of experience taught you about growing your wealth?" Because I could use some tips.

"Commercial real estate. I dabble in day trading when I'm bored. It's the modern version of gambling—sometimes it's fun to blow off some steam, other times it could be destructive, but I have excellent self-control. Except with you."

My heart skipped a beat. I wanted to ignore where that train headed because I had more questions. "When you compelled my boss to give you the paramedic's job, you had no need in the world for that paycheck."

"The paycheck wasn't enough to justify that itchy polyester punishment."

I frowned at his use of the past tense and realized what he said hurt. "You quit?"

Oliver chuckled. "I'll be your partner forever, but you were right. You're capable of taking care of yourself, and with your witchcraft, you'll always be able to make your own decisions. You're free to do whatever you want, and..." Oliver's hands cupped my face.

"And what?" I asked on a breath, mesmerized by his words.

"Free to decide your future. That's all I've ever wanted for you. Although next time I ride along in an ambulance, I'll be in a suit."

I smiled. I'd pictured myself mastering control while strictly motivated by bringing Oliver back to life, so I could have this very thing. I never expected him to be at my side the whole while. Now I could protect myself, and he'd be my backup. I would always be safe, and he would always love me. Things were working out okay.

"If you ever end up in my rig, we have bigger problems to worry about."

Oliver glanced outside, seriousness returning. "You seem to be adjusting well to your father's death."

My vampire deserved the truth. "When Pierce staked you, my dad tried to kidnap me. Since I became a witch, he wanted to make a new serum."

Oliver tensed, but respectfully, he patiently listened.

"When he'd ordered the elf to physically cart me off to the lab instead, despite my objections, and the elf had obeyed without hesitation, that was my breaking point. If I didn't stop them, where would it end?" I pressed my palms against Oliver's firm pecs. "You said I am free to do what I want and make my own choices because of my magic. You're wrong. It's because of you, Oliver. It's you who gave me strength, meaning, purpose." *A magic ring.*

Oliver smiled through teary eyes. I had to keep going, or I was going to start crying too.

"You never gave up on me, and I did what I had to do to keep us safe. No more lab. No more experiments. No more serum." Killing made me sick, but I couldn't change the outcome, and even if I could, I wouldn't. The guilt still rode along on my conscience. Oliver and I could be happy now, and that was worth the sacrifice to my soul.

"It never goes away," Oliver said, searching my face as if he could read my mind.

"What doesn't?"

"The guilt of taking a human life. I want you to know you're not a monster because of it. You taught me that." Oliver's wistful smile melted me.

"Evangeline?" I prompted. It couldn't have been easy.

"Among others. That's why I bought the blood bank. I can subsist without hurting people, without the risk of losing control. Sometimes I have to do what I have to do, but I think you understand that now."

He might believe I wasn't a monster, but when the wave of guilt crashed over me, I felt like one. "I could use a drink."

"Allow me." Oliver crossed the expansive, cushy suite and pulled out bottles of red wine and glasses.

I followed him over and teased, "Only four bottles of wine? Someone forgot to restock."

Without missing a beat, Oliver lifted the handset of the landline and pressed a key. "Lauren, I need more wine up here."

I couldn't hear her reply, but I expected it was super bubbly. He hung up. "Where were we?"

"Lauren sure is friendly," I said, taking a glass of red wine from him.

"I pay her to be." Oliver sat next to me on a barstool and lifted a glass.

My brain misfired. "You what?"

Oliver sipped. "I own this establishment."

I leaned back, wide-eyed. Truthfully, I figured the owner was a corporation or a private equity firm. Snarky student-loan brain said, "Wow. You know what? Don't send me the Shelby's bill."

Oliver laughed. "You needn't worry about money with me. This vacation and everything included is on me."

The mystery of Oliver Rockwell's world just kept getting deeper and deeper. "Is there anything else about you I should know?"

The vampire set his half-finished drink on the shiny bar, careful to use a coaster. Oliver rose and held out his hand, urging me to join him, and I did. Pale gray eyes lit with a glow of excitement. He pulled me gently into his embrace, and I locked my arms around his neck. His cute smile was contagious. "There is one thing."

Warmth curled down below. "Oh?"

Oliver grinned deviously as his hands slid down and cupped my butt. "My car hasn't gotten a ride in a while. I'm afraid the battery is going to drain if it doesn't get a jump start and a good, long run."

I tilted my head. The Shelby just...oh, car metaphors. My favorite. I leaped right in with him. "Did you bring the jumper cables?"

Oliver popped his eyebrows suggestively. "A clean pair awaits in the drawer of the end table in the primary bedroom. Ready at your service."

I laughed at his thoroughness and then grimaced. "Wait. Why did you specifically say 'clean'?"

"Because...they're clean," Oliver said, confused.

"As opposed to used? How do you know they're clean? Did you ask the staff to sanitize them?" I was teasing. It was fun to watch Oliver squirm with confusion.

"I called ahead and had all our favorite things stocked just for us. The handcuffs, and all the other toys in there, are new and...clean."

That was quite a list of specific details to get right, and he'd called the receptionist to deliver extra wine. This was a little more than a weekend getaway. "Why all this trouble? What's the real occasion?"

Oliver sighed. Something was wrong.

"What is it?" I pressed, now worried.

# 33
## The Truth

**Oliver**

I'D HIDDEN WHAT I was from Evangeline, never brave enough to show her the truth, until the option had been taken away. The cascade of events since had been devastating. I gazed into Daisy's worried eyes. Once again, I hid a devastating truth. My attempt at a stoic facade to hide my melancholy mood failed. If I told her the truth about the onyx ring on her finger, she would fixate on finding an answer, but she wouldn't succeed before I lost her again.

To remove her immediate concern, I snuffed out my gloom and changed the subject to something far more pleasurable. With my sweetest flirty smile, I said, "I have something for you."

Daisy tilted her head with curiosity, and I brought her to the flower-covered coffee table. Pulling open the small drawer in the front, I removed a velvety jewelry box and gripped it as sacred. Nicole had encouraged it, and she'd succeeded in convincing me, despite my reluctance over her known regrets. This was something I'd declared I would never do again, but

I simply loved Daisy too much. She had experienced enough of my world to make a wise decision. I couldn't be the one to take the choice away from her.

I held the box, delaying giving it to her. "I made a promise to myself over a century ago, but I'm willing to break that promise this once, only for you. We had discussed this before, and I firmly believe we're still in agreement, so please understand, I'm not making this offer because I've had a change of heart or mind. Think of it more like an insurance policy in case something happens, and I'm not there, and you can't see any other way out. A life preserver."

Daisy frowned at the jewelry box. "I don't understand."

I lifted the hinged lid and showed her a handcrafted Victorian locket with ornate scrollwork and a garnet gem in the center, hung with a draping double chain. It wasn't her style, but neither was the last necklace I'd gifted her, which had since been made obsolete. This one still held a purpose.

Daisy touched it with her fingers. "It's a beautiful necklace, but I don't need vervain or black nightshade anymore. Vampires are going to need protection from me." Daisy smiled.

Sooner than she thought. I gave her a sad smile in return. "This was my mother's locket, and it contains the ultimate protection—one that still helps you now, even as a witch."

"Like what?" she asked slowly, suspicion on the tip of her tongue.

Nerves swirled in my stomach, a feeling so rare I had to swallow thickly before continuing. "The first step in the process of becoming a vampire is ingestion of a sufficient quantity of a vampire's blood. But it's not something you can pick up at the local grocer's." I gave her a reassuring smile.

"Thankfully."

I hoped I wasn't making another mistake. "When a vampire attempts to save a human life using their healing blood, you can imagine how easily such a thing could occur. But if that human were to die anyway with the blood still in their circulatory system, the human will reawaken from death to make an important choice: feed and accept a new life or deny the hunger and perish forever."

"The basketball player. I remember the process. Where are you going with this?" Daisy shifted, uncomfortable with the magnitude of the offer.

I continued explaining the full process. Then, if she needed to use the insurance policy, she'd know what to do. "The amount of vampire blood that triggers the transition is insufficient to maintain that new life. To complete the process, more blood must be ingested. This locket hides a vial of my blood. If you're ever in danger, and I can't be there for you, drink it. My blood alone won't make you a vampire, but it will heal you. And if you sustain a mortal injury, it will allow you time before making that important choice. Since we both know what your choice is—to decline the immortality of vampirism—drinking this will give you one last day with me. Can you wear this for my peace of mind?"

She paused, staring at the necklace, thoughts twisting her features. Her brows knitted. "If for some reason I get hurt, that necklace will protect me, but you'll be with me, and with this ring, there's no problem, right?" She held up the hand displaying the magic-stifling onyx ring.

I hated lying to her. I smiled. "No problem, of course, but since I quit the EMS department, you'll need a strong partner, especially while you learn to master your magic."

"That's a good point." Daisy considered. "So, it's a healing potion and, worst-case scenario, a resurrection spell with a timer. I can do that." Daisy lifted her hair off her neck and turned around.

Without a sizzle at all, I slipped the necklace free of the box, eagerly draped it around her throat, and fastened the ends. I sighed with utter relief.

Daisy lowered her hair and faced me. "Would Pierce know what it is and try to take it?"

"Only other vampires can smell it, and since our blood is less desirable than human blood, they won't pay it much mind. Since it's hidden behind the garnet, no human would otherwise notice, but I wouldn't announce it to your roommates."

Daisy perked up, the way I liked her. "Got it. I have something for you too, but it pales compared to this." She dug in her bag resting on the couch and brought me a bright white and green cardboard box. "I didn't have time to wrap it, but I think you'll still be pleasantly surprised."

I read the label and laughed while I opened the box and pulled out my new cell phone. "I've been missing the word games. You promise not to destroy this one?"

Daisy crossed her fingers. "I promise to try really hard not to."

I set the box down, and a delicious grin crossed my lips. "Deal. Now, come here." I hooked my fingers into Daisy's belt loops and tugged her close. So close, I could smell her shampoo. I reached for her hips to slide her shirt off. "There's a whole drawer of toys waiting to be tested."

"By alphabetical order or by size?" Daisy unfastened my belt and pants while my fingers freed her from the confining shirt.

My lips found hers, and I kissed her with feverish need, never more excited for our future, however short it would be. We stumbled into the bedroom, clothing flinging everywhere, and at last, Daisy drew back and freed the tented silk confining my erection.

I squeezed the low muscles to bounce it in a welcoming wave and answered her playful question. "Size. Definitely the size that counts."

"I'm pretty sure how you use it counts way more." Daisy panted against my lips. "Everything about you is beautiful, like a fairy tale too good to be true."

I intended to keep up the fairy tale as long as possible. "Sometimes wishes come true."

Daisy snorted. I loved that little noise she made. "I've wished for a million dollars nearly every day, but the bank account is still like squeezing drops of water from a cactus."

I squinted at her, translating her problem. "You're broke?" Such a foreign concept to me.

Daisy laughed. "I'm an EMT with a mortgage, and I'm drowning in student loans from failing out of medical school. Why do you think I have roommates? I don't enjoy giving up my privacy or my personal home, but that's what I have to do to pay the bills. I suppose you may have forgotten what it's like to live paycheck to paycheck over the centuries."

"My memory can be dusty." It pained me to think of how much she struggled and how blind I'd been to it. "Let us indulge ourselves with my credit card. Anything you want is on the menu—the room service is at your beck and call."

She raised a brow and her sneaky lips. "How about limes?"

"Whatever you want." I'd always have limes stocked in the bar. Her requests were too easy, but I loved pleasing her.

"Can you lick up whipped cream and chocolate syrup?"

I brushed my fingers along her jaw. "I'm sorry, but I cannot."

"Is that a vampire thing?" Disappointment tinged her question.

"Lactose intolerance."

Daisy blinked at me and barked a laugh. "Are you serious?"

"Took me a while to figure it out, since it feels like vervain poisoning, but that's why I prefer my blood bagged. Less chance of drinking unwanted dairy sugars. But vampires cannot ingest food or similar products. Our diet includes blood, alcohol, and black coffee only."

Daisy's thoughtful face appeared. "Do you miss it? Food, I mean."

"Sometimes." I tried not to think about it.

"The way you talk about vampirism leads me to believe there is a cure out there, that your condition is medical in origin, but my roommates said there's a long-lost spell."

"Magic did create us, and trust me, if witches knew of a cure, they would've used it to destroy the plague of vampires a long time ago."

"But isn't all magic just science that's not understood yet?"

I brushed the hair out of her face and planted a kiss on her lips. "If you could cure vampirism, you'd be a billionaire."

"Why do you say that?"

"Because I'd give you a billion dollars for a cure."

Daisy squinted. "I can't tell if you're joking."

I released her beautiful face. It wasn't like I hadn't played the 'what if' game dozens of times before, but a cure didn't exist, and every second that ticked by was another second closer to our inevitable separation. "Kiss me."

Daisy refocused on our naked bodies. A mischievous grin lifted her lips. I loved to see her happy. "Where?"

I laughed, and my erection bounced, submitting its vote. "The engine's fired up and ready to hit the open road, but the shifter is jammed. I think it needs some rough handling to loosen up the gears."

Daisy pushed my shoulder, tipping me onto the mattress, and she climbed over me. "You mean this shifter?" She gripped my erection, and a surge of pleasure roared through me. I arched my hips up and groaned.

She said, "It is a little stiff. I think I can take care of that."

As Daisy's lips closed over my flesh, my head tilted back in a swell of excitement, and I groaned again. Pulling myself together, I watched her stroke with her hands and take my head into her mouth. Her hair tickled. The pendant with my blood around her neck swung free on its chains. I loved this woman so much. I would do anything for her. She had my heart forever.

Until the ring wore out.

I kept my focus on Daisy Barrett while I was lucky enough to be in her presence, happy with the world at her fingertips. I was happy with her fingertips on my world.

Warmth pooled under her amazing stroking touch and quickly gathered steam. I clenched, and as my engine burst with the pedal to the metal, Daisy pulled free, allowing my fountain to erupt all over me and the bed.

I'm fairly certain I called her a god, and then it was her turn.

*To be continued...*

DIVE INTO THE FINAL chapter of Oliver and Daisy's story in **Vampire's Promise**, where Oliver's worst nightmare becomes a reality. And don't forget to check out **Vampire's Distraction**, the prequel short story where Oliver and Daisy first meet at Abby's wedding.

As an indie author, I'm thrilled you shared your time with me, exploring the crazy worlds and voices living rent-free in my head and keeping me up at night. Your reviews are very important to me, so if you enjoyed this book, please consider leaving some stars at your favorite retailer for the second part of Oliver Rockwell and Daisy Barrett's story, Vampire's Secret.

If you found any typos or errors, I blame my cat. Rat her out at: support@stephanieflynn.com.

Thank you for your support!

# Also By Stephanie Flynn

Find my catalog at StephanieFlynn.com

**Immortal Protector series**

0.5 Vampire's Distraction

1 Vampire's Deception

2 Vampire's Secret

3 Vampire's Promise

3.5 Elf Bound

4 Vampire's Demand


**Immortal Protector Side Tales**

Deer Holiday

Love Claws

Depths of the Heart


**Matchmaker in Time series**

0.5 Minutes to Live

1 Seconds to Act

2 Hours to Arrive

3 Days to Hide

4 Years to Savor


**Pirates in Time series**

1 Pirate's Prize

2 Pirate's Treasure

3 Pirate's Plunder


**Time Travel Romance Shorts**

Fateful Time

One Crazy Time


If you like your urban fantasy without the romance, too, check out Stephanie Flynn's other name, Marie Flynn!

# About Stephanie Flynn

Stephanie Flynn writes action-packed paranormal romance filled with adventure, suspense, and danger. She lives in Michigan, USA, with her husband and kids, and she spends her writing time surrounded by a herd of normal cats who bat everything off her desk, including her coffee. Check out her website for more books: StephanieFlynn.com

www.ingramcontent.com/pod-product-compliance
Lightning Source LLC
Chambersburg PA
CBHW061046190726
48286CB00006B/1626